The Casino

The Casanova Papers

Carl MacDougall

THE CASANOVA PAPERS

Secker & Warburg
London

From *Summer Farm* by Norman MacCaig,
reprinted by kind permission of the
estate of the author and Chatto & Windus.

First published in Great Britain in 1996
by Martin Secker & Warburg Limited
an imprint of Reed International Books Limited
Michelin House, 81 Fulham Road, London SW3 6RB
and Auckland, Melbourne, Singapore and Toronto

A CIP catalogue record for this book
is available from the British Library

ISBN 0 436 20293 X

Phototypeset in 10½/13 Sabon and 10½/13 Bodoni by
Intype London Ltd
Printed and bound in Great Britain
by Clays Ltd, St Ives plc

For Euan and Kirsty

ONE

Blessed is he that readeth . . .

Revelations 1:3

Your mother is dead. She was cremated more than six months ago.

I chose Lambhill because I wanted away from everything. I also thought Janie could show up.

When the ashes arrived two weeks later, the undertaker put an envelope on the kitchen table. Can I take this opportunity of rendering my account? he said. I'll just leave it here.

I paid by cheque. He seemed surprised.

Are you moving?

Yeah. I've bought a flat more or less in the centre of town.

Good, he said, then paused, as if there was something he'd forgotten to say. Good luck.

The move came two days later. I left the keys with Mr Patel. He had written instructions for the Salvation Army. I'll ask to see their warrant cards, he said. And I am very sorry to lose your custom. Small businesses now have a hard time and I always enjoyed keeping your newspapers.

I expect the new folk'll take a paper, I said. They'll be here next week, Tuesday I think.

But they won't take three, sir. Three newspapers to the one house is very unusual. I envy the newsagent who gets your business.

The idea was that I would leave Fenwick Road in the

morning, the removal men would take the stuff to the new place, fit it up, and I'd arrive that afternoon. The Salvation Army could take what was left.

I changed my mind.

Irene's ashes were in the car I had used to drive her to and from the hospital, a tartan rug around her legs, another over her shoulders like a shawl; the car I drove to visit her, the car with the tissues in the glove compartment.

I went to the new place, picked up the keys, told the removal men to pull the door behind them and headed out the Great Western Road, up Loch Lomondside and through Glen Falloch, round by the line of the Highland Railway and the Caulfeild road, past Black Mount, Loch Bà and across Rannoch Moor to the King's House Hotel on the edge of Glencoe, Irene's favourite place. Just to be here is enough, she said.

I took a room and drank whisky in the bar, listening to the walkers who crossed the moor on the West Highland Way.

I was awake at six and the first for breakfast. I paid the bill, then set off for Altnafeadh and the bridge across the Coupall, taking the path into Coire an Tulaich; scrambling the pink and grey scree on the edge of Buchaille Etive Mor, pulling myself up the ledges, over the *bealach* and on to the ridge. Pink boulders and cairns on the way to the top, and the view from the summit was handfuls of air and light. My eyes watered slightly in a trickling wind.

Nevis and the Lochaber hills leaned across the light, the spine of the Mamore forest turned me west to the crinkled tops of Bidean nam Bian, then round to the

4

other side with Schiehallion in the corner. The lochs and gullies glistened from Bà to Rannoch Station, where a small train rested, then pulled away.

I unscrewed the cap, held the urn above my head, and Irene tumbled out. The wind carried her. She did not shift even part of the landscape as she moved from the vase to Lochaber, Rannoch, Glencoe and beyond. A speck of something caught my eye and then was gone.

It was the speck that did it. I had been closed, but now it tumbled from me like innards from a butcher's hook, screaming against the wind in gulps.

I shut my eyes and saw Irene's skin, the surface changes, watered purple marks, the bruising on her arm, her diluted smile as she opened her eyes and saw me, reached across to take my hand, tried to speak, then shook her head, breathing slightly, her gestures shadows of themselves.

The last thing she did was lean across and kiss my cheek. She said one word.

Janie.

Then there was AnnA. We met in the rain.

Café windows were misted by the heat and smoke inside. Only the Café des Sports on the rue Mouffetard was clear. It was usually empty, as cold inside as on the street. There were no tops to the houses; shining streets, closed doors, leaves lay sodden in the Jardin des Plantes. Tourists looked sad. Signs of spring were unexpected, like crabs and seaweed left by the tide. A dour, lustrous sky with a chill in the air. March, and Paris is shabby.

AnnA now seems indistinct, as though I am trying to recall an image or a photograph taken with a white light to obliterate blemish. My memory divides into what happened and what I wanted to happen. I invent the way it should have been. She had dark skin and shiny hair. She smelled of honey and Miss Dior.

Rain penetrated everything. More debilitating than heat, it persisted, a sound that hissed and flapped in your ears.

Every day some hopes were dashed. The morning sky was bright. By ten o'clock it had grown dark and the wind got up. It always felt bitter, personal, some sort of criticism. Days now seem the same, determined by rain rather than light.

Sundays were suffocating. People were caught on their way to church. The front of the men's shirts, trousers and jackets were soaked before they could unfurl their umbrellas. The women covered their hair with their hands and screamed, a softly controlled scream of anguish and disappointment. Everyone was uncomfortable, and knew they would stay that way throughout the service. Trousers would go baggy at the knees from kneeling. The women's hair would be unkempt. No one would look their best.

By afternoon the rain was a hush, like an engine or a low, salacious whisper. I was living on rue Censier in a small attic room with a backward view. The rooftops now seem permanently wet, but I remember thinking I could lie outside in summer, sunbathing on the roof, reading to improve my French. The idea seemed exotic.

Everything was accidental. The room had been advertised in a café window. The proprietor gave me a wooden block with keys on a ring. He pointed to the end of the street. The number 8 had been painted onto the block in red like the start of a child's drawing. One key turned the outside door. The room was poky, on the fifth floor with a window opposite the door, a bed to the left, chair and wardrobe on the right and a sink beside the window, opposite the bed. There was a rag mat and no cooking facilities.

Back in the café, the proprietor looked up from his newspaper and jerked his head. I nodded. He made a gesture with his hand, ruffling his fingertips and thumb together in a way that suggested I should come towards him and pay at the same time. I took some notes from my pocket, gave him two. We smiled and shook hands.

He took a dusty bottle of Macallan Glenlivet from the shelf and poured two whiskies. He lit a cigarette as the glasses snapped together. The whisky was good and stayed warm in my stomach as I unpacked my books and clothes.

I eventually met the four others who shared the landing, living in rooms the same as my own. We passed in the morning or late afternoon. We nodded and smiled, shrank into ourselves.

The smell of rosemary came from one woman's room. The other woman's room was dry and smelled of polish. She was always elegant and I imagined she worked in a *tabac*. The men were reclusive. Their rooms smelled of smoke and hair oil.

This is a black Bic pen, and a Zweckform jotter of recycled squared paper. This is me trying to write.

I have decided to do it the way I did the translations, roughly at first by hand, then checked and copied on a disc to ease the spelling and determine length.

7

The room is cluttered. There are too many books, and pictures are stacked below the surfaces they are supposed to occupy. The carpet is old and the furniture friendly. You, my sons and daughter, used to have music whenever you worked. If there is music, I am forced to listen. I work in silence, mostly at night.

I am assuming you will read this, that it will become important to at least one of you, that someone, I don't know who, maybe Colin, though given his appearance at the funeral it seems unlikely, but say that Colin felt he wanted to get to know me better. He would feel terrible. He would feel he had wasted a great opportunity.

I can see him, rinsing his mouth in beer, ponderous, maudlin-drunk and sorry for himself. I know what he was like, he'll say. I bloody well know him better than any of you.

And you'll emphasise the word *know*. You'll roll it round your mouth. And the fact that you never liked winning at games because you always felt sorry for the loser will prevail. He can't be all bad, you'll say.

And when you get this far, somewhere near this point you will turn away.

Colin. This is the only way I can hold your attention, the only way I can let you know this is for you, all of you. It is neither explanation nor confession. Some of it will be tediously familiar. This is me passing time, imagining you were here, pretending to talk to you now and then, all of you, trying not to interrupt or argue, trying to let you have your say.

I want you to know how I came by the Papers. I want you to know how they saved my life. I would like you to know what happened when I went to Paris, that trans-

8

lating these papers helped me deal with my grief and my guilt, because I loved your mother and I love you too.

This is a plea, a shot in the dark, the way we send pulses into space, hoping they will be understood elsewhere.

Your photographs are in front of me, framed and smiling.

Read on. Please. Look at it this way: my wife is dead and I live alone. This is the story of some of my failures, of things as I see them, which makes them neither right nor wrong, it simply makes them mine. I will tell you what's happening as we go along.

Having mentioned the difficult bits, I feel compelled to continue.

It's time for some of The Pages which have ruled my life since I found them. I have translated and arranged them into a kind of order, which explains why they more or less sound the same. The voice you hear is probably mine. I was more concerned with accuracy than with reinterpreting character, establishing voice or narrative flow. When I consider the time they took, the hours I spent revising and trying to get them right, they must be a failure. There is no central voice and they bear little relation one to the other. They are no use here. They will probably interrupt the text and cause confusion. But I've nowhere else to put them. The intention was to make a book of them alone, but that failed for the reasons I have stated. And now they are here. They are justified, I think, because they relate to AnnA. Were it not for her they would still be lost and were it not for them I would never have known her.

AnnA.

Will you read this? That one thought has kept me going, you in your flat with this little book, curled on the sofa with a mug of tea and Alan Stivell, shards of rain girning at the window.

PROMINENT FEATURES, DUBIOUS AGE

Simply, the head and shoulders of a young man, drawn in profile; a pastel portrait, which could be the study for a medallion.

He has prominent features. The age is dubious. Perhaps he is 20. No more than 25, he could be 18. The eye has a slight sparkle, suggesting the portrait was drawn by daylight, in the sun. The lashes are short and the contour unlined. His eyebrows could meet in the middle.

He has a full mouth and slightly sags below the jaw, suggesting a round, chubby face, maybe even boyish. The lips suggest a rosebud mouth and a heart-shaped upper lip; they seem warm enough, sensuous. On second glance, for we naturally move from the eye to the mouth and from the mouth to the eye via the nose, the eye is slightly enlarged, as though the subject was given to thyroid trouble. A second glance at the mouth invites us to turn the drawing onto its side; with the lips facing upwards it could be a heart.

The nose is bent. This, with his darkened eyes and features, as well as his Venetian origins, was later taken as the mark of Cain, a sign of Jewishness. He also has a high forehead, said to signify intelligence. His youthfulness and forehead suggest he was drawn

unwigged. The fluff of hair at the side of his face, below the curl and before the ear, suggests he hardly shaves.

This is a difficulty. The complexion is fair, the eye is dark. Nor does he wear a shirt. He is unclothed, save for a ribbon tying his hair at the back. It is reminiscent of how one would draw a woman of similar age, her hair in ringlets down the side of her face, rather the way his hair rounds across his neck and shoulder.

Hair is the problem. It is elegantly coiffed at the front and side, worn straight back to exaggerate the face, another indication of its fullness, and the curl at either side of the head would certainly draw attention to the eyes. Then the hair is long enough to be tied at the base of his neck and curl across his shoulder. What kind of young man has hair of such length?

This young man has a long neck, an elegant neck with no Adam's apple. He seems sturdy. One can imagine a good body, strong legs.

We search for meaning. Is the dark aura round his face a decoration? Is it a shadow intended to highlight the face, or is it indicative of a deeper component known to the artist? The portrait was done by the sitter's brother.

There are other likenesses. The bust which supposedly came from the Waldstein Castle of Dux, though how such a thing got there I cannot imagine. Casanova was thoroughly miserable in Bohemia. He kept leaving to find better conditions and was forced to come back. Waldstein himself barely stayed there. The bust, incidentally, has also been ascribed to his brother Francesco.

There is also a miniature by Anton Graff, which I have seen described as Mozart, an unhappy mistake; another by Pierre Antoine Baudoin, which is too severe; and there are two haughty portraits, neither of which look like the same person though they were reputedly executed by the Venetian, Alessandro Longhi.

Finally, where would we be without the Johann Berka engraving of Jacques Casanova de Seingalt, aged 63? It was done in Prague. Place the Francesco pastel beside it and similarities are immediately obvious.

It is the same person, apart from the mouth. This is because Francesco's mouth is an exaggerated travesty. Berka has drawn an old man's mouth, yet the lower lip is as full as before.

The Berka skull is skeletal. The jaw has collapsed, the cheeks and brow have wrinkled, but the hairstyle, eye and nose are the same: the nose may even have become more prominent. The shoulders have stooped and the body thickened. This is an old man with spindly legs.

Berka has drawn by candlelight. The light comes full into the face. Francesco's Casanova faces left, Berka's to the right; Francesco faces life, Berka faces age.

The eye does not move across Berka's face. We know what we are seeing. Yet there is something wrong. This was the age when, on Meissner's evidence, Casanova was in Prague, prior to the first performance of *Don Giovanni*. This was ten years or so before he died, the year when he published *The Story of My Escape From The Leads* and began work on *L'Histoire de ma Vie*. Look again at the Berka mouth and eye; travel from one to the other and back again. What do you see?

This was a low point, though he was to get lower. Old and forced to accept charity in abhorrent conditions with servants who despised him and a master he never saw, his world destroyed by revolution; yet Berka has drawn a merry face with a roguish smile and a twinkling eye. Was this an advertisement? Who paid Berka and why was this engraving done? Was this the frontispiece to the *Escape From The Leads* or some other publication? Did this portrait decorate the servants' lavatory at Dux?

It would be fair to say Francesco Casanova is remembered because of his elder stepbrother, yet his is the more interesting parentage.

Francesco was born in London in 1727, two years after Giacomo. Francesco was conceived while their mother, Zanetta, was mistress of the Prince of Wales, later King George II. Did royal blood course through Francesco's veins? He appears to have studied in Dresden, where another brother, Giovanni, later became Director of the Academy of Painting. The pair are said to have collaborated as forgers in Paris, where Francesco painted battle scenes with clouds of billowing smoke to hide the difficult parts he could not paint. Like his brother he was constantly in debt; unlike his brother he appears to have been impotent.

I have made enquiries and believe he is dead. His brother makes frequent references to Francesco in his manuscript and I thought it would be interesting to commission a drawing of Giacomo in a more characteristic pose, neither young nor old. I feel it is better to imagine him as we imagine his life.

And now to another, more tedious matter. You will, of

course, be aware of the costs such a project could incur. I need hardly remind you, existing costs are quite considerable and are being entirely met by us. Should we go ahead with what I think is a fine idea for illustrations, then further costs are inevitable.

I am sure

The manuscript peters out at the end of a page. It seems to have run out of energy, but reads as though there were more, as though the writer had another agenda he was about to address.

I think the fragment is from the Brockhaus offices in Leipzig and was addressed to Carlo Angioloni, whose emissary had sold the twelve bundles of manuscript in Casanova's hand, bundles that eventually became *L'His-toire de ma Vie*, to Brockhaus for 200 thalers in 1820. Carlo Angioloni's father was present when Casanova died at Dux in 1798. The first bowdlerised volumes of Casanova's text were published by Brockhaus in 1826–27. As far as one can tell the engravings were never commissioned. Berka died in 1815. How I came by that letter and other similar documents is the purpose of this memoir.

AnnA used to cover her mouth with her hand and giggle. Occasionally I found it hurtful, though she seemed oblivious.

The first time may have been something I said, but I remember she laughed at my clothes. I had a shirt with a Dior logo on the pocket. She pointed and giggled.

Another time she looked at me and said, I am not going out with you dressed like that. I changed. She giggled.

Why don't you tell me what to wear?

What good would it do? When I'm not around you would simply buy the same as before, Yves St. Laurent and Valentino logos. And don't get so sulky about it. Is that right? Sulky?

It'll do.

What is the word you use?

You mean what word would I use?

I think that was what I said.

Not quite; but the word I would use is huff. I would say, Don't get yourself in a huff.

Is it Scottish?

Don't think so; it may have started life in Scotland, but like many such things it has moved elsewhere.

Doesn't the giant say he'll huff and puff and blow the house down?

The wolf says it. And that's another meaning.

So it means to become angry and to blow?

Uh-hu.

What started this?

You did. You suggested I was sulking.

That's right. I was only telling you for your own good. Then she giggled. I sound like my mother.

I got an opportunity when her hair turned green. It was black and shortish, roughly cut, slightly punk. I asked why she wanted it blonde. I like blondes, she said.

But your hair is black.

I know the colour of my hair. Anyway, this is just a little blonde. It will not be my head, just little strands or bunches of hair.

16

Streaks.

I thought that meant to run.

That's what it means in children's comics. It also means a strip or a line, which is presumably what you are making.

If you want to use the bathroom, do so now. I will be busy. I've never done this before.

She came out two hours later with green lines down either side of her face. I said it looked like straw hanging out a midden.

What's that?

What's what?

What you said.

Straw hanging out a midden?

Uh-hu.

You know what straw is?

Of course.

Is it the word midden you don't understand?

What is it?

Literally a dunghill, but usually a rubbish heap.

So, I'm a dunghill?

It's an expression.

Scottish?

Of course.

Is that the best you can do for someone whose hair has turned green?

It's for your own good.

She giggled, looked in the mirror and giggled again.

It's easy to minimise waste or quantify regret, but I know my loss. It's the grieving I find difficult. Just when you think it's over, back it comes. Some times are worse than others.

And then there's the way guilt merges with grief. The grief for Irene and missing AnnA, staring across this city from my desk by the window.

The editor came to the funeral, though he met Irene only once. Next day he telephoned and asked if there was anything I needed or wanted, time off and the like. I went back to work when I returned from Glencoe, had moved in here and was on my own.

He'd ask how things were, how the kids were doing and so on. He called me into his office and asked if I fancied a move. I said I thought things were fine, but I'd maybe think of moving in a while.

This is coming up, he said, and handed me the brochure. I thought it would be of some interest. You can go if you want.

He really does talk like that, really does use phrases like, I thought it would be of some interest. The effect is in the last two words, which are spoken evenly, without emphasis. He has also said, That must have been terribly frustrating, which I remember having something to do with traffic on the Kingston Bridge and me suspended in midair, listening to a radio announcer telling people to avoid the Kingston Bridge. Bits were falling off and it was in danger of collapse: another casualty of the 1960s.

Back to the editor, who has trouble with his adjectives: some interest, terribly frustrating.

The paper paid for my trip to Paris. I was supposed to be covering a conference at the Sorbonne where a number of Scots were speaking. I think the editor arranged for me to speak so that I wouldn't feel bad about the trip. Have a nice time, he said. I had the notes and references I needed and would have considered it a cheap holiday but for the weather.

I had been compiling a book about Glasgow, and while I was in Paris thought of researching the last of the town's Roman Catholic archbishops, James Beaton, adviser to Mary, Queen of Scots, and her ambassador to the court of France. Beaton left Glasgow in 1560, fleeing the Reformation. According to the *Registrum Episcopati Glasguensis* he took a golden image of Christ, the apostles in silver and all the church vestments. Portions of the Cross disappeared, along with the Virgin's hair and milk, part of her girdle, Christ's manger, St Mungo's scourge, parts of his body and bones, as well as various phials, boxes and two linen bags containing the hides, bones and hair of a number of saints.

He took the city records, which were in the Scots College until the French Revolution, were removed for safety and never recovered.

My research was completed within a day. The Scots College seemed used to questions about Beaton. I wrote the conference piece very quickly and phoned it over. It was mostly based on hand-outs. It's fine, they told me. I think we might cut the reference to your own speech. It'll depend on how much space we've got, but we ought to be able to use it in Saturday's paper.

I felt surprisingly free, was due to speak the following afternoon and leave at the weekend. I sat in a café on the rue St. Jacques, reading until the guy in the story made me restless. I crossed over to the Sorbonne and, sheltering from wind rather than rain, attended a lecture by Louis Bernard, whose name was familiar from a connection I could not recall.

19

Life in the City Between 1780 and 1800 turned out to be a series of anecdotes and quotations, interspersed with details that sounded exactly right. He introduced me to a world of washable leather condoms and encouraged my restlessness. I think it had to do with the asides, placed near the beginning to settle his audience, to make them smile and feel at home.

The finest women in the world are French, he said. This is a fact upon which all nations are agreed. And the finest French women are the mulattos imported from Senegal, or those who come to Marseilles from Dakar; which is surely what the colonel meant when he said service in the *Légion Etrangère* carries its own rewards.

When the lecture finished, I walked up one side of rue St. Jacques and down the other; a dreich prospect. Paris, like New York or Venice, is a city of the mind. This real thing did not match up.

I tried to picture what was missing, what I expected or what was lost. This was nothing like the first time, when Les Halles and the Mouffetard seemed unchanged from when Hemingway lived at the top by the place de la Contrescarpe and rue du Cardinal Lemoine, in the hotel where Verlaine died. I thought of Degas and the horses in the Musée d'Orsay, a railway station converted into a triumph of bourgeois art administration.

They sabotaged the Jeu de Paume to create a new museum in the enormous *fin de siècle* Gare d'Orsay. It does to Impressionism what contemporary critics could not do, it emasculates the paintings, removes the vitality, degrades their dimensions. In this setting, these small rooms, spectators automatically reduce the pictures.

Most of the Impressionist pictures were painted when

the artists were poor, though many subsequently became rich. These paintings not only revolutionised the way we see light and colour, they revolutionised subject matter, removed art from the patronage of church and privilege and democratised their subjects. Not that you would learn that in the Musée d'Orsay. The impact has been cosmeticised by placing forceful pieces alongside works with which they have no sympathy, the big Salon paintings the Impressionists despised. There is no sense of what carried us into the twentieth century. Out of context most art becomes meaningless, and no one knows that better than gallery administrators.

These were more or less the notes I made for a piece I thought of writing, a piece about the gallery. I phoned the paper and they said, Maybe. Get back to us. Have another look to firm it up.

I went back and found the white bedroom furniture, the hard, narrow bed Charles Rennie Mackintosh designed for Househill. This was a seventeenth-century mansion Glasgow Corporation bought in the 1930s, intending to use the house and policies in the Pollok housing scheme. Hous'll was abandoned during the war, though the land was used for council-house development. The mansion was vandalised, set on fire and eventually demolished. Contents were scattered. Mackintosh – *L'exemple de l'Angleterre* – is sequenced between Vienna and Frank Lloyd Wright.

I told the paper about the Mackintosh stuff. Okay, they said, do the piece.

I wondered what the artists would have made of their work being exhibited in a disused railway station. Some Degas dancers are in with the Monet poppyfield and

Van Gogh's *Eglise d'Auvers*. It was like going to a place where I spent my adolescence. There is a room for Degas pastels and another for Lautrec.

Degas paints tension, as though the horses, bathers and dancers were preparing for a performance. His work is preface to most contemporary photography. I thought of the psychological overlays, the way he positions people, their faces, looks and glances.

I heard the Bernard lecture with Degas' images in mind, while thinking about Mackintosh and the politics of art, while wondering what to write in the piece no one wanted.

I wandered along the rue St. Jacques turning somewhere around the Petit Point to look in the bookshops, then sit by the deserted fountain, beneath St Michael killing the dragon. Paris was the same as ever, except for plausible Front National posters and the new graffiti.

LE PEN = FILS DU PUTA

FN SALOPES

FN = 卐

Fictional coincidences have become such a part of our imagination that we undervalue or ignore the force of coincidence in our everyday lives, infusing it with mystical significance.

I passed a café. Bernard was smoking, staring onto the street while his wife chatted with a couple of students. It was the hair I recognised, fine, like baby hair, and pure white with a cow's lick at the front, the hair and the circular tortoiseshell glasses.

He was in the Café de Cluny, on the corner of boulevard St. Germain and the rue Dante, the first in a warren of foreign restaurants and *le selfs*, open counters, burger and kebab bars, Tunisian, Greek, Russian, Chinese, Thai and Moroccan restaurants between boulevard St. Germain and the quais de Montebello and St. Michel, a lively place in the evening, especially around St. Séverin, in the area known as Little Athens.

The coffee was finished. He was smoking, with three stubs in the ashtray, when I sat opposite, near the window. He was building bridges with the sugar cubes. The waiter brought my coffee and the bill for a *crème chocolat*.

Paris.

This close Bernard looked frail, as though he had been fortified and tidied for the lecture. His skin was pallid. It lacked brightness. He seemed restless, even anxious, as he stubbed his cigarette into the ashtray, brushing aside the other remains.

I tried to catch his eye, but eventually had to talk.

I enjoyed the lecture.

He looked across, as though he had been expecting me to say something, disappointed I was so obvious. He shrugged, smiled and nodded, shook another cigarette from the packet, lit it and immediately snapped ash into the tray. His wife looked relieved. I could entertain her husband.

Anglais?

Ecossais.

He smiled through the new cigarette. Not the same thing at all, he said in English. He was clearly trapped.

I told him I was interested in his Casanova references. He smiled and moved a cube of sugar support from one bridge to another. I said I had become interested in

23

Casanova while working on a St Valentine's Day piece for the paper.

And why are you still interested?

Because he's bigger than me. He's almost Shakespearean. Bernard smiled. I'm interested in the mythology that surrounds both him and his reputation. It's the one name everyone thinks they know. Say you are working on something about Casanova and people will ask how the research is going.

No wonder your work has come to nothing, he said, smiling as an afterthought. I do not think you are a writer. Your material has taken control of you. If you were a writer you would have taken control of the material. You must learn to work within your limitations. Do not over-reach yourself. Remember Icarus.

He stubbed his cigarette. His wife had finished talking. The students respectfully left. The professor stood up.

You were talking about Casanova? she asked, hoisting the overcoat onto his shoulders.

Did he tell you about the papers? she asked when he was in the lavatory. I was waiting for my change.

She tutted and shook her head. I'm not surprised, she said. He tells no one anything. He is the professor, which means he either reads what students have written or listens to what they say; in either case he delivers pronouncements.

I left my change in the brown plastic tray, pocketed the bill and we moved towards the street. The wind was noisy as the traffic. She pulled her scarf together and looked up to confirm it was not yet raining.

For forty years or more he has been collecting references to Casanova, she said, documents where he is mentioned, anything on paper which has something to do with him. He even has a laundry list and promissory notes in four languages. It is, of course, uncatalogued like everything else.

What does he intend to do with them?

I do not know. Are you interested in what was happening in Europe then?

In a way. Europe was in a revolutionary mood, and Scotland was just as revolutionary as elsewhere, but we had recently undergone a huge change, Union with England, which meant we could turn our minds to matters that were revolutionary in areas other than politics; I mean the Scottish Enlightenment.

Her husband came out of the restaurant and walked past us, towards the pavement, as though we weren't there.

In that case Casanova will be no use whatsoever, she said. He hated all that. He was a traditionalist.

I'd still like to see what's there.

We have had people in and out of the house like workmen, all to organise his material. One week after they've gone, and it's back to what it was; all he ever does is complain that his papers have been scattered. It's worse now. He has been very ill. The thought of lecturing has kept him going until today. Now he is tired. He should sleep.

She wrote a telephone number on the back of my torn bill. Phone tomorrow. There's nothing at the conference.

I'm speaking.

Then phone when you have finished.

The professor had hailed a taxi on boulevard St. Germain. A grey Citroën stopped. As his wife ran towards the car, the professor opened the door.

When Irene died I grieved for myself, having imagined I would die before her.

Months later, I thought of myself as a lamplighter out on the moor, putting light in a window no one could see.

There were times I thought I'd collapse in the street. There was neither preamble nor warning; no wind to stir the leaves before a storm. It is thin as cooking smoke. I would be shopping, walking, doing what a normal citizen does on the street, when the hand would grip me.

I was in the midst of life. The only way to cope was to create myself and my surroundings. This is a street. There are buildings along the edge of this street, traffic in the middle and people on the pavements. This is a table. There is bread and wine on the table. There is salt and an empty plate.

Then I said, It's hidden, filled with love and terror, like a children's game. It is gentle and sleekit, hides in closed rooms and cupboards, lies in drawers and envelopes ready to pounce. It is patient and persistent. Just when you think it's gone, back it comes, like midnight.

It tightens its grip, then releases, knowing it can wait for you to wonder, to look in the places where it might be lurking when you feel strong; but it knows you are never strong enough.

I have found it in places I could never have imagined. It threw itself at me in the men's lavatory of a none too fashionable restaurant. Driving my car, reading the newspaper, eating, sleeping, drinking. I have moved house and stay away from certain districts. I may move city, could conceivably leave the country, find a place I've never been; a cottage on the Sligo coast sounds fine.

I avoid conversations with strangers; ever since a woman asked me to pass the milk while I was doing the crossword. An ordinary request. Yet the combination of me doing the crossword and that woman's request caused a tremor, like writing for an hour or a day without a pen in your hand, like finding that the meaning of Christ's parable to the rich is that they should condescend to the poor because it's all they expect.

This morning I heard her voice, clear and very distinct.

You know the way she delivered her question, complaint and judgement simultaneously? Where were you last night? What were you doing? I think it's horrible of you, I really do, and all before you've opened your mouth.

It happened this morning. I was looking for something I must have lost in the move, a sale catalogue for dabbed ware by Seaton Pottery of Aberdeen and some Cumnock jugs with the prices marked in the margin. I wanted to compare their quality and cost with a sale last week. I looked through the desk drawer where that stuff was kept. Underneath the wallpaper she used as lining I found a small bundle of letters.

Pathetic, really. Four letters, all from the same pad of Basildon Bond blue paper, written in pale blue ink, sent from Hamburg more than twenty years ago. It was in the days when newspapers had industrial instead of business correspondents, when your mother was working for a firm of architects.

They were pitching for a building, maybe a complex, let's say a shopping centre in the middle of Hamburg. They employed your mother as translator. She did their letters, made the phone calls, and when they went to Germany, she went with them. Four trips in all, a week at a time; going to the same place, seeing the same people. She sent me one letter a week while she was gone.

The first was eight pages of chatty news, who she had seen, where she had gone, down the Rhine by water taxi and so on. I am writing this at two in the morning and I miss you, darling, she said. I wish you were here in bed with me now. I need a cuddle. I am lonely and feel continually out of my depth in this busy place. At the end she wrote, Kiss my darlings night night from me.

The middle letters were five and four pages respectively. Things are getting better. I am tired at night, she said. So much socialising with the clients and such intensity during the day. It all depends on me. If I get it wrong, they could lose the contract. They might not know it, but I'll know it.

The last letter is written on two sides of a single sheet. No address. Thursday, it says at the top. She enclosed a photograph. Having a lovely time, she said. All well. Miss you and wish you were here.

The photograph is of a group of five; the sixth, a man, took the picture. Three women and two men in an almost straight line, the women more or less in front. A man has his hand round your mother's waist. You'd barely notice it; he could be drawing her into the edge of the picture, making sure she's in the shot.

I know your mother. The photograph is a message.

She sent it to tell me, This is my lover. I am sleeping with this man.

His name was Dieter. I know because the firm lost the contract. Later that year we went to a reception. The managing director was back from Hamburg. A group of us were standing, drinks in hand. The managing director kissed Irene on the cheek. Guess who I saw in Hamburg and he was asking very kindly for you? I said that if we got the job you'd be part of the team, which seemed to be some kind of incentive.

Irene smiled. Very kind of you, Charles. I don't think you've met my husband.

Oh, said Charles.

And how is Dieter? said Irene, knowing it was the only thing to do. I excused myself and left them to it, wandered round looking at things.

She caught up with me. You all right? she asked.

Fine.

You sure?

Absolutely.

And that was it. She had sent the photograph to say, This man is my lover, because she felt guilty and could not tell me. Why did she stay? You lot, rather than me, I'm afraid.

I don't know how it happened and it's hardly important, not now, if ever. But I know it happened and am telling you because I have to tell you the most shameful thing I ever did. I am afraid of myself; when I think of this I feel humiliated.

Your mother was no more capable of having a wee fling with Dieter or anyone else than of having an abortion. She loved him. I am sure of it. I imagine she told him they could have a little time together and that was it. He was certainly more attractive than me, obviously fun to be with; he would have made her laugh. But she was a married Edinburgh lady with responsibilities and she would never leave her children, nor could she put them, or herself come to think of it, through a messy divorce, and if you don't believe it would have been messy, think what your grandma would say, far less what she would do. She and Dieter had a tearful farewell and she came back to face her responsibilities. I knew that then and am certain of it now.

I think I realised it driving home.

You're very quiet, she said. Are you sure you're all right?

If I had said anything she would have told me, and then it would have been up to me, my decision. By saying nothing, I kept her. Had I said anything she would have been forced to leave; was probably waiting to leave, I'm sure, and would have taken you with her, for I am also certain Dieter would be waiting. She would have made sure of that long before she left her bedroom door unlocked, or whatever happened.

I'm just tired, I said. It's been a busy week. I could have done without going to the party. This was in the days when I was still at the university as well as doing the television stuff.

She sighed.

The moment passed and never returned. The sun set. A three-masted ship entered the harbour; golden and rose, it sailed in silence. The prow was gleaming, everything was light. Three buttons on the front of her blouse shone in the headlights of oncoming cars.

My shame?

She was, I guess, in her early twenties. I had passed her and others like her every night, driving up St Vincent Street from the office, heading for the motorway and the red sandstone villa on the Fenwick Road, Giffnock, up the hill from Eastwoodmains Toll, the house we should never have bought, on a busy road. Irene was terrified while you were young, which is why you were confined to your own and other people's back gardens.

She devoted herself to family life with the emotional fervour of someone intent on making amends. She and I were distant. The only way I could let her know was to detach myself emotionally. I figured four or five weeks where I kept myself to myself would be about right. She would not have to comment. More than five weeks and she would have to say something. I was pleasant, happy and attentive, a man with a mission. It all came to an end when I was late home. Are you all right? she asked.

Fine.

I was worried sick. Where have you been?

Sorry, I meant to phone, I said, and told a little of what had happened. I brushed my teeth and went to bed. She touched my chest.

My shame smelled of drink when she got in the car. Right, darling, she said. We're going straight on here.

Where are you taking me?

Someplace quiet. Nice and safe. What's your name again? No, straight on. Keep going till I tell you to stop.

The first place was one of the lanes near St George's Cross, an office car park with security lights. Then we went to a hotel car park.

She took the money I gave her and put it in her shoe. That's twenty pounds, she said.

What for?

Whatever you want. She turned away from me, staring out the window. Twenty, dear. Twenty pounds. And don't fuck about or I'll smash your windscreen. Now, are we doing business or not?

I did not drive home immediately, but went eastwards on the motorway, driving to rid myself of nerves and the memory of humiliation, to feel clean; turning to a place I barely knew existed. It is obvious, behind the gas station to the left on the motorway on the way to Edinburgh, but it was a grimmer, darker place than I had known.

Buildings were crumbling, waiting for demolition. Rats ran in front of the car as I turned. Bonfires were lit in the middle of the road and on the edges of the vacant ground. Children threw stones. Dogs barked as they chased the car and I knew I was lost.

Turning took me further into the maze. I was in a long street where broken glass was reflected in the orange sodium light from the motorway. Shapes and figures turned from around the fire as I passed, their faces suddenly caught in the flames, sparking on the bottles some held in their hands. A few houses were inhabited and figures stretched from the windows to watch my progression.

I had to stop. There was no way I could have taken the car through the bricks and rubble and broken glass, through the rusted corrugated sheets, slabs of timber and stone. I tried to turn. Straddled across the middle of the road, a group approached.

Just pull in, he said.

There were maybe six or seven men, with some dogs and three or four children. They had been standing round the fire, obviously watching, awaiting my arrival, knowing I'd get there sooner or later. The dogs barked and snarled by the door before the rest of the men came down. They stood, silent, staring at me and the car, two already smoking, one rolling a cigarette.

I must have taken a wrong turning.

Happens.

Could you tell me the way out?

Out where?

Back to the motorway.

The motorway's back the way you came.

I could not see their faces, only the children and dogs were visible.

Hey.

Nor could I see where the voice came from.

Tommy. Lea that man alane. He's here tae see me; i'n't ye, mister?

The spokesman sniggered: You here tae see Mary?

Right, ya fucken bunch o idleonians, beat it tae fuck oot o here. Come on, mister. They'll no bother ye.

He's here tae see big Mary, said a child, who pulled his trousers down and wiggled his genitals in my direction, thrusting his hips back and forward. The men laughed and went back to the fire. Mary shook her head: He's a cheeky wee cunt, that wean, she said, and laughed.

Mary's was a shebeen. I don't know what I drank, a syrupy, sweet kind of wine that made me retch. I drank it with lemonade, then on its own.

There were two other women around Mary's age, difficult now to describe them properly, dressed in dark clothes and aprons, their hair short and stubby. They drank from a cup and occasionally sang.

Two girls flashed their eyes when I entered, put their hands to their mouths and giggled. On you go, said Mary about two hours later. Take your pick. You can have the two if you like.

It was a sour bed covered in coats and blankets. No light bulb in the socket nor linoleum on the floor. My bare feet stuck to the floorboards. The street light came through the curtains, tied together with a safety pin.

They undressed me and laid me naked across the bed. I saw the smaller of the girls leave the room with my clothes, while the other said, Here. Come on now. Here you are. She pushed a small breast towards me and raised her skirt. The second girl came back and I heard the skreich of laughter. Come on, she said; then they were gone.

I think it was Mary, but it could have been someone else. They've gone for something for your own protection, she said. Do you know what I mean? You don't want to catch anything. They'll be back. Here now. Here. Take this.

I came to on the open ground, dressed and penniless, shivering in trousers, shirt and shoes. The car had gone, fires were out and the streets deserted. Light was flickering, as the sun rose grey and golden over Edinburgh. A police car found me. They sniggered as they took details of the story. If I was you, I'd stay in Giffnock, the young one said.

This was all so long ago, before cheque guarantee cards and cash dispensers, in the days of the unpaid fare

34

card. I got home by bus, firstly from the police station to George Square and then to Giffnock. Folk were going to work. They looked at me and smiled.

I walked home. The back door was open. Irene came downstairs. Are you all right? she asked.

Fine.

I was worried sick. Where have you been?

Sorry, I meant to phone, I said, and told her I'd been robbed.

Did they take the house keys?

Everything.

Where's the car?

It was found in Manchester four days later, burned and abandoned. We changed the locks and never mentioned what had happened. I told her I'd given two men a lift. I'm not sure she believed me, but knew she could not ask.

We assembled and observed our small decorums. We settled.

Looking back it is a room. The Fenwick Road sitting room haunts me. I will carry that room for the rest of my life. Yet I closed the door so easily.

In the mornings it was empty, even at weekends. The door was always open, but the room was never used. The cat slept there till the children came home from school.

How many times have I tripped over schoolbags and shoes, wellington boots and raincoats, dumped on the tiled floor behind the storm doors. And who moved that pile of stuff from around the table in the long lobby, the telephone directories and address books, the gloves and scarves?

Run from the front door through to the kitchen, take a drink of juice from the fridge, make a sandwich, just bread and jam, later a cheese and ham toastie, then, with a handful of biscuits, go through to the sitting room, move the cat from the sofa and pile in front of the television until forcibly moved.

And later when everyone's in bed, when I'd come back from the office, having left for work before you lot came home, I would always find Irene in the downstairs sitting room. I'd say, Hello. She'd turn and smile.

I'd move to the kitchen, refuse the offer of food, pour a drink or make some tea while she told me how you got on at school, what would need to be done next day, who she'd seen and what she'd heard.

Then she'd take the next day's paper I'd brought, kiss my cheek and tell me she was off to bed. I'd go into the downstairs sitting room, wait till I heard the lavatory flush, go upstairs, brush my teeth and in dressing gown and pyjama bottom go into the bedroom, to my side of the bed with the pile of books and soft pillows.

Irene liked biographies and travel books. I liked political biographies, which I read for work, but usually read thrillers. She put the light out and I'd read on for a while, until she'd turn.

This is the sort of thing your mother liked, taken from the work of an Edinburgh lady such as herself. It is from what I presume to be a series of notes made by Margaret Montgomery during a conversation with Wilhelm Roth, then thought to be aged about seventy, and believed to have been a servant at Dux when Casanova was librarian. Irene liked women like Miss Montgomery, matter of fact, punctual and perfunctory women. Miss Montgomery brooks no nonsense. She seems to have intended these notes to be the basis of a travel book which, as far as I know, was never written. Miss Montgomery appears to have returned to Edinburgh in 1855 or 1856 and married shortly afterwards.

CONVERSATIONS AMONG THE BOOKS

7 May, 1855

Back in Dresden, and dizzy from the last two days. We decided to travel to Prague, braving the coach again and going by way of Teplice and Dux. Teplice was well known to us, and well remembered; was this not where we lost a wheel travelling from Leipzig at the invitation of a member of the de Ligne family whom we had met in that charming city, someone who had not only invited us to call upon him at Teplice, but had told us about the castles and their association with the notorious Casanova?

Time was of the essence. Our previous visit to Teplice had been in the rain, hence the muddy roads and broken wheel, the interminable wait in a draughty inn, the tired horses and appalling coachman who took us back to Dresden rather than on to Prague, all of which contrived to make us doubly anxious to see Prague on this journey, ever mindful as we were of also wanting to visit Linz, Vienna, Bratislava and Budapest, before deciding where else our wanderlust should take us.

The weather being fresh and springlike, we decided a coaching jaunt would do us good; and since we were almost passing the door of Dux Castle and had received no reply to our letter to the Prince de Ligne at Teplice, we decided to visit the home of the Count Waldstein and locate the grave of his ancestor's librarian.

The trip to the castle at Dux was very worthwhile. It is a pretty place, both front and back; one could hardly detect its lamentable past from the outward appearance. I believe we have its kind in Scotland, though not so romantic and imposing as this. Scottish castles are more obviously fortresses; this is a palatial residence, more reminiscent of Holyrood House than the great edifice of Edinburgh Castle.

In truth, it reminded me of an English castle. There is a lake and a stream, more of a river, though I cannot say what the river is named. There are many woods and meadows, while the chateau and the town of Dux itself are surrounded by countryside which I should say gave excellent sport. There was evidence of some coal and iron-ore minings to blot the landscape, so who knows but the place may well become increased.

The chateau is in the centre of the town and opens onto the market place. The frontage is very imposing, though not so imposing as the Prince de Ligne's castle at Teplice. From the market square there are huge figures atop the massive stone gateposts which stand on either side of the castle path. The figure to the left seems to be digging while the figure on the right clubs an animal to death. We felt such a public display of barbarism was quite unnecessary, irrespective of the Classical allusions which could no doubt be mustered in their defence.

I had to remind myself I had travelled to discover the remains of the melancholy Casanova. He is buried in

St Barbara churchyard, outside Dux and beside the lake. A footpath through the churchyard takes travellers from the lake to the village. His grave has no headstone, though many do. There is a cast-iron crucifix over Casanova's grave. Iron railings used to surround it. The guide from the chateau told us the railings had been removed because they caught the skirts of the girls as they passed.

The present Count Waldstein was not at home. We were fortunate to find a servant who could not only speak French, but was also familiar with the history of his surroundings. How could he be otherwise when these surroundings contained someone who had not only seen and conversed with the lecher whose account of his life has scandalised proper society, but who could remember these events with astounding clarity? Meeting Wilhelm Roth was like meeting a Jacobite; in truth, it was to my mind more reminiscent of the time one of Robert Burns's children was pointed out to me on an Edinburgh street. He looked the very presence of his father.

This aged Bohemian was brought into the great Dux library, where Casanova worked and where he himself had witnessed the events he was about to relate. He was in no way overawed by his grand surroundings, indeed, he seemed more at ease there than I, who was anxious to inquire upon the great volumes, to touch a part of history. He was like an apple which had fallen from the tree, had lain in the grass for a winter and was discovered by children playing in the spring. He did not know his age, but he must be very old and must have been here all his life. Casanova died in the early summer of 1798.

Roth's head was almost hairless, save for a froth of white mane which covered the sides and back of his head and gathered beneath his ears in two great muttonchops, like Grandpapa's dundrearies. His face was tanned and wrinkled. His eyes were blue and merry, especially when he talked of times past, and though his gums were toothless his face was full.

He refused refreshment and sat with his hands clasped together on the desk, was at all times thoughtful and respectful, nodding and smiling towards me as my questions were translated, as though to signify comprehension and approval.

He well remembered Casanova, because, he said, of what happened while he was here and because of what happened after his death, and though these events were significant and important, and though his name was often heard, Casanova was remembered mainly for himself, because of his looks and what he was like.

'I believe he was a lonely man,' said the servant Roth. 'You will know that much without my saying. It is true his years here were far from happy, but that is not why I believe him lonely. I believe he was always lonely. He seemed to be melancholic. He had the air of a man who had learned to keep his own company, who had come to enjoy his own company because it was forced upon him. Years ago, we had a coachman at the stables who reminded me of him for that very reason. He had spent hours riding great distances. It gave him a melancholic air.'

This I thought was especially profound from one

untutored and unskilled in the greater arts. I sat
opposite this man looking at his face, noticing now and
then as he spoke how the stubble on his face was
uneven around the chin and upper lip; that he
obviously had a cheap and probably rusted razor, one
that had been in the family since his grandfather's or
even his great-grandfather's time and had been
handed down from one man to the other, was shared
and passed round like a communion cup; and that he
had used it specially and probably recently in honour of
seeing me. He had used it too quickly, it was hurried
and his stubble remained in patches. The places where
his razor had passed over once or perhaps twice were not
so smooth as the other places, the places which had
been well shaved; and he had forgotten how to do this.
This old man had forgotten how to shave, not because
he had not shaved regularly – such a skill once learned
is never forgotten – but because he was used to taking a
certain time with his toiletries and of proceeding in
a certain order. He washed his face with warm water,
soaped his face and stropped the razor. He shaved and
then repeated his processes, dried his face and ran his
hand across it, soaped his face once more, the upper lip,
chin and below the chin, then he stropped his razor
and, for the last time, he shaved; and this was why his
face was smooth, why his skin was brown, this was the
way he had shaved every morning for most of his life
and had plenty of time to do it today. He had simply
forgotten. He had run his hand around the chin and
had forgotten to strop the razor, forgotten to lather
and shave his face for a third and final time. The soap

marks that lingered on the lobe of his left ear were all the proof I needed.

'I find it hard to describe him now,' he said of Casanova. 'I have not thought of him for years. There was an air about him. He was very grand. He had not adjusted to the times. He bowed low and with a great flourish when he entered a room, in the old manner, and we found his dancing very funny. Of course, he disdained the likes of me and even when he was desperately in need of my help – his last weeks and maybe months were terrible – he did not like accepting aid. He could barely bring himself to speak to us. He may have been a leech on the flesh of society, but they are leeches on the likes of us, and he considered himself far superior to any servant. That was the cause of the trouble. He thought he was a guest, a scholar. We treated him like a servant. I don't regret it now. It is horrible to treat an old man so and he was seeing things at the end. He was deluded. He told me he saw a dancing girl. He told my sister also. He said she was young and beautiful and she danced away from him. He told me that when I mocked him. I told him Napoleon had taken Venice and was coming for him. He considered Napoleon an upstart. A terror, he said.'

This speech was too familiar. He had made it many times before. It may be true or it may be lies. It may never have been true nor held any semblance of truth at any time, but he had told it so often, whenever anyone asked about Casanova, he did not have to think, had nothing to remember, he simply had to repeat the formula. He could sit anywhere, even in this hated and detested part of the building, he could sit in the library with his hands together across the table, in his boots and breeches, sit in a library, the great Library of Dux, and speak without thinking.

'Were you with him when he died?' I asked, for I wanted to know how Casanova came to be buried in an individual grave. In Vienna, having walked for more than an hour to the St Marx Cemetery, which is well beyond the city limits, on a lovely summer evening we were shown the part of the grounds where Mozart was buried, though obviously the exact spot had been forgotten, and having read von Nissen's account of the great man's life, I concluded that if he was not accorded an individual grave, why was Casanova, a far lesser personage who had died in a far remoter part of the country seven years later, why was he given a marked and public interment. I know all about Emperor Joseph II's reforms for the dead, but surely they extended to Dux.

He looked out the window and sighed. Questions about Casanova's death were new. Here he would have to think. This was not the usual questions about girls, Faulkircher and Wiederholt, known as Viderol; this was not about the kindness of the Duke to others less fortunate than himself, about the French Revolution and Marie Antoinette. This was not about Prague. Did Casanova ever mention them? I could hardly have cared less.

'I was not with him when he died. He died in his room. I think there were gentlemen, and a priest, of course; I think there was a priest. His brother-in-law, another Italian, was there. I do not think I ever knew his name. He left with some papers. I know that

43

because I knew the girl who cleared the room. She told us he took some papers and the rest were put in boxes in the Library. They may still be here for all I know. I only went to the Library to take his food and when he died I never went near the place again. I have no use for books. Horses I have use for, horses, not books.

'I have no schooling. I came to the chateau when I was old enough to work. I do not know when I was born or where. It was on the estate, I think. I must have been born on the estate. We worked here, all of us. My mother and father worked in the stables, my mother supplied the horses' feed and my father was a groom.

'We were inside the castle at first. Children are good for fetching and carrying. It is like a game to children, not like work at all. I started in the kitchens, which meant I was lucky. I was well fed; or at least I was fed regularly. Then I was in the garden for a while. I hated that work in winter, almost as bad as a woodsman. Thanks be to God, I never was a woodsman. I was a gardener and now I am a groom, as my father was a groom.

'My sisters came to work here. They could tell you of Signor Casanova. They knew him better than I.'

I wondered if his grave was robbed. There is a terrifying story of poor Josef Haydn's skull being taken from his tomb at Eisenstadt soon after his burial. Schiller's skull had gone. There was no point in lingering. I had been told the official story. I thanked the servant Wilhelm Roth, paid him and left.

TWO

Self under self, a pile of selves I stand

Summer Farm,
Norman MacCaig

I did not phone Mme. Bernard.

My talk was well received. Later in the downstairs *self*, six or seven students discussed what had been said.

They had an intensity, where everything is important and unimportant at the same time, a way of switching from Sonny Rollins to Utrillo, Mitterrand, the Métro, Magritte, *les flics* and Serge Gainsbourg. It was tough going. They soon tired of me.

I thought of going back to the hotel. I had finished the Mackintosh piece and phoned it over. We're waiting for some pictures, then we'll use it, the deputy editor told me. That's what they say when they have no intention of using the piece immediately, when it joins the queue of other stuff that's easily forgotten.

Going to the door, the girl by the drinks machine smiled as she put a Bali can in her bag. She'd been part of the earlier group.

On your own? I asked.

She smiled. I'm going to the *cimetière de Montmartre*, she said. Have you ever been there?

This was AnnA.

She asked if I had a *Paris Visite* card and when it expired. This is the only time I have gone from one Métro station to another, changing lines, negotiating tunnels, without a map. It was a liberating experience.

The cats in the *cimetière* looked rabid as we walked

among the dead, the shiny granite and sentimental plastic photographs, Zola by the entrance, darkened in the rain. We saw the Berlioz, Stendhal, Offenbach and Nijinsky monuments.

I love it here, she said.

Why do you come?

To read.

And do you read in the rain?

She giggled, blushed a little and looked at the path, skipping sideways to avoid a puddle.

Your English is very good.

My accent is not good.

It's not as bad as my French accent.

Again she giggled. Your French accent is *terrible*.

You mean terrible.

Yes. *Pardon*. I mean pardon.

Where did you learn to speak English?

At school. Is it at school or in school? I never know. I also stayed in England. For three months I had a school exchange to High Wycombe. Do you know it?

Never been there.

It's what I imagine as very English, you know, the shops, the pub and so on.

There was a delicacy about her movements; even walking she seemed fragile, in need of protection from more than the rain. She caught me staring, smiled quickly then averted her gaze, as though she had been caught doing what was forbidden.

And what about this place?

Here? This is my favourite place in all the world. Down the road is Pigalle and all that trash, but this is like an island.

48

The rain had stopped, but the air was moist. She pulled the collar of her raincoat up and around her head, then tightened her belt. Do you like Brahms?

I like him best in small doses.

What is doses?

I'm sorry. It's a colloquial expression.

Now I am very lost.

I'm sorry. Shall we start again? You asked if I liked Brahms and I should have answered, Yes. Now, why did you ask?

They are recording the piano quintet tonight at the Radio France studios on avenue President Kennedy. Would you like to go?

The musicians were casually dressed, giving the performance an incongruous visuality; I remember a red sweater, jeans and a blue shirt, a floral skirt, a corduroy jacket, suede waistcoat and a pair of brown boots. I hardly remember who was wearing what, or the sexes of the players. From the opening notes, mysterious, angry, becoming suddenly grand, I was wrapped in the music.

She said nothing until the steps of the Passy Métro, where the track passes wrought-iron balconies, then rattles across the Seine. The steps were dark. She had been crying.

When will you be free tomorrow? she asked.

Any time, really; though I'll certainly be free by evening. Will I phone you?

No. Meet me in the *cimetière*.

What time?

Six o'clock.

Where?

You choose.

Zola.

It might have been the moon or it could have been a shadow. The first time Irene and I slept together the room was locked in a pale, insipid light, but our shadows on the wall were sharp and strong.

She was a second-year student and I was her tutor; a disgraceful state of affairs, as popular then as now. I was attracted by the difference. My own background was poorly genteel, with Scottish qualities of hard work, thrift and hypocrisy. She was an Edinburgh girl away from home.

I noticed her in class, head down, taking notes, anxious to do well. She was pert in seminars, arguing the need for social change, suggesting we could vote for revolution.

What the fuck do you know about it? said Thomson, fresh from the beer bar, loud and belching. In those days he had a beard and was a leading light in the Socialist Society. He is now a Liberal Democrat MP.

I could tell she was shocked. A single word had floored her. For weeks she moved in and out of class like a shadow. Her moment came during a discussion on the Fabian Society.

Reformers, said Thomson. Tinkering with the edges, helping to make capitalism work. The whole thing needs to be swept into the dustbin of history.

Hardly an original phrase, to say nothing of the idea, said Irene.

I bow to your superior knowledge.

No need. As you have previously suggested, I might not necessarily know what's wrong with society nor how to change it, but I certainly know what's wrong with you. I don't think you get enough sex. In fact, I'd be surprised if you get any at all.

We saw each other twice a week for most of that term. We went to the pictures or the theatre on Wednesday night and she stayed most Saturdays, arriving with a small case at the back of four. I remember the football results on radio, followed by a programme of Scottish country dance music, while the chips were frying.

After tea we watched television, read, did a cross-word, played backgammon or Scrabble. Around ten o'clock Irene would have a bath, change into her night-dress and get into bed.

I bet your mother thinks you're having a wild time every weekend, I said. She didn't answer.

We cooked breakfast together on Sunday morning. The sandwiches were packed and we were on the hills by ten. We were back by six and I dropped her off at the halls of residence.

Thank you for a lovely weekend, she'd say before getting out the car. I'll see you tomorrow.

And so it went until one Saturday night when she said, We're going through to Edinburgh tomorrow. My mother said she'd like to meet you.

How does she know about me?

I told her.

Told her what?

Nothing. She asked if I had a boy friend and I said I think so. That's all there is to it. Look on the bright side: we can have a long lie.

I remember a soft and uncomfortable sofa in the

drawing room of the New Town flat where her mother lives.

We married a week after Irene's graduation. The black and white photographs don't tell much. I remember hiring a morning suit with a hole in the pocket and a cigarette burn on the left sleeve. The trousers were too tight. I remember floral patterns and pastel shades. The bride wore white.

During the 23rd Psalm a sudden bolt of sunlight illuminated the windows of the Memorial Chapel:

> *For thou art with me and thy rod*
> *And staff me comfort still.*

I had read somewhere the stained glass windows symbolised life as a spiritual quest. The sunlight and verse gave the ceremony an added significance. For long enough I thought the marriage had received some sort of blessing. We honeymooned in Paris.

When I visited her in hospital, she wanted to remember. What were we like? she asked.

When?

When we were younger.

You mean together?

Of course.

When we were married or when we first met?

The beginning, whenever that was. How did you recognise me?

You mean notice you; how did I notice you?

That's right.

You were very studious.

Everybody was studious.

No they weren't. And if they were they weren't as pretty as you.

Did you think I was pretty?

Oh yes.

You never told me.

Yes, I did.

I don't remember. When did you tell me?

The first night we slept together.

I didn't believe you.

You should have.

I thought you said that to all your students.

What do you mean?

Well. We thought you slept with a lot of girls.

Who's we?

The girls, other students. My friends.

Surely not?

We all thought you were very handsome. The least that could be said was that you were attractive, so we thought you could probably have any student you wanted.

I wasn't like that at all.

You were with me.

I wasn't.

So you were.

You mean, You were so.

That's what I said.

Sorry.

We sat in silence in the pale afternoon, her hand on the cover. She sometimes slept. Conversation tired her.

I have a photograph of Irene as a student. It is how I imagine her. She has long blonde hair, rather than the shortish greying hair you knew, her face is fresh, without make-up, and she does not wear glasses. You'd recognise her eyes and smile.

The photograph was taken on the drovers' road across the Rannoch Moor, now part of the West Highland Way, on the bit by Coire Bà, where James VI saw the white hind. She is leaning on Bà Bridge with the fringe of Clach Leathad on her shoulder. She is smiling a warm, lop-sided smile. She looks slightly louche, a bit careless, unconcerned.

I think the sun was in her eyes. Just after the photograph was taken she sighed and smiled properly into Black Mount, at the cloud and sun and the shafts of light that fell with spring rains, bringing yellow and white flowers as far as the eye could see; either that or the shining green of the heather and bracken, the froth of curled leaves and the wind that smelled of spring and pollen in the sun, light and rain.

She did not say much for the rest of the day, walking lightly in spite of the rainwear, looking round her, staring at the Buchaille, sighing every once in a while. Later in the King's House bar, when we swopped stories of routes and equipment, she was alone with a whisky by the window.

You okay?

Fine.

I don't think I'd known her long, maybe a month or two. I had, of course, seen her in class and that was all there was to it, until someone, I think a girl on a foreign-exchange thing, invited me to a party. It was near where I stayed and easier to go than devise an excuse.

I arrived as a drunk was leaving. It's the same old

54

fucken tragedy, he said, pissing on the stair. Take a wee drink yoursel? Aye?

I barely knew the others. No one expected me to come. I was the only member of staff. It was a first-year party. The men got drunk.

Irene was trapped by an earnest young man with a pipe and cravat. She was drinking lemonade. I caught a glisk of her over his shoulder. She held my gaze and smiled.

I figured on staying an hour, but got into a discussion about the Fred Quimby cartoons that always raised a cheer in the men's union beer bar; or that was where it started: by the time I noticed Irene we were wondering if Dylan's political statements in *The Hour That the Ship Comes In* had been sparked by Che Guevara, Father Camillo Torres, Martin Luther King or simply by the burgeoning political awareness of people across the world, rather than an individual or his action. And was it deliberate or had he unwittingly tapped into this awareness, giving it musical articulation?

Irene was having a lousy party. I saw her turn and knew she was going. We met on the stair. Are we walking in the same direction? I asked.

Along Kelvin Way and down Bank Street; late autumn, sharp and frosty.

We talked about the party and we talked about the course. Somewhere near the top of Gibson Street, she asked what I was doing at the weekend; walking on Sunday, from Wanlockhead more or less to Beattock, skirting Daer Reservoir, coming off the hill on the edge of Holmshaw, meeting the bus on the A74, near Egypt.

Do you go on your own?

Not at all. There's a club.

I'd love to go sometime.

Are you free on Sunday?

Which was more or less how we fell in with each other. The folk in the walking club thought we were a pair because we'd turned up together. As far as I know, the department never found out until we were married.

Her mother, your Grandmama, was first to say it. School then university, she said. And as soon as that's over, you're off to get married. I've done my best, kept you till you found a husband.

She seemed to be thinking aloud. When she looked at me, she smiled. It's always hard for a parent, especially the mother of an only daughter, she said. Irene barely knew her father. He died when she was twelve, she told me every time I visited.

Irene said, He left you well provided for.

More tea? asked my mother-in-law.

The only thing Irene told me about her schooldays happened in primary during a playground game, where girls make a circle and sing. Someone goes into the middle and dances around, eventually picking another girl to take her place in the centre. And so it goes until no one's left. Everybody picked their pal, she said. I was new and no one was going to pick me, so I just went into a wee dream. I stood there dreaming till I felt a touch on my arm. It was a school monitor. I was standing apart from everyone else. The circle had moved and I hadn't noticed because I'd been lost, away in my dream. I often wonder if my life would have been different if that hadn't happened, she said.

We were walking downhill, from the Glasgow Film

Theatre into Sauchiehall Street. It was a Thursday night, we had seen a French film in grainy black and white, having walked from Kelvinbridge to the cinema. Outside the McLellan Galleries she took my hand, pulled me to a halt and grabbed the lapels of my jacket. Folk stared as they passed, women turned their heads.

I was brought up in genteel deprivation, she said. We lived in a nice house, in a nice part of Edinburgh, but we never had any money and never went anywhere, not even to the free museums, because Mother was suspicious of such overtly intellectual activities. You might get ideas above your station. No pictures on a Saturday morning, or at any other time, no theatre except perhaps a pantomime at Christmas and no television. We had a car that sat there because we could hardly afford to run it. Ever had the pleasure of going for a Sunday run to Fife, of sitting starving on a beach because there wasn't enough bread to make up sandwiches and anyway there was a big pot of stew waiting to be eaten when we got home, so we mustn't ruin our appetites, stew that would have to do us another couple of days? And driving back worried in case we ran out of petrol. That wasn't once or twice, but every summer Sunday. Two miserable weeks' holiday during the Edinburgh Trades Fortnight, a cheap boarding house in Dirleton, Elie, Dunbar, that sort of place, a short drive away. The car was sold when Daddy died. Sitting in the dark to save electricity. If you were cold, then put on another jumper. I had a cold and hungry childhood in the service of a gentility I now resent. School was a series of rules: Don't chew in the street, Don't drop litter, Don't draw attention to yourself, Don't use slang. We were constantly reminded of what we could not do. Rules for life. These things stay with you. But everyone you knew was more or less the same. No socialising, very few friends because they lived far away. All these bland men with pink faces and their pale wives in flowery patterned frocks. Church socials; we had a lot of them. And amateur dramatics.

A lot of this sounds very familiar.

In Govan?

Yeah. We didn't stay there very long. We moved across the river to Partick.

She took my arm and we walked down Sauchiehall Street and up towards the Bath Street bus stop.

And was that better? she asked. Was it better in Partick?

I think so.

Why?

We lived at the top of the hill in Gardiner Street, on Partickhill Road, but my mother shopped in Partick, along Dumbarton Road. I think it killed her, lugging messages up that hill.

How was that better?

The house was bigger. I remember the rooms; well, two rooms were empty for a long time. They gradually filled with second-hand furniture. We had more space and we had a bath.

Did you miss Govan?

Yeah. I wanted to go back. We hardly knew our neighbours. We kept ourselves to ourselves; we listened to the wireless and read the *Glasgow Herald*. My father left for work in the yards as though he was going to the office. He walked down the hill and got the ferry across the river, all weathers. But he'd done well for himself. He had given his family a start in a nice bought house.

What about school? What school did you go to?

The local school, Hyndland Academy.

And your brother and sister?

Same. They were older so they went first.

We waited for the bus in silence, sat opposite each other on the Rexine benches along the window by the door, looking up and smiling every once in a while. We walked to the house in silence. Inside, she pulled me down from the back of the neck and kissed me with the house in darkness. We rolled across the floor, struggling against zips and buttons, laces and clips. We fumbled with each other and ourselves, scattering clothes along the lobby, not making it into the bedroom, frantic with wanting it to go on forever. I remember holding back as she arched her hips towards me, holding back as I stared at a clump of dust beneath the table, looking for something to interest me, saying the six, seven and eight times tables until it was useless. And as soon as it was over we were twisted and uncomfortable. Oh my God, my leg, she said; extricating each other slowly, gathering our clothes in silence, brushing our teeth now the sudden thing was done. We lay in the unlit room with the curtains opened. Sometime in the night, I told her about Tommy Aitchison, the first person I heard use the word Socialist.

Miss Fernie saw her duty to instil her belief in King, Country, God and Empire and the inextricable way all four were linked into every child in her classroom.

There are, even as we speak, she said, people who are

59

dying for freedom, dying so that we can walk these streets with our heads held high.

In Partick? said Tommy Aitchison.

We laughed.

Miss Fernie ignored us.

And there also are, even as we speak, those who were too cowardly to fight, those who would rather have better, braver, younger, more able bodies perish so that they can slink from the public house to the betting parlour, where they will squander their own and the substance of others.

That's definitely Partick, said Tommy Aitchison.

We laughed.

Miss Fernie waited till the laughter subsided.

I am especially thinking, she said, of someone whose son sees fit to mock those things other people hold dear. It is an honour to die for your country, in the service of God and what is right.

Tommy Aitchison walked out the classroom.

She screamed. Her face turned red, her mouth a black mass of noise with her eyes shut tight.

Do not leave this room. Stay, boy. Stay where you are. I command you. Stay.

The door slammed shut. The little brass handle bounced in the silence.

Another teacher finished the lesson. We did not see Tommy Aitchison for four days. His father visited the school. Andrew Cowan said he saw Miss Fernie run away when Mr Aitchison approached her in the street.

When Tommy Aitchison came back we were afraid in case Miss Fernie would wreak some terrible revenge.

He later died in Northern Ireland. I saw his picture in

the paper. He had married a girl from County Tyrone and went to live near Carrickmore. He looked the same as he did in school, a married man with four children. God knows what he's done, she said, his wife. Nothing. He's done nothing, nothing at all. Absolutely nothing. He was going to his work.

I looked at the photograph and remembered how I loved his silly face and the way he did not know how to be dishonest.

He sat in the class. Miss Fernie ignored him. They both knew what the other knew, but only they held the information. It was the Clydebank Blitz that did it: And how brave people who were going about their peaceable business found their way and in some cases their very life impeded by the bomb, she said. This was the last hour on Thursday afternoons. Local history, which for Miss Fernie meant the war.

Please, miss, said Tommy Aitchison.

She looked at him and the room went still.

Why do you think it happened?

What happened?

Why do you think Clydebank was bombed?

Don't be stupid.

I don't think it's stupid, he said, an eleven-year-old boy. My father says war is evil and those who profit by it are the most evil of all for they hold human life as worthless, only fit for filling their pockets. My father says the most precious thing we have is life.

Silence.

And that the best thing that we can do is to live it the best way we can. That we must stick to our principles, we must respect our women and look after our mates, that all we've got is each other. My dad is a Socialist and that's why he is also a conscientious objector who did not fight in the war. We have to show them dignity, he says. We have to be better.

Silence.

From somewhere in the building a piano played The Ash Grove, and a class sang. It was almost precisely the end of the verse when Miss Fernie spoke. You'll never amount to much, she said.

What makes you think that teaching me is such an achievement? said Tommy Aitchison.

We looked at our home readers till the bell rang at five to four. We got into lines, marched downstairs and into the playground. I walked behind Tommy Aitchison as he ran home with sandshoes on his feet and the wind in his face, running downhill.

This, whatever it is, has nothing to do with him; but I told your mother and I'm telling you because I'd like someone to know he existed.

I suppose this is something of a record. When I am dead, or have left the country, when I am finished, you will not have to do what you did with your mother, sift through the scraps of her life trying to find her in the ribbons she kept or the jewellery she wore. It is an attempt to say that you have a history, that this is a little of what happened before you, this is what I have done and what I am doing. I am your father and I love you more than I have been able to tell you, more than I ever thought possible to love.

I have always considered my life a private affair, the business of no one beyond those I love, and even they do not know everything. There are secrets I have tried to maintain, sometimes for my own reasons; more often, I believe, to protect those I love from hurt or shame. Now, and entirely for the reasons stated, I am trying to tell the truth. I would like my children to separate my truth from their truths, to take my side of the story into their consideration, or reject it in the light of evidence they already have or which will doubtless be revealed. They may be able to see their mother and me in a different light. I would be very upset if this turned out to be an exercise in self-justification. If it does I'll be the last to know.

Thinking what I might say, I went into the kitchen. The table holds a patterned cloth, a bowl of fruit, a white teacup with coffee dregs, a spoon and today's *Guardian*. There is a red lamp above the table. The light from the city reflected upwards and bounced from the ceiling into part of the room. I paused with my hand on the switch. Everything was ghostly, pale and lifeless, but I could see the kitchen. When I switched the light on, the table and its contents were illuminated brilliantly, the rest of the kitchen was dull, red and warm. Neither was the real kitchen or how the kitchen would look by daylight. Both were an illusion, an impression of the kitchen. Nothing shifted, nothing moved, a light above the table changed the appearance and my opinion. Both were correct.

I think this could be something similar.

It is very early in the morning, or late at night. It is dark and the end of September. The wind is shifting and the clocks will soon go back. Geese arrive and the nights are fair drawing in.

I am looking across the city, which I think I will leave.

Sodium lights shimmer in the cold. There is condensation on the window and a haze across the motorway. The night birds are out in darkness, police and ambulance sirens, taxi doors and heavy lorries make their mating calls.

What can I see?

Magic.

I am on a riverbank, staring into the water. I can tell it is dark and flowing because reflected clouds scud across the sky. The lights in the water are reflected stars illuminating small stones and reeds. Minnows scurry in the darkness. Parts seem brighter, but they only make the darkness more intense, the stone squares and circles, birds and dying leaves.

What would I give to feel another hand.

Today I saw a tramp with a blanket round his shoulders. He had been sleeping on a bench. A woman with wrinkled, fallen stockings and dirty legs scuffled towards him with a hot drink in each hand, two polystyrene cups, her grey hair streaked and her face covered in smudges.

He had torn shoes, wrinkled hands and face. He carefully combed his hair as she approached. She put his white and steaming cup on the bench, sat down, took a sip from her own cup and smiled.

A young man and a girl with a dog on a string, torn jeans and leather jackets, coloured hair and studs in their faces, a couple who had been selling the *Big Issue*, stopped beside the older pair, exchanged glances and gave the woman a couple of £1 coins. As she looked up to smile at them she clenched her fist round the money and raised her hand to her face to shelter her eyes from the sun.

This is a new pen. The old one had ink but refused to write, leaving an imprint on the paper. I find it strange and inexplicable how I attach myself to writing implements. I will use one pen until it is done.

When my mother died, I did not know what to do with the detritus she gathered, a life's accumulation. Tom was in Carnoustie, Jean in America.

Sell it, said Tom.

But I could not.

Burn it, destroy it, give it away, said Jean. What are you calling me for, asking stupid questions like that, wasting your money? Do what you like. I don't care.

I wanted to talk with my brother and sister about the violence of objects, how owning is an obligation we cannot meet. I cannot discard something my mother loved for fear I discard part of her, the love she had for the object. No matter how tacky or cheap, no matter how trivial, I cannot discard something my mother loved, myself included.

It is extraordinary how we are able to do this. Would someone from another century recognise the Bic or the impression of a dead Bic on a sheet of squared paper the way I remember this document? Mostly I remember the ink, which changed from darkest black to almost brown. I remember how the handwriting changed, in places making it difficult to decipher. I have tried, but still know nothing. This is a document from an unknown source. I think it could be part of an investigation into masonic activities held for the Duke Karl Theodore, Elector Palatine at Mannheim. I think that because it is written on a note by one of Bernard's researchers. Having no other explanation, I am forced to agree.

AnnA liked it.

A CLEAN, WELL-LIGHTED PLACE

Heidelberg
September, 18–?

The vipers are with us still. They have penetrated every area of public life. We have seen the results of their plotting in France, where they rose from the sewers of Paris to spread their pernicious influence across the continent, moving like a plague from country to country, carried by travellers and spread by discontent.

The American illness remains. Bonaparte and his followers have carried it across Europe and now we hear it survives in secret. I ask Your Excellency to forgive me. Your Excellency is, I am sure, aware of these facts. I feel I must elaborate to give a true account, not only of my recent activities, but why I embarked on these activities and how I have reached my conclusion that we who love our liberty and freedom, we who value our lives and who serve a nobler cause, must be ever vigilant. I know Your Excellency will understand my concern and forgive my attempts to absorb his time.

We must remove the Lodges and those who frequent them. They and their kind, their influence and teachings should be eradicated from society. There is only one way to deal with those who wish to destroy our civilised society. Should we offer them civilisation in return? Should we meet their barbarism with a reasoned response? Look at what such a policy did to previous empires, which some may say were greater than ours. We have one opportunity to make our nation pure, to rid ourselves of this scourge, this menace, this blight. We should not be seen wanting. Others will condemn us if we do not accept the challenge. They will have to live with our mistakes.

It is my duty to acquaint Your Excellency of my findings. They concern the Venetian Jew Casanova, who is mercifully dead and who styled himself de Seingalt while alive. Your Excellency may not be aware this man belonged to the Grand Lodge Ecossais, that he was a gambler and therefore utterly unscrupulous about money which did not belong to him. To satisfy his cravings for the tables he conducted public lotteries. He is also said to have known many women and a combination of this and his other activities is further said to have been the chief cause of his wanderings. I know he visited Your Excellency's court and is known to have been acquainted with the functions of the court as well as many of its attendants. I fear a further discourse which went into greater detail would be more suitable for His Excellency's ears than his eyes and I will do my best to acquaint Your Excellency of my intelligence when I return, which I hope will be with God's speed, and when I do return I hope the Almighty will have seen fit to bless Your Excellency's every endeavour.

Knowing my sources to be strong and reliable and

trusting them implicitly, I undertook to discover further, given my limited time and experience. The details I give must be scant, for reasons similar to those already stated, but that should not render them any less valid. Neither will it, I am sure, decrease their relevance.

In Leipzig I accompanied a corpse to the place called the Cemetery of the Nameless, where the poor are buried in pits of lime or where remains are burned in times of plague. I had recently arrived, had no lodgings and desired little other than a clean bed and a wholesome meal. I had come to pay my respects to the one who taught me, a man whose sorcery and trickery would have graced any theatre, whose chief legacy was my understanding that truth and eternity are without end and that service in one brings reward in the other. The reduced circumstances of age forced his end.

I arrived too late to thank my old master for his many kindnesses. He passed from this world to the next before I could offer my blessings and my thanks. I was relieved to learn he died in God's grace, the last rites having been administered by a priest whose nature is the soul of discretion and who I know accompanied my friend on many errands in the service of truth and the maintenance of justice.

I arrived after a five-day journey, in need of rest and sustenance, sore from the wooden seats, since this is how I am forced to travel. Four days of wood make one of horsehair insignificant. I was relieved to learn my mentor's body had not been sold to the dissectionists, but lay in a pit which was recently filled. Tired and aching, hungry though I was, I demanded to see where this man had been laid. I wished to utter some *Aves* and appeal to the One who is Without Beginning and whose World is Without End to carry the soul of my friend to the throne of the Lord. I knew some comrades would be guarding his grave against robbers who for a few coppers would remove the very means whereby we enter heaven.

Two pits were recently filled. There had been a burning, whose stench was in the air while the stink from the pit rose from the ground. The smells met where my nose probed the darkness for a penny candle to light my way with the tread of the earth to direct me. I avoided soft earth and walked on what was already firm. There were ember glows of dying fires in the misted evening air and the priest accompanied me to the spot, where we met two others who, like us, were there to see the mortal remains installed. Someone had the dregs of a bottle of brandy, which I fear had been mingled with another spirit. Its fire nevertheless warmed me, though when its flames had dulled I found I was colder than before. I feared this was due to a lack of food and when I expressed this belief to my companions, food was miraculously produced.

We sat between graves in the darkness, surrounded by the smell of putrefying flesh, a bowl of spiced apple sauce, some bread, cheese and spirit between us. For a while it was as if the souls of the dead were drifting, rising towards judgement with the smoke and the smell, with the rancid evening's undertaking. Then, subtly, it changed. When all is still, one becomes accustomed to one's surroundings and is very aware of a change in the circumstances. I caught the whiff of another smell, which was at the same time both disturbing and adventurous.

Firstly, the smell of lime. I was shocked not to have noticed such sharpness until now and could only blame the cold and the strength of the spirit we had been consuming. Then came another smell, or many smells, the smell of woman, or the smells of many women.

Black is many colours and the evening dark and stillness has many lights and movements. At first there was not a sound to be heard, nothing moved, not a blade of grass nor a pebble turned. There was nothing, not a glimmer in the clouded sky. We whispered for fear, to protect ourselves from death, that those in this city of the nameless, those who were buried with no memorial, those too poor to be remembered, were shouting their names, crying out for recognition, desperate to ascend to heaven. The noises came from within us, the sound of our breathing and the beat of our hearts.

There was a rustling, satin and muslin collided as leaves in the undergrowth. We heard the noises change, and watched the colour emerge. Four women stood together sobbing and staring at the earth.

'You may have found your lodgings,' Rudolph told me. At the hiss of his whisper, the women, who obviously thought they were alone, huddled together.

'Forgive us,' said a friend. 'Forgive us for frightening you against our wishes and in such a place. We too have suffered loss and have come to communicate with who-knows-what, simply to be near the place where surely something of our friend remains. Please let us not disturb you.'

There was no reply. They stood with their handkerchiefs pressed to their faces. Already, their presence had altered the place, as if they had brought new air and surroundings. In that place with its smells and remains, where there was little or nothing of life or the living, a place where few ventured, especially after dark, knowing they would go there soon enough, where criminals took refuge, sometimes hiding in the graves pretending to be dead, knowing the police would not venture beyond the gates. It is said some criminals have lived there for years, among the dogs and cats, the rats and insects who grow fat on the corpses then carry their disease and plague, bring death from the cemetery into town, infecting the living and ensuring a constant food supply. Even there, at dead of night, these women appeared like a rainbow against snow. Their rustlings were mysterious, their perfumes changed the air, bringing a breeze and a warmth, their presence like breathing, sobbing statues.

'They are from an establishment,' said Rudolph, who works in a restaurant and knows everyone and everything in Leipzig. 'They work for a woman called Sophie d'Agneux, obviously not her real name. She may even be with them; I cannot see. They have reason to mourn. One of their number, a pretty girl, not yet twenty, died in the arms, it is said, of Zdenko, a Bohemian financier, the house's greatest protector and patron. Then Zdenko died soon after; the girl on the evening and Zdenko the following afternoon, which caused the stupid authorities to cry plague. They have put a notice on the door, barring entry. There is no plague. The girl died because she was a whore. She was constantly crying, blessing herself, praying to statues, giving money to her younger sister, to their parents, or paying the lodgings of beggars in the streets. She stayed, she said, to save her sister. Now the sister will have to whore. The whores are mourning the girl, who day and night prayed for death. Her parents thought she had come into service. Zdenko died because he was fat and ugly, old and guilty. The house is not plagued. The mistress of the Police Commissioner has opened an establishment at the Riga Café, so while they cry plague in one house, she makes a fortune in the other. Everyone knows there is no more plague than usual and will not go to the commissioner's whore. They will return to Sophie in a few days. Because you are a man, she will give you accommodation, the run of the house I am sure for free, providing you walk around Leipzig telling everyone what a wonderful time you had at Sophie's, which was empty. Tell them you had the pick of the house, tell them there was a black whore, tell them anything. I will have a word with Sophie.'

They must have heard his voice, and may even have been able to make out what he was saying. Yet they neither moved nor glanced in our direction.

I am constantly surprised how people alter in times of crisis. I am equally amazed at how a change in circumstance makes one forget how they were before. What confounds me most of all is how quickly a person alters when he feels he will benefit from a change in his habits, style, demeanour or position. It is usually as certain and lasting as a shower of rain.

The presence of women, no matter the type of women, had altered our company. We were four men who immediately became more gallant, who hung around the graveyard longer than was necessary. Where there was darkness, now there was light from two candles, produced more quickly than the bread and cheese. When the ladies lifted their heads and glanced around the fetid darkness before turning to leave, arms were offered, voices schooled in refinery warned where to step as they were solicitously led off, their noses wreathed in handkerchiefs. I was told to follow.

There were two carriages, one blue, the other yellow. The door of the second was held open. I had hoped not to enter such a contraption for several days, at least until my body could deal with the contusions, at least until I felt repaired.

The seats were satin and stuffed with feathers. There was room to stretch. I was offered the leg of a roasted chicken, pastries, a glass of Steinberger and a tray of sweetmeats. Though we bounced and sparked across the cobbles, there was no need to grasp the straps or apologise to my fellow passengers. It would be an exaggeration to say we floated towards Sophie d'Agneux, but neither did we ride in a carriage. The noise of the horses, the crack of the whip and the roar of the wheels were there to remind us of where we were. Otherwise it could have been a dream. The carriage was dark. No one spoke. I could barely see the faces opposite, but watched the movement as they lifted their hands to dab their eyes. I tried to guess where we were by the changing sounds and echo of the wheels, but was

73

only aware of entering a courtyard. The noise was dulled and echoed when we went through an archway.

I followed the women into a hall. They ran upstairs and I waited below. Even though it was poorly lit I could see the place was far from ordinary. For a reason I now cannot explain, and I fully recognise this will shock, almost immediately I was aware of my shabbiness. I had been travelling, it is true, and could hardly attend to my toilet as regularly as I would have wished, but this place was like no other I had ever entered, it smelled like no other and looked like nothing else. My dirty, wrinkled stockings, filthy coat and shoes, my stubbled face and hands, my smell seemed to defile it, the way priests say such things defile the presence of the Lord, that when entering a holy place we should be clean in body as well as spirit. I know what I am saying. I do not mean to be blasphemous. I remember where I was and that I was suddenly aware of the smell from myself. I realise how unusual this must sound, but it was the place that made me think of it, as I hope to explain. I have been in stews and bagnios. I know the way these places survive and the women who work there; young women chasing money, old women chasing drink. I have seen their chains and apparatus. I know what they offer. But this was unlike anywhere I had ever been, unlike anything I had ever experienced. Again, I repeat, more like a church than a brothel.

'This way.'

The voice was calling from the top of the stairs. I have said the entrance hall was dimly lit, no more than two or three free-standing candles, giving unreflected light. The stairway to the first floor consisted of more than fifty steps. The way got brighter the higher I climbed until, at last, on the landing I found myself in a blaze of light, lit by as many as a thousand candles, from chandeliers, walls and tables. I was in ornament and colour. Plaster angels prayed and danced across the ceiling, bowers and classical gallantries and a village frolic adorned the walls. These were hardly the usual brothel wall adornments: laughing girls with bands of flowers, children dancing at the feet of their parents, cupid's arrow piercing the heart of a shy and single, pale young man. There were black iron pillars, columns of veined and coloured marble, whose shades and texture were reflected across the floor; there were glass and mirrors to reflect the light and bounce a rainbow across their surface; there were wall and ceiling decorations of fruit and flowers, leaves and grasses, small tables with waxed fruit and floral arrangements; and there was Sophie d'Agneux, waiting to greet me at the head of the stairs.

The place and her presence made me conscious of myself, though I was treated as nothing other than an ambassador come into the kingdom, as though I brought a message of peace, carried something from which mankind would flourish, as though I came with more than riches, for riches she already had, as though I was the source of her pleasure. My ease began with her smile. I could neither look around me, nor at the floor as I would have wished; I was forced to look at her. She was neither fat nor thin, young nor old, but a woman preserved in an age of her choice.

'You seem in need of some attention,' she said. For an

opening statement from the madam of a brothel, it was the most unusual I had ever heard.

'I have been five days travelling and arrived in Leipzig less than two hours ago.'

'Tell me if you are aching, hungry and in need of rest.'

'I am absolutely as you describe.'

She gave my baggage to a servant, crooked her finger for me to follow, then led me down two corridors, to a room which was mostly blue and crimson, with velvet draperies and a feathery bed, a room that smelled of lavender and roses. Again, the walls were covered with scenes of pastoral beauty.

'People come here to be repaired,' she said. 'Someone will call when your bath is ready.'

I had never been in a bath before, considering it an idle pastime, though I never had access to enough hot water, never had the means to immerse myself completely in anything other than a pond or stream.

Two girls removed my clothes. One carried them off; the other brought a long, open robe which was tied round my middle. The first returned with a pot of coffee and chocolate mint. When I finished the refreshments, my bath was called.

There were perfumes, lotions, steam and girls. The bath was sunken into the floor. One girl was already in the water. Two others led me down. They soaped and sponged my every part, floated me in warmed and perfumed water, poured pitchers over my head, pared my nails, cut my hair, shaved my face, brushed my teeth with paste and bristle, dried me entirely, perfumed my body, put ointments and unguents on

76

my chafes and sores, then combed my hair and, in a dry robe, led me to a room which may have been the one I'd been in before. If so, there was mulled wine and coffee on a table by the fire; and a change of clothes, which fitted but for a few tucks here and there, were warmed and laid across the bed. I was dressed in stockings and underdrawers, blue breeches and shoes with a white laced shirt, opened at the neck. My hair was tied with a silk red ribbon and a deeper blue sash twined round my waist. I was taken to dinner. Not a dinner as I had known, rather a choice of food.

Sophie d'Agneux stood to greet me, standing by a table in a room that was dominated by an open fire. 'You seem improved,' was all she said, and motioned me to sit opposite, away from the fire, I am sure for fear I would fall asleep.

I cannot remember what we ate, though we did begin with a warmed soup, made from tomatoes with a hint of citrus and chopped cress leaves mingled with chives and basil across the top. There were also what seemed to be stuffed pigeons, certainly a stuffed small bird, omelettes and vegetables, three kinds of wines and more sweetmeats, vegetable pastries with spinach and potato, roast pork slices, some hams and melon, nuts and fruit. I do not remember details of the food for trying to recall the conversation.

Sophie d'Agneux told me the story of the place. She spoke in a soft voice which seemed to console, indeed seemed incapable of being raised. 'I have eaten,' she said, 'but please continue. I want you fed. Men are easier to handle when their stomachs are full.'

I smiled. She did not.

'I believe you met in the graveyard. I am told you lost a friend, that you travelled to see his remains were safe, and that is commendable. I commiserate with your loss. We also have suffered a terrible tragedy, one we cannot yet believe.'

'I have heard something of your loss.'

'One hears a little and assumes a lot. This child came here as a servant, to clean and polish, that is all. I believe she was possessed of a Biblical innocence. They tell me she met a young man who asked where she worked. She, of course, told him. He said he wanted nothing to do with her. I have often wished I could meet this young man, for I don't know if his actions were a blessing or a curse. The child thought she may as well become what she was branded. She could have become a musician or an artist more easily. She is the only woman I have ever met who was incapable, absolutely incapable, of performing the functions expected in this place with anyone who chooses to be a customer.

'No one takes to this life by choice. It is like converting to the church. You reach a point in your life where you cannot stand still. You must go forwards, must change, and usually turn to that which is easily available and seems to offer a simple solution. This child was born and died a virgin. She was never anything more than a cleaner.

'Yet the paradox is that it is she, rather than I, who is responsible for the place you see around you. She went to the nuns, who also rejected her: no bad thing for a girl who wishes to retain her virginity. They urged her to find God on her own, that she pursue her vocation where God had placed her. She found God in the service of others. She found Him here.

'Very quickly I noticed a difference. The place was cleaner. I have never seen a person so devoted to soda, soap and water. She washed herself I don't know how many times a day. She washed floors and ornaments, walls, curtains, tables, everything. Nothing was dry for long. She continually washed, objects or herself, and when everything was cleaned she ran water through her hands, admiring, she said, the way light changed the texture. She was always working and within a year had convinced me I should change direction, that I should offer something different, warmth and consolation, comfort, cleanliness and light.

'This has never been the usual sort of house. I will tell you why later, but the arrival of this child made things complete. People come here because they want to be clean. We offer an alternative. What they find in other houses they do not find here. It is true we are what we are and sexual exchanges do take place, but this is neither a brothel nor a drinking den. You must be feeling better since your arrival; and think of what took place, innocence itself really. I think we provide the same service as an inn, without the straw and flea-riddled beds. No one bathes alone here, nor do they want to, and they seldom sleep alone. Sexual congress should contain an element of mystery, so we wait until our customer is nearly asleep then slip into bed beside him. That way a man gets what he wants. He is comforted. In the morning she is gone. He will remember it forever. Every night just before sleep he will imagine a firm body slipping in between his sheets. We offer an experience, rather than satin and filth. I learned that from her. I watched what she did, and, as I say, she devoted herself to the service of others.

'She was especially fond of the banker Zdenko, who missed his home, though he told everyone he hated Prague, and bored us with stories of how he knew the singer Zardi. He said he had helped arrange the finances for the concert to launch Mozart's son, who was also called Wolfgang, when the child was six years old and living in Prague with Duschek and his wife. She was a singer and a friend of Mozart whom Zdenko heard sing in the first performance of *La Clemenza di Tito*. He attended the first Prague performance of operas by Mayr and Paisiello as well as something earlier by Mozart, which the little maestro conducted in a blue coat. He also went to the Duscheks' concerts in a music conservatory they had specially built onto their house at Betramka. Zdenko said the child's concert was the only worthwhile thing he had done with his life, and even then he did not do it alone. It allowed him to shake the hand of Mozart's wife and son and to meet great singers like Campi and Benedetti. Mozart's manuscripts of course were sold here and Zdenko tried to buy something or other from Breitkopf and may actually have done so, for he obviously loved music and never wanted to be a banker. He often wept for his wasted life.

'This was a business venture. He came to check my accounts. I borrowed money at a usurer's interest and he came here monthly to collect his pay. Our dealings were cordial, nothing more.

'She found him at night, downstairs, alone and

weeping. Rather than leave with an embarrassed hush, she asked if there was anything she could do. Zdenko was prone to melancholia. He shushed her away, but she would not go. She got warm water, removed his shoes and stockings and bathed his feet. He told me this himself. He told everyone. That was the start; from then he virtually lived here, would have married that child and left her his fortune, would have done or given whatever she wanted.

'When he came here she bathed him, gave him chocolate and tucked him into bed, sometimes reciting parts of the Bible. She blew out the candle and, fifteen minutes later, slipped in between the sheets. I would have raised a memorial to the child myself, would have buried her in a vault. She wanted her body scattered for the birds. I compromised, having her laid in a common grave. I believe Zdenko died of melancholia, could not live without her and took his life.'

I had finished eating. The table was cleared. A dish of fruit, some cheese, coffee and brandy, as different from what I had drunk in the graveyard as horse piss is from Rhenish, was what remained. She peeled an apple and ate the slices with an occasional black grape, washing it down with dry mineral water.

Her eyes never left me. I was lost for what to say. 'Have you been doing this long?' I asked. 'How did you start?'

'Men always want to know; how long have you fallen and do you think you will ever rise again? And women always lie; a month or two, I'm only doing this until I'm back on my feet, or I started because a friend was doing it, first of all I collected her money, and so on.

Have you ever heard of Casanova, who styled himself de Seingalt?'

I may have nodded.

'They tell me his *mémoires* have been published and now he is notorious. He was always famous to me. It's wrong to say he got me started, but his influence caused me to appraise my position. I will have to be frank. You, I know, will have no objections. Women are used to being frank when discussing bodily matters and functions in a way men usually find distasteful. They like it when women are frank because they cannot do it themselves. Women's frankness has nothing to do with what men consider; anyone who has witnessed a birth, where women leave their dignity with their lover, will be aware of that.

'Were I to ask you to describe your earliest sexual experience, it would be over and done with in as many sentences as the deed took minutes to perform. Women, on the other hand, could talk of such a thing for days, a sad and lonely, frightening time for everyone.

'My proper name is Emilie Hauptmann. I knew Casanova and was the last, or one of the last, to see him alive. You may have gathered, the reason Zdenko and I got on was that I am also Bohemian. That was why he gave me the loan. I do not know where I was born, nor do I know anything of my parents. I was given into service at the Castle of Dux sometime around the American war, for I remember them saying revolution would never come to Dux.

'As a child, I swept the floors and cleaned the excrement from the corridors, along with anything else they left, by throwing water across the stone. This was all I was trained to do.

'When Casanova came we knew all about him; if not everything, then as much as we needed to know, for the fat count fell for any Freemason, especially one who knew the cabala. We assumed Casanova was both these things and, of course, we were right. We also assumed he would be younger, for the count's taste in men did not usually run to an elderly poseur with bleeding piles and loose teeth.

'I was a child when he came and grew up to the sound of his feuds with Faulkircher and Wiederholt. He left and came back, left and came back; and every time was worse than before. Of course, he won and they were forced to leave, but there were continual rows before that happened.

'The first time he addressed me was to complain and almost every time he spoke he complained about something. He complained about Caroline and complained about Paris. He was back from Prague and the count was trying to force Caroline to marry Wiederholt. His mother objected to her son's occasional lapses with a servant; had she known of his other lapses, she would have been delighted that the servant he lapsed with was female. If she wishes to marry, let her marry Wiederholt, then her ideas will be in keeping with her station, the old woman said in everyone's hearing, which of course made Caroline even more insufferable. Casanova asked if I served her. I told him I did. Does she enjoy her food spiced? he asked. I nodded. Then spice her food with grounded glass, he said.

'His rooms were in a wing which led onto a courtyard, far away from everyone else. In retrospect, I find that very symbolic. He was isolated. Which was for him a good thing. Any time I saw him he was writing, sometimes reading, but more usually writing. His room was littered with papers. He gave me a copy of the *Icosameron*, the first book I ever owned, which I have tried many times to read. It is a very tedious work. There were copies in his room, piled by the window. He had paid for the printing and since no one wanted to buy them, there they stayed, apart from a copy which Wiederholt attached to the door of the servants' lavatory for people to use when they wiped their arse. Casanova did not know this, nor do I believe he ever found out.

'I was in his room as usual, he was by the window, writing. What, you may ask, was I doing in his room? I am afraid I cannot provide a simple answer. I have, until recently, believed I was working. I was, after all, a servant girl. Until the moment I am about to relate, he had never taken the slightest notice of me, as I fetched and carried the water for him to wash, emptied whatever needed to be emptied, laid and lit his fire and so on. Normal duties for a girl in my position.

'As I have grown older I have thought about him and thought about myself. I have tried to explain what I was doing and why I went, purely for my peace of mind. I have come to some interesting conclusions; at least, they are interesting to me.

'Remember, I had no background. I was unskilled and untutored, could neither read nor write and had no hopes of ever being able to do so. Yet I loved learning. I loved books and I loved stories. I loved thought and I respected anyone who was able to compress their thoughts onto paper. I did not know who he was, nor did I care. He was hardly kind or considerate, the opposite if anything. He was irascible and selfish. But any time I saw him, he was writing. God knows what he was writing, for I certainly never knew; perhaps it was the infamous *mémoires*; but whatever, I was presented with something I had never known. I had never seen anyone writing before, so that was one thing.

'There were others. I felt sorry for him. I do not know what age I was, any more than I know what age I am now, and it is highly unlikely I will ever find out. I never learned to read or write; if I need to know something a girl will read to me. I believe there is a time, a time I have noticed, especially in the life of the poor and saintly child who died – saints, you will have noticed, are always poor – there is a time in early adolescence when a child, especially a girl, feels things very strongly. We want a fair world, are captivated by life, by its sights, sounds and smells, when an air of joyous discovery is upon us, when we feel all things are possible, when we feel more intensely than at any time in our lives, before or after. The sight of playful kittens brings tears to our eyes, and poverty turns us into revolutionaries, determined to fight for a better world. We will redress wrongs, the mistakes and follies of the previous generation.

'I felt sorry for him. I felt it was wrong that this skinny old man, this pathetic and pompous, shambling creature, was alone and unloved. I came from nowhere, but I believed we ought to have people around us, friends and relations. I felt all humanity was good. If they did not show it, all that was required was for another to show goodness to them and that would restore whatever was lost. If not that precisely, then something very like it. I could not have articulated such a thought. It was hardly a thought, or not a thought as I understand it, more of a feeling.

'So, I certainly felt sorry for him; but there is something more, something far more powerful and far more important. I had been told to stay away. Even then, in some ways more then than now or at any time since, I was a girl of independent spirit. Tell me not to do something and I immediately did it. Tell me I could not enter and I found a way in. Tell me not to think or do and I thought or did. Wiederholt had made Casanova unbearably attractive; and there was something about him.

'If I was to compress the elements, it would not do, for he was more than the sum of his parts. He was all I have described. Age had not been kind, but it was as if he did not notice these things about himself. He saw himself as a young man and acted in the way he acted when he was young. His world had been swept away. He was a relic.

'Men who have been attractive usually retain something of their appeal. Charming men are always charming. But it was more. There was a physical presence. For all his arcane mannerisms, his foppish ways and antique posturising, especially when he entered a room or, God help us, danced; despite these things and many more, he had a presence, a way of standing, a demeanour that was entirely captivating. When he walked, one could see a young man struggling with an old man's body.

'He never seemed to notice me. It was as if I were invisible, but he must have noticed, must have been aware of my presence when he did what he did. His desk drawn to the fire, writing. The room was clean. There was a sharpness in the air and a warmth in the room.

'I was doing what I often did. I was transfixed, watching him write, the way a child is fascinated by work, can watch a farrier or a wheelwright for hours and never tire. I was watching him, amazed at the way he wrote. It was almost demonic. He slouched over the paper, guarding it with his left arm, as though someone would read or copy what he had written. There was the scratching noise, punctuated by silence as he dipped his quill into the ink, scratching and silence, the fire in the grate.

'He looked up and saw me. Girl, he said, placing his quill on the paper. I turned to face him and he lifted his hands upwards, like this. I did not know what he meant. Your skirt, child, he said. Lift your skirt and let me see. Of course, I did as I was asked, or tried, but could raise my skirts no further than my calf, perhaps my knee, I do not know. I was frozen. I wanted to burst into tears and run. Thank you, child, he said. Thank you. And he gave me the book. I can tell you I thought about it often and when I was alone I raised my skirts to see what he had wanted to see.

'His words were chilling. I will never forget them. He sighed. I have performed as my reputation demanded and cannot even seduce a servant. My conquests forget me. You take this to remember my failure, he said, and gave me the book. I wanted you to remind me of myself, for all I have left, the only thing here is my reputation. Thank you, child. I am sorry if I offended.

'It did not happen again, though I sometimes thought it might, just the way he looked at me, the way he always seemed to be wanting something. Ask anyone who knew him and they will tell you, any woman would tell you, he always seemed in need of something.

'People were coming and going, in and out and around the castle, always someone going somewhere, coming back from someplace else. The count told all his friends that if they were passing they should drop in and stay a while, and, of course, that is what they did. This was how we got our news, how stories circulated. Around this time there was a terrible scandal when it seemed Europe, and his servants, were laughing at Casanova. We heard it from a coachman who arrived with some frightened, impoverished nobleman or other, someone who spoke French and claimed to have escaped the revolution with nothing but his head. An impostor more likely. They usually turned out to be Russian.

'Anyway, this was someone who happened to be passing and had come in search of the fat count, who was away, in league with other Bohemian royalists working to restore the French monarchy, and him a Freemason. The reason his marvellous scheme did not take place was that if his servants knew he was in England trying to raise money, presumably others did too. I can never see him as a fighter, though I can see

88

him carrying gossip from one court to another and thinking he was a spy.

'The coachman told us the Paris mobs were publishing papers the *ancien régime* considered secret. Among those nailed to the Bastille gate was a letter from Casanova to some prince or other, telling him how to make the Philosopher's Stone. I thought it was stupid and that this French prince deserved all he got if he believed such a thing. What I did not know was that someone, perhaps one of the coachmen or a stable boy, told Casanova the letter had been published.

'I saw him next morning and he had not slept. The fire was dead. He sat with a blanket across his shoulders as though it was winter, huddled in his chair, a spent old man. I was used to being ignored, well used to his complaints and blusterings. He did not stir when I entered and remained motionless while I was there.

'Had I known I would have washed his feet. Instead, I lit the fire and fussed around him, chattering about things which held no interest. I remember he stared when I told him a stable mare had given birth to a foal. I thought he was going to shout, but he did not. I fetched a pitcher of warm water and left it by a basin on his table. I went to the kitchen and stole some food, especially coffee, and these I carried on a silver tray. This was particularly dangerous, for Wiederholt was still around and, needless to say, we had been told Casanova had to eat in the servants' quarters like anyone else. On no account was food to be taken to his room.

'I helped him wash, wiped his face, made his bed and opened the windows while he sharpened his razor. I told him to eat the food, then went to the garden and picked some flowers. When I brought the posy into his room he was asleep. I built the fire, took the dishes back to the kitchen, where I waited until the way was clear, and when I was certain no one would see or find me, I rushed to the cellar, a horrible place, wet and dark with slippery walls and floor, horrible, where I took an armful of the first bottles I could find, rushing back to where he lay, running all the way, going the long route, hiding in rooms and using ways known only to servants, for fear of being caught. To be caught stealing the fat count's wine would have meant a very severe flogging. Greta Linn the orphan was crippled for less.

'In his room, I waited for him to wake. I gave him bread and cheese and a pot of fresh coffee. He still had not spoken. He ate the food and drank the coffee. Then he stared at the flowers for a very long time. You have saved my life, he said. I was at the door. He was weeping, staring at the flowers. Please, he said. Do not leave me.

'I told him I would soon return, then ran to the kitchen. I told Wiederholt I was cleaning rooms in another part of the building, preparing for the fat count's return with gentlemen and servants in need of accommodation. This is on top of your other work, he said. I stole more food and coffee, went back to Casanova and sat by the fire, waiting for him to waken. He slept all day, then wakened at night, when he ate a little soup and fruit and, of course, he drank coffee; he always drank coffee. The wine had made him slightly drunk, neither sentimental nor maudlin, rather intense. Drink simply increased the tension that was already there, he got no release. Drink allows some people to shed their inhibitions. It gave Casanova inhibitions, screwed the anxieties he already carried even tighter, with neither remission nor remorse.

'He told me he wanted to take his own life, that he had wanted to die many times. The troubling thing about this bout of melancholia, as with recent bouts, was that he felt there was no alternative. His life was pointless. God has gone, he said. He felt deserted and angry.

'Do not tell me what the stupid priests tell me, he shouted. If you are distant from God, then you have moved. God is no more fixed than a firefly. He is not human. We are made in His image, yet we continually remake Him into ours. He is our creator and what I dislike is the way He uses that power to His advantage.

'You will have gathered, child, he said, I am not speaking of churches. They are there for those who need them and no one needs the church as much as those who serve them, priests and nuns, the principal players of ritual and mystery. Do you honestly think the creator of the universe needs us to sing to Him? Do you think God needs to be reassured, to be continually reminded of how mighty and wonderful He is, how much we revere and love Him? Do you think He is interested in how grateful we are? I refuse to have anything to do with a God who needs my worship.

'I had never heard anyone speak like that. This was blasphemy, though I found it funny, mainly I suspect from embarrassment. I remember thinking he was drunk and tried to stop myself from laughing, for I

91

knew he would have been offended if he saw me smile, far less quiver on my stool.

'I know what I am saying. I was a monk, he said. That did it. Laughter burst through everything. He stood there, stiff and formal, terribly proud, red-eyed, drunk and angry. Your name? he asked. I told him. Well, Emilie, he said. You may call me Frère Jacques. We laughed. He was a crafty old devil. Come along, child, he said. Let me hear your confession. Who's been lifting your skirt? A naughty friar, I said. Oh dear, a man of the cloth, and we laughed again, a small laugh, no more than an interlude, an attempt to change the mood.

'It didn't work. He sat for a while. When I think of how I was then, he said, and how I am now, I think I have been two different people. More than two, certainly, but two extremes, north and south, hot and cold. You could say I have lost my innocence. I will disagree with myself, he whispered. If God can do it, so can I. I was ignorant then and have lost that ignorance. I believed and trusted; followed blindly. I was younger then. He sat back, his anger gone. He was old and pathetic again.

'He had tried to believe, had wanted to believe; then, in the middle of prayer, he said, during the holy mass, I found I was speaking to myself. In the midst of devotion I was thinking of other things.

'God had led him to the monastery for an education and that was all. These very teachings were the source of his unrest. They opened his mind to a world he wanted, a world of books, music and theatre rather than devotion. When he left the monastery he was forced to throw himself on the mercy of others, who could fulfil these needs in return for having their own fulfilled. Some were kind, others were not; though they all got what they wanted or had paid for, he said. He had seen his plans frustrated, his life was ruined, turned to a mockery.

'He had become what he despised. He'd be remembered for things he neither cared about nor wanted. He would gladly die, rather than continue with the misery of constantly borrowing, repaying debts, of always owing, penny-pinching and scrounging, of being dependent. I would rather have thrown my liver to the wolves, he said, than have ended in Dux. That way I would have known when it was over. This way could go on forever.

'The problem was confusion. God's will. There had been times, he said, many times when he believed, when he felt as certain as if he had been asked his name, that he was doing God's will. He claimed these assertions had been confirmed; small things convinced him, tiny acts of certainty had made him aware he was doing what he ought to be doing. I did not know, he said, that when God was most gracious, when he seemed to be smiling sweetly, when He was at His kindest, He was actually resting, plotting and preparing another torture, another disappointment, another glimpse of something he could not have. He could watch others pick up things, achieve and succeed for less than half his effort, and with less than half his skill.

'He told me he had been promised plenty. Many times he thought eternity lay in the palm of his hand, only to watch it fly away. He cursed God and pleaded to be shown His will, to be shown His way. He restlessly prayed for forgiveness and guidance, for a sense of order and direction, promised to do anything, whatever God wished him to do. This was both during his time in the monastery and later. When he was a boy, fifteen or sixteen, he was admitted to the four minor orders of the clergy, but much later in life, in his mid-thirties, with debts of 100,000 francs and after spying for the French government in a vain attempt to repay these debts, he took refuge in a Benedictine monastery in Einsiedeln.

'He told me that during these times he believed he had truly repented. He had prayed for God to show Him the way and always believed, in every single instance, whatever he did with his life, whatever move he made, whatever journey or enterprise he undertook, he always believed he was doing what God had wanted him to do. This was because he had been shown the door to the monastery. Yet when each enterprise was ended, he doubted God's will and sought reassurance. He knew what God had not wanted him to do only after he had done it.

'Think what such talk could do to someone who since childhood had been cleaning what others left behind in case they stood on it when they woke in the morning. Consider what I have told you and picture the scene, dying stumps of candles, a high ceiling and a darkened room – warm while I knelt, cold when I stood – a low fire, this old man, his corset off, wig away, make-up undone, sunken cheeks, red-eyed from crying, half drunk and maudlin now, or pretending to be maudlin so's I won't take his confession seriously and he can apologise in the morning, can reasonably look at me again, another bottle of wine in his hand and me afraid of him; not because of what people thought, what he was said to have done – proposed marriage to his own daughter and fathered her child because her husband could not – that incidentally I believe to be true and thank God I did not know it then, I who never had a father thinking of myself as his daughter. These things were fearful enough, but I was frightened because of what he had wakened within me. Show me, he said. Show me. Lift your skirt and let me see. The fact that there was something to see surprised me, that he should want to see it scared me, but not half as much as the fact that I enjoyed him looking and wanted him to ask again.

'I was terrified and can say honestly, now, between us two, us together, here, like this, as in a confessional – and if this house is not a sort of confessional I don't know what it is – I can say honestly, as it was then, that I wanted to run. I simply wanted to stop him talking, did not want to hear these things, especially his stuff about God. I wanted to stay as I was, especially, yes, especially when he stared with those dark brown eyes, angry and placid, warm eyes, the eyes of a saint, as though they'd been painted on an icon of Jesus, those eyes that pierced through me – why did he want me to lift my skirt with eyes like that? Could he not see through me? – his eyes never moved, in the dark they were blackness itself, darker than anything in the room.

'He made me want what I never could have and I think I loved him for it. He believed himself cursed

95

because God let him recognise ability in others, yet never possess it in himself. He did not want what others had, did not want to do what others were doing. He wanted his own worth recognised. They could have their success and he would have his. And that was why he wrote the book.

'I lifted my skirt again and again. I was his dancing girl. It was me he saw when he was dying. I danced through the room and took his soul to meet God. We agreed it would happen, that he would stay, help and protect me. That I would have what he had never had. He showed me everything. I was at the window when he said, Come over and play. He taught me cards, then taught me to gamble. Gamble for money, he said. Nothing else is worthwhile. Coins are proof of immortality. When great thoughts are forgotten, when books have been burned, great art ignored, great wars pacified, buildings demolished, Venice returned to the sea and monuments to the dust, money will survive. Indeed, it will be money which will cause these things to be done and undone. And finally, he said, always use someone else's money, never your own. Hence my involvement with Zdenko.

'Did you know he was Venetian?' she said. 'I have never seen Venice. They tell me it is very beautiful.'

Sophie d'Agneux was as fresh as when we met, yet she had been talking for at least two hours. My body was becoming cold again. The fire was all but out. The candles had been replaced and I needed sleep.

'You were not with him when he died?' I asked.

'No. The gentlemen were there, the Prince de Ligne and so on. I sat by his corpse when the priests and morticians were done. I sat all night. In the morning I kissed his forehead and left. I could not cry for my loss. No one would have understood. He was taken to the St Barbara churchyard, wrapped in sacking and covered with soil.

'His body was barely cold when those who spat on him, spat in his food, teased and taunted him, ransacked his quarters. By the time the gentlemen returned, only his papers were left; obviously useless to those who cannot read. There were boxes filled with letters he wrote but never sent to Faulkircher and Wiederholt, as well as anyone else with whom he was angry. He vented his anger in an imaginary correspondence. There were bills in the boxes, parts of the operas he had seen in Prague. There were his writings, essays, philosophies and so on, his alchemic formulas, scientific and mathematical formulas and experiments, diagrams, letters he wrote to the fat count – who always welcomed him back to Dux, I think because he kept his visitors amused – letters from his ward in Cassovie, to whom he left the manuscript of his life story. There were poems, equations, calculations and papers that made no sense at all. These things were there when I left. I bribed a clerk to tell me what they were. He gave me a paper in Casanova's hand, the receipt for a bill of sale. A strange souvenir, rough paper covered in small, cramped writing.'

She smiled: 'And now they tell me Brockhaus has bought the manuscript from Angioloni, or it must have been his son. What I have heard, I do not remember being written. The truth is I remember little of what he wrote. I remember him. I remember the way he stood and the way he walked, the way the sides of his eyes crinkled when he laughed and his snoring. He was a wonderful snorer.'

What else is there to tell? She apologised for having spoken so long and showed me to my room, which was warm and airy. The bed had been heated. Fifteen minutes after blowing out the candle the sheets were lifted. I put my arms around her and, with my hand on her breast, we slept till morning, when she was gone.

I have taken this opportunity of tendering my account for this and previous services, which I hope Your Excellency will see your way to settling.

And this little note must have accompanied the above. It was stapled to the bottom of the last page. Was this the work of a librarian for whom this document had become an object? The staple was rusted. I removed it when I returned the document. The mark of the staples and the rust has been photocopied along with everything else.

Can you urge that tub of lard, the Jew Landsberg, to pay me. The enclosed is true in every detail and has taken almost a month to write, on top of the time it took to compile. I know the commissioner will not read it, though if he did I am sure he would enjoy the account of the brothel. If he is anxious for this work to continue, I must be able to settle the many bills I have raised on his behalf. I am with Sophie d'Agneux – where better to discover the secrets of Leipzig? – and will let you know what arises, no pun intended, or what intelligence I receive. Can I suggest you have someone check the Casanova book for references to His Excellency. I have referred to him exactly in the term she used. Such disrespect cannot continue in times like these.

THREE

In Kyoto, still
longing for Kyoto: cuck-
oo's two time-worn notes.

Matsuo Basho
(1644–94)

Mme. Bernard did not remember me. She opened the door, stared and eventually shook her head.

You were supposed to telephone yesterday, she said. We thought you weren't coming. With her hair gathered at the back, she looked as though I had interrupted her cleaning the bath.

The flat on the rue Jean Nicot, at the corner of quai d'Orsay, overlooking the white Presbyterian American Church, was grand and impeccable. A small glass and golden chandelier dominated the hall, while a wide and ornate matching mirror almost covered the wall at the far end. There were black and gilded tables for the telephone and flowers, a small chiming clock and a lamp with a pale blue shade. There were prints of eighteenth-century Paris, two sixteenth-century maps and a print of Napoleon. A small marble bust of the emperor and a photograph of the professor were on a table by the door. A grey Persian cat sniffed and went into another room.

The library is here and the door is locked, said Mme. Bernard, producing a key from her apron pocket. When Mathilde is here she may offer you refreshment, but please do not wander unaccompanied. This is where you will work.

She opened the door with a flourish. The room was small, with a carpet, a table and a chair. A large cardboard box, saying *Joker Jus de Pamplemousse*, was on the table. Otherwise it was warm and empty, situated to the side of the house, looking into the American Church library. Other rooms must have overlooked the Seine.

Because the professor is not here, you can come and go as you please. You will not be expected before 10.00 a.m. and I would like the room clear by seven each evening. You may use the lavatory, but no other facilities. We will take no telephone messages and please do not eat in this house. The professor will be back in one week. I would like you to be finished by then.

What's the cat called?

Dolphie.

That morning I slept late. The hotel room was filled with light; the white net curtains like a cinema screen, suddenly billowing into the room.

There were noises in the corridor, a chambermaid singing, a vacuum cleaner, voices.

I enjoyed the hotel; the warmth and the coffee smell in the blue and yellow dining room.

Every morning I was kept waiting by the door, while a previous occupant's crumbs were dusted. A fresh cup and plate, a basket of bread rolls, sachets of butter and jam, kiwi fruit halved in an eggcup, *fromage frais* and a sachet of castor sugar were placed on the table; then I was called with a flourish. Seated, I was offered tea or coffee.

There were new arrivals every morning, with their guide books and maps, articles clipped from newspapers which were consulted like astrological charts. They were obsessed with changing money or buying presents.

They wanted to see and do the same things. No one went to the top of the Eiffel Tower, but they all had a trip on *les bateaux mouches*. Most of them smiled, and wished me a nice day; there was no conversation.

That day I breakfasted alone. The dining room was cleared when I went down, but the girl looked at me and smiled as she pulled a chair away from the table.

Monsieur, she said.

She brought fresh coffee, butter, rolls and jam. The staff ate with me, trying out their English.

I like Princess Diana, said the waitress.

Prince Charles does not, said a woman, and we laughed.

These early days fell into a pattern. I usually went over the previous day's notes, then walked from the hotel to the Bernard house, where I never heard another voice, nor hardly any sound. When I left, which I sometimes did at lunchtime, I heard nothing. When I came back, Mathilde opened the door. I varied my times and attendances. Some days my concentration was better than others.

It took maybe two days to empty the box, to arrange the material according to language. The prints and drawings, maps and plans were easily classified; and even though I was aware of what I had discovered, I often lost myself in a document, reading the previous researchers' notes and comments, looking for substance, meaning or interest in the works themselves.

They seemed to have been randomly assembled, tied with string or ribbon, often crammed into folders or envelopes, with little or nothing to indicate what they contained; sometimes a sentence, sometimes a label.

One long and rather complicated document had been broken into sections, presumably divided into digestible passages. When I put the sections together on the basis of the handwritings, I realised how much was missing, that papers had obviously been stolen or destroyed. There was no way of knowing what the box once held.

I tried to assess the relation between the *pamplemousse* box and others on the grey metal shelves. Again, there was no indication. The first two boxes I opened were empty, others had typewritten manuscripts, books or notebooks, often what looked like account books or ledgers. Another held newspaper and magazine clippings.

Nor was there any way of knowing what was in my box, other than trawling through the material. Mathilde seemed not to know. This room was never used, she said. Most of the professor's papers were kept in his study, which was always locked, and, as far as she knew, my material was put in the box when they knew I was coming. Madame could tell me more.

And yet it was exciting. I never got used to untying a ribbon or opening a folder, never dragged papers from an envelope without a sense of being midwife, that something was about to be reborn. I looked upon it as compensation for the lost Beaton papers, that Bernard had offered a replacement for the Glasgow treasure. For the first few days I was fine, lost in a blissful seclusion.

The office told me all was well. I left messages with the editor's secretary, whose voice reminded me of home in a way I could not have anticipated, like night in the trees, the smell of running water or a cow swinging its belly home from the field.

Well, said the editor, his voice disarmingly close, that's wonderful. Things are much as they were when you left. We still have that wee matter to consider, but I don't want to rush you into anything yet. The terms are, I think, pretty good, but I understand if you'd want to stay.

This was when I had phoned about the Mackintosh piece.

I think you should be direct. Bring that up front and use Mackintosh as an example of what you mean. The d'Orsay disease seems fairly widespread. I suppose these things come and go in cycles. Look at the pig's ear they've made of Kelvingrove; every exhibition you see nowadays is packed with rubbish that makes intellectual sense to the folk in suits and flowery ties who compile them. Personally, I agree with you. The art world's in a mess. You can't see a decent exhibition or gallery any more, everything has to be classified, contained, selected, specially chosen, as if that was how artists worked. It's cost, of course, money. Many exhibitions are there because they've got a sponsor rather than an idea. Say that. It's a good piece and we'll use it on Thursday. I think you should do more stuff like that; look around, see what you can find.

The rewrites were easy. Later, walking round St-Germain-des-Prés, past Brasserie Lipp, crossing to the Café de Flore and round the corner at Les Deux Magots, I remembered how he changed the subject quickly and did not say, had never said, he wanted me to stay with the paper, never mentioned politics at all. It was cold. I sheltered in a bookshop where a jazz funk tape was changed for Wynton Marsalis, *Uptown Ruler*. After the first side I crossed to the Magots and asked for a table. The headwaiter managed to be both contemptuous and apologetic.

I was obviously near the St-Germain-des-Prés Métro station. I crossed the river, changed at Châtelet, got off at Bastille, where the opera house was lit like a department store, divided by the July Column. I walked around the Marais, eventually eating steak and salad in a restaurant near the place des Vosges. It had small wooden tables and uncomfortable wicker chairs, low lights and taped music.

I was glad when the meal was over. The waitress was too pert and attentive. She smiled all the time. No one could be that happy. It took more than two hours to walk back to the hotel.

When I was married, I continually longed for time on my own. Irene did too; we talked about it, like most things, never in a definite way, rather as something we'd get round to, the way married people talk, in the same category as the trip down the Nile or renting a cottage somewhere nice with a view to moving into the area now the kids were gone, going to see my brother in Carnoustie, or my sister in America who talked like a budgie, her accent neither here nor there.

It could have been I was a stranger, dealing with a foreign language, however familiar. It could have been I was alone in a city which still felt strange, a place that kept itself to itself, always with something new to discover, was simultaneously aloof and genial, suave and rude. I was most probably experiencing that feeling of uncertainty mingled with impending doom, but to me it was a little like being in love. I wished Irene was with me and kept seeing things I wanted her to see.

Simply, the smell of roses in rain.

I found them in a garden by a churchyard wall, the Cathedral Church of St Mary the Virgin on Great Western Road, the heavy flowers melancholy, huge and glistening. The perfume was trapped. When I shook the rose, the scent escaped.

It rained today. Just a little. After lunchtime it was no more than a drizzle, but by three o'clock there it was, full pelt, teeming down, and over by four.

I worked in the morning, went for a walk, got soaked and shook the roses coming home. Had Irene been buried, I would have visited her grave, would have stood on the cinder path and read the remains of her life.

I rowed with her mother. Irene wanted cremation, I said.

I want her buried. I do not want my daughter's body burned.

I feel it's my duty to respect Irene's wishes.

It's a pity you didn't respect them while she was alive.

And she replaced the receiver. Which is how most of her arguments are resolved. She injects a little barb and goes, places herself in the role of the victim, simultaneously trying to make you feel guilty, pretending she does not understand what you are saying, asking you to repeat yourself, to go over what you said, so your argument is lost in explanation. Irene used to come off the phone, put her head in her hands and stare at the table.

What's wrong?

Her. That's all, it's only her.

I think of my wife and her skin is glowing, her eyes are cobalt and strands of her hair catch the light, bits that turn on themselves.

She is wearing a patterned, floral dress and flat shoes, baking on a Saturday afternoon, the table a contradiction of flour and dough, bowls and forks, the kitchen warm as soon as you enter, a curtain of heat and Radio 4. Her arms are floury, her fingers sticky and there's a white blob on the bridge of her nose.

Don't, she says. Go away. I'm busy. Stop it. I have to get these things in the oven. I haven't got time. And don't get in a huff about it either. Finally, she says, See if the kids are okay. I'll be up in a minute.

Then she always has a piss and feels obliged to let me know she's doing me a favour, disparaging me for thinking such things in the first place.

Look at it, lying there. Look at the snigger.

The kids usually come in to be told we're having a cuddle, which means they want one as well, especially David, so we all end up in bed in the middle of the afternoon, talking and singing, telling stories until Irene remembers the stuff in the oven, jumps out of bed and runs downstairs naked, just to check.

I cannot understand time, neither do I accept its shrinkage, the way it concertinas into itself, becoming nothing. I do not understand the passage of the seasons. Autumn always surprises me, with the daffodils and crocuses, which are no sooner flowered than it's time for the tulips and then it's summer. New Year is an ending. I feel older. Birthdays are meaningless, but the celebratory nature of New Year cries of helplessness, of how the substance of our lives is compiled of waste and mystery. The important things take so little time. By simply recording your mother as she was then, remembering my wife and yourselves as children, I am not remembering myself, I have rather committed an illogical act. So much time has been taken. It is natural I should remember when my body was strong, when I was young and in love with a woman who was in love with me, that I should remember making love when our bodies were tuned to the charge of sensation. If I were to compile what happened between then and now I could barely muster three or four events a year. The rest is obsolete. I choose to remember not a whole afternoon, but five or ten minutes' worth, half an hour at most.

Irene's mother did not acknowledge her daughter as an adult. She was always a child. The mother looked at the moon without acknowledging night.

How long was it before you started sleeping together? she asked us after Sunday lunch.

Irene had dealt with this type of question before, and the way it was delivered, giving her mother maximum control, springing from surprise.

You don't want to know the answer to this, Mother.

Why not?

Tell me this, said Irene. I loved the defiant way she flicked her hair behind her ear. Tell me this, Mummy. Why did you ask a question like that? It could have been a year or it could have been five minutes, maybe it didn't happen at all, but I know this much, it's none of your business.

I find it extraordinary that my daughter should act in

a way I find disgusting, should abandon her upbringing and jump into bed with someone she barely knows, then have the audacity to tell me it's none of my business.

Let me tell you something worse than that. I did it because I love him and I did it because I wanted to make love with him and I believed he wanted to make love to me. Now, isn't that an extraordinary concept?

On the M8, beyond Livingstone, a huge tear rolled down Irene's cheek. We had barely spoken since leaving Edinburgh.

And though the incident was never regurgitated, it clearly developed in Irene's mother's mind into something disgusting which could not be discussed.

I know how she feels. Who doesn't?

You like this, she would say. Not any more, Mother, Irene told her. You do this. I do not, said Irene. She persisted in buying clothes Irene did not like, clothes she may have liked when younger. Every incident she recalls is from the time before Irene met me. There were handsome men who came a-courting, lost opportunities.

She took little joy in her grandchildren and was in perpetual arguments over their lack of manners, poor dress sense and bad taste. When she was three, Janie came back from a party. Why is my granny so horrible? she said. Karen Thomson has a nice granny.

Irene broached the subject. I have to, she said. I must say something.

You can't tell her what Janie said.

I don't think I should protect my mother from my children.

Neither do I, but at this stage it would be needlessly cruel.

Maybe I'll go through this Sunday then. Or Saturday; I'll go through on Saturday. We can go shopping; afternoon tea in Jenners, she loves that.

It was late when Irene got back. The kids were in bed. I'd bought a bottle of Glenmorangie and had a couple of glasses watching the football. She'd bought a skirt and a dress from Marks and Spencer, both of which were later returned, and stuff for the kids.

Did they go down all right? she asked.

Fine. We went ten-pin bowling and ate hamburgers.

Was that their supper?

The deal was they get a hamburger, come back here and do their homework. Then we made toasted cheese after bathtime and curled up with chocolate by the fire to watch an awful TV show.

I know the one. What about you? What did you have to eat? She kissed my forehead.

Leftover soup while they were watching TV.

Soup's better on the second day.

I take it you don't want to tell me how you got on.

Don't ask. I need a cup of tea.

Fancy a whisky?

No; I'm too tired. I'll have my tea in the bath. You watch the game.

I sat on the edge, the mirrors steamed over, Irene's face pink and shiny, hair in a fog and eyes closed, while she told me, in a voice that disbelieved her own experience, that she was eventually forced to tell her mother what Janie had said.

She was probably tired and didn't mean it. Poor little thing.

And later, when our children went their separate

ways, when Janie succumbed to hormonal bombardment, when the boys grew sullen and dour, even though she never said so, even though it was barely mentioned, and even though she seemed sympathetic, her attitude suggested she always knew it would end in tears, but hadn't told us to save the pain.

She asked me how work was coming along. Doing anything interesting? she said.

The fact that I work for a national newspaper, that my work is available for all to see, scarcely seems to have occurred to her. Don't you think it would be nice if they had him back on television? she asked Irene.

Thank God she's not around to see this. Towards the end, say for the last four or five years, I protected Irene from the worst of the office excesses. I also protected myself. For she would have insisted I see the editor, make absolutely certain he knew my position and my worth. She always thought someone was trying to undermine me, trying to usurp my abilities. In this case she could have been right.

Have a think about it, he said. Take your time; there's no rush. We can always use your skills and expertise, but this frees you, doesn't tie you down to one thing, and will certainly give you more time for writing. We've got a new political set-up here now, so maybe you could think of some other stuff you'd like to do, general features, that sort of thing. Have you ever thought of doing book reviews?

And it's important you know two things, he said. First of all, it isn't personal. We have always admired your work, the way you can cut through a speech, look at it for what it's worth, recognise a hidden agenda. And your contacts are, in my opinion, second to none.

I suppose these things come from experience.

Absolutely. Secondly, you are not the only one involved. Doubtless word will get round as to who the others are, I don't suppose it would be too difficult to find out if you put your mind to it, but it would be improper of me to mention anyone else at this stage. It's been a tough time for everyone, especially those of us with long-term responsibilities to think of, but decisions had to be taken and we thought it was time to freshen up certain areas.

I know what you mean.

A new approach would be better for all concerned. So, as I say, the terms are generous, have a think and let us know what you decide, in the fullness of time, of course.

When we married I was a rising academic. Change came with the 1964 General Election. I got a phone call from a television producer who wanted someone to comment on Wilson's victory north of the Border. I was well paid and recognised for about a week. Strangers smiled and said hello.

Eighteen months later I did the same again and in 1970 repeated my triumph, with almost weekly appearances in between. My academic colleagues were openly hostile, so when the call came three editors ago, I took a job which paid almost twice what I was making from every other source.

Since then technology has cleared the caseroom and switchboard, turning the editorial floor into a silent shadow of its former self. There used to be the clatter of typewriters, ringing telephones and open hostility. Now there's carpets, hushed telephones and computers. No one shouts, not even for a copy boy. Most of us have rooms which are generally shared with another person, so even the arguments, which were always a good source of entertainment, take place in private. There is also news management.

Irene was delighted when I moved to the paper. We got a bigger house and a bigger car. We went on foreign holidays and increased our family.

Spillage again. That list gives the impression that Irene was materialistic. It avoids intimacy, which is what I now recall, that it was a miracle to find love in my grasp, but to find it accompanied by material advancement, by comfort, when I had been so diffident, slow, thwarted by the poverty of my own beginnings, was something I could never have anticipated and cannot even begin to relate. So I spill a little time.

Old photographs.

Who are these strangers smiling into the sun? They hijack us with mystery and speak of things we can never understand. If only I could burn them. They are a shifting landscape. Why did we want to remember so many views of Italian cities, French chateaux, Majorcan plains, North African markets or Greek tavernas?

We photograph our children to protect the things we think their childhood represents, their sweetness, their innocence and unswerving ability to surprise. Photographs of birthday parties now break my heart. Yet we could not have avoided them at the time: the camera became as necessary as the cake and candles. Do we know what we are doing to ourselves, do we know what we are storing?

Every generation tells the next and is ignored. So we photograph that which is slipping away, like a ship to the sea, what remains are the chains and supports that held it erect and unfinished, the structure that supported whatever it was while being built.

The newspaper euphoria did not last. I moved to the wrong medium at the wrong time, had left a rising medium for the poor relation. I never fancied living in London, where no one wants a specialist in Scottish politics anyway. By the time we realised I should have pursued my academic career, done a few text books and the occasional piece of journalism, made myself available for election commentaries, by the time we realised the move was a mistake, it was too late. We were used to the dosh.

I saw more of the children when they were young, because I was around during the day. When they went to school, Irene often said, This man is your father. No one smiled.

It isn't funny, I said.

She said, You're telling me?

At the time I was sure she thought I was a failure; that she wanted to be the wife of an academic, the man she first admired.

It was as easy as wandering around in fog. We did not decide to do this, we made as few decisions as possible. We simply watched the landscape change, saw the hollows fill with vapour, the rooftops disappear and the spider's webs turn heavy.

Driving home at two o'clock of a summer's morning,

through the avenue of larch and birch when the sky was darkly blue and clouds the colour of the sea rose like rocks around me, the lonely beginnings of the dawn chorus; with the window down and the wind on my face I realised I was going home because of the children rather than myself.

But I never got used to being wanted. Driving home was always exciting. I loved the intimacy that came from sleeping together; two minds alive with separate dreams, yet their breath mingles above the counterpane, rising as one breath. I felt stronger, the closer I moved towards home. I never felt it was a sacrifice; that my wife and our children lived there, which made my leaving necessary. So I loved coming home, would phone from the office, to see how things were or say I was coming.

Home was Irene's natural habitat. I have watched her make something like scrambled eggs many times, yet they were always new, perhaps a touch more pepper, less salt, more cheese, different cheese, a little fresh herbs. I have watched the way she compiled a casserole, or better still, apple and blackcurrant pie.

Her face rapt in concentration, running her hands under the tap to make them cold enough to knead the pastry, the way she tucked the mixing bowl under her arm, rotating the other, biting her bottom lip, the way she measured the fruit, always dropping what seemed to be the same amount from every spoon.

It was a ritual, like a religious service. Can you forget the trips to the country, the way she'd scream for the car to stop and out we'd go to pick autumn blackcurrants, the way she turned a Pick Your Own Fruit trip into an adventure, reciting where each strawberry, raspberry, gooseberry would go? Everything was useful. What could not be baked or turned to jam was frozen, mixed and whipped into ice cream, a fool, or simply bottled. The Giffnock garden was her own creation.

I rarely saw her consult a cookbook. She sometimes watched television cookery programmes, but never copied recipes and often disagreed with their methods. She liked Delia Smith. I bought the Cookery Course books one Christmas, but never saw her use them. Now they're part of my kitchen equipment.

Nothing was too big, no dish too complicated, nor were there ever too many people. She loved Christmas, a miracle of sponges and sauces, starting with the Christmas cake in early October and finishing with turkey soup and barley in the middle of January.

I knew she was ill when I found her crying in the kitchen. She often did that, for no reason, yet perhaps our lives were reason enough. I wish I could see Janie's baby, she'd say.

But this was different. She was confused. I've forgotten what to do, she said. I've forgotten what I was doing.

That wasn't the worst bit. I held her as she sobbed, stroked her hair and ran my finger down the support muscle at the back of her neck.

Don't, she said.

I made tea and she said she was tired.

I tucked her in and cleared the kitchen. Putting away the cooking things, wiping down the table was the worst. Defrosting a ready-made quiche, heating it in the microwave was the worst.

Two days later she told me she was going to the doctor.

I have enough money. With insurance, redundancy payments and selling the house I am, at last, comfortable. I live in a building that used to be a church. There is a large living room, several small bedrooms and a view across the city, stretching on a clear day to Ben Lomond; sometimes light catches the loch like glass on the pavement.

I still work at night, rise late, eat little or nothing until afternoon and have too many clothes. I have taken to collecting Scottish pottery, mostly Bell's jugs, some Cumnock ware and almost anything from Portobello. I have some Wemyssware, but it has become too expensive, worse than Staffordshire. I take great delight in shops and salerooms. The collection is uninsured and mostly scattered around an old mahogany bookcase. Buying the sort of furniture I like, old and well used, was my second act of freedom; getting rid of the stuff from Fenwick Road was the first.

I have turned a bedroom into my workroom, stare out the window, watch the planes come in and the Campsies change, surrounded by notebooks and dictionaries. I am suspicious of the things I longed for: I want companionship rather than love, comfort rather than fashion, care rather than desire.

The present is peopled with characters from The Pages. They are like the products of my imagination, who do what I have never done. I love them, which is why they are here, they are as much a part of me as anything to do with Irene, the paper, AnnA, Wemyssware or Scottish politics. Ignore them if you think we have no imaginative dimension, that our lives are external happenings.

Last week I met a man I worked with for more than twenty years. He had also taken early retirement. After the polite and formal greetings, we had little to say to each other. He told me he had won the club championship medal and I had to ask, What for?

Golf.

Never knew you played.

I didn't until I retired.

We said we were in a hurry, he had to meet his wife, had heard about Irene's death and was very sorry. He promised to phone and we'd go for a drink, or maybe I'd like to come out to the house one night. There was a golf club dance coming off if I fancied it. I took his number and said I'd phone.

William walks round the West End. He's had three homes since leaving hospital, but had never previously lived in a house, never paid a bill, so he forgets what to do, closes the door and walks away.

He doesn't mean to; he likes the idea of living in a house and wants a place to stay because he doesn't like living on the streets, especially when it's wet, but William forgets things.

The first time he forgot his keys and did not know how to get into the house nor who to ask. He waited for someone to tell him. The police found the man with the key and let him in; he had left a pot on the stove.

Lucky we wurnae burnt tae death, said the woman downstairs. That boy's no right in the heid. He could've had us roasted alive.

William waited in for the Carer to show him what to do, or rather to remind him of what he should have done. She phoned to say she'd be along another day, but when she came she was already late for another appointment and left a video.

He enjoyed the hospital's Training For Living Programme. They showed him how to make his bed and use a washing machine, how to cook and clean, sweep and sew. They took him shopping, where he had to buy enough for one, take it home and cook a meal.

But William forgets things. He's all right when you remind him, but he forgets to do the things he was taught because there's no one to remind him.

He'd sit in the house, knowing he had to go shopping and cook, but not knowing how to do it. He usually ate dry bread or biscuits.

The second time he lost the house was when neighbours hadn't seen him for more than a week. They phoned the police, who broke the door down because William was sleeping.

The Carer said the house was unfit for habitation and took him back to hospital. But there weren't any beds, so they sent him home. He couldn't get in because the house was being fumigated, so he walked back to the hospital and said he wanted to stay. They found him a bed in the geriatric unit.

Then they gave him his last house. He forgot the keys. The man in charge of the building gave him a row. So when he forgot to take the keys next day, he didn't go back because he didn't like getting rows. He liked that house because it was next door to Margaret, who sometimes made him a cup of tea and a biscuit and always asked if he was all right.

Now he wanders and forgets to eat. William stands in church kitchens, in where it's warm. They give him tea and sausage rolls, sandwiches, biscuits and whatever's left. Then he walks.

If he sees the side door open, he goes in; the church folk always ask if he's well. The warden telephoned the hospital. William has been allocated a house, they said.

People on the street sometimes give him money, sometimes a fish supper, sometimes cigarettes. William doesn't smoke.

He doesn't like beards. Men with beards frighten him. His father had a beard. William doesn't want to grow a beard, but he forgets to shave.

He sometimes gets new clothes, people stop to give him things, but he forgets them, leaves his new clothes in the carrier bag. He likes his brown duffel coat and corduroy trousers, but they're warm in the summer, though it's sometimes cold at night. He sleeps up the park during the day, except when it's raining, and he spends the rest of the time walking round the West End.

I dreamed about Rhona last night. I rarely remember my dreams, but can recall this one all too clearly, so it must have come when sleep was running out, which is sometimes first light for me these days. I rarely sleep more than four or five hours and hit a low in the late afternoon when I read the paper, do the crossword, watch television or a little of them all.

Rhona came in the morning. It was that time, which happened every time we were in the car, but was never again like the first time, the time we always tried to recapture: a dark country road, only the headlights, Rhona lit by reflection, she'd had a couple of drinks, enough to loosen the tensions of being eighteen years old and trying to impress. She was wearing a black skirt and a chiffon shirt, her jacket in the back, and we were talking about I don't know what when, changing gear approaching a bend, I noticed her knees were close, almost touching my hand. Next time they touched. And the time after that. Then, on a straight stretch of road, while she was talking and I was laughing, I put my hand on her knee. She opened her legs and kept talking, acting normally. I love that bit and play it over in my head, when I'm driving, walking, sitting on the bus. Do you mind if I smoke in the car? she asked afterwards, and we laughed.

Next time it was us naked in her room. I want to see it scoot, she said. I've never seen it. She screamed. That's wonderful, she said. Do it again. Make it skoosh again.

What can I say? I did not deliberately manufacture this, nor do I seek to embarrass you. The Rhona bits may be awkward because they concern an aspect of me you could never otherwise have known, and because of what happened.

I haven't thought about it for ages, certainly not since AnnA, and presume they occurred because of the material, not this bit especially, but other bits which I may not show you.

This is an extract from an unsigned letter which may have been addressed to Faulkircher, though it is more likely to have been addressed to the Count Waldstein

124

and have fallen into Faulkircher's hands. Its destinations thereafter are unknown. The paper has what is thought to be a Rome watermark and the letter was sold to a Prague stamp, coin and curio dealer in Mikulandska, Stare Mesto in 1938.

FROM THE WATERFRONT

May, 1795
   Excellent Sir,
   I ask you to forgive me. Your time is far more valuable than mine, your presence far more worthy and I do not wish to intrude upon your excellency's presence. My plight is desperate and I would not have bothered you with my troubles were it not so. Hear me, I beseech you. Listen. Do not burn this letter. Do not throw it aside. Please read on.

Sir – whoever you are: if you have any sense you will do what she asks you not to do. She is a mad woman who has had me write this letter then write it again and again and again all to no avail with the same message as before differently put for no extra money; she is a witch and a hag who looks spent; forget it. I will write the letter because she asks it to be read back line by line and makes corrections backwards and forwards each time she hears it. Never again will I or any other letter-writer do her a service of any kind. She is crazed. Burn this.

My enquiries concern a gentleman. I am a lady of sorrows who shepherds the night, a shepherdess of

125

loneliness and misery, which I have known in my life. Punctual as twilight, I roam the streets, returning with the dawn when I will not be seen. I am not a dreamer, a lazy wanderer through midnight fields. Sir, I am a seeker in the mantle of darkness in all seasons and every weather. I roam the streets and alleys, never knowing what I find, searching for what I most desire. That which I seek is lost and dead yet alive in my heart. I know he lives. I know my love is alive and pray he is well.

I have prepared for him a garden of my heart. I have planted little seeds of blood from which my love will grow. I have taken dust from the moon and scattered it across the wind so it will find his eyes and make him sleep, render him immobile until I alone can wake him. Where is he? Tell me if you know.

I have saved to get this letter written by a priest who hangs on my every word. I saved to pay the reverend father rather than use a common letter-writer outside the church, in the squares or by the coffee-houses, those who deal in debt and commerce. What would they do for me? They write with hands like implements of torture, hands like tools or branches, hands like the pendulum of a clock. Hands that dwarf the pens they hold. What could they write with such hands? They would take my money and go to the poorest brothels.

I have asked the father who has heard my confession, who has seen me light candle after candle, though a continuous candle burns in my heart. I have asked because I trust him and because he knows me and my pain and can put this pain into his writing. He can make his writing more magical than it already is. I am a woman of no education, unlike yourself or the reverend father. I cannot understand how marks made on paper can be understood by someone they have never met, someone who has never heard their voice, someone they will never know, someone who may even be dead, how can they understand what they say through marks? I believe the marks are magic. I believe it is the spirit of the marks that talks, so I ask the priest to let the marks reveal my pain as though they had been planted on my back by a whip. Let the reader, you, sir, feel my anguish as you read. This I have asked the priest and this I know he will do. I ask you, sir, beseech you, show him. Show him the letter. Tell him it is me. He will come when he knows this. If he does not come he will be dead, or be dead inside and better dead than cause this grief, dead though walking and alive for he is dead inside, without a heart, without a conscience, without feeling or remorse, without goodness. If he knows it is me and can feel the pain in the marks and does not come then he is dead.

Please. Tell me he is well.

I desire to know his whereabouts and am writing to you as someone who will help. He has often spoken kindly of you and I know would be ashamed if he knew I was writing, which is why I can only whisper his name, can ask you to ask him if he remembers when we met in a place that shines like silver in the rain. This is something he will remember for he is a man of great memory, warmth and tenderness. He cannot look after himself and blusters, but is good at heart.

It is winter and I am cold. The money which could have warmed my body is being used on the love who warms my soul. I have searched this place and looked for him by the wharfs and the river, searched for my love among the stars and whispered his name to the friendly dark where I remember smelling him and tasting his breath.

He is fearful of the cold and will go wandering. He left and promised to return. My heart is locked for him alone, sometimes howling like a dog at the moon, like a hound from hell it tears my flesh. I will tell you how you know him. He never says goodbye. He is in a room then he is not in a room. He simply gets up and goes. He did not say goodbye. I know he will return.

Tell me he is well.

FOUR

For trouts are tickled best in muddy water

Samuel Butler (1612–80)

We haven't had this cold for twenty-five years, he said when I came down for breakfast. The proprietor was wearing two sweaters.

The rain was weak, then rattled at the windows, hard and strong.

After the Brahms concert, back at the hotel, I wakened suddenly in the night. The room was cold and my breath stained the air. I lay thinking of Robert throwing stones into the sea while I stood on the shore wishing there were things I could discard so easily. I read for a while, eventually slept and missed breakfast.

I had something in a café, walked along St. Dominique to Jean Nicot, where I worked till after four without feeling hungry. I ate a sandwich, took the Métro north, then walked around the *cimetière* till AnnA came running, fifteen minutes late.

Did you think I wasn't coming?

It crossed my mind.

Je m'excuse. I was working and had to stay late.

Have you eaten?

A little. You?

I had a sandwich.

You need more than a sandwich, she said, and kissed me.

I hesitated, just too long.

Sorry, she said, and turned away.

There's no need, none at all. It was wonderful. I'm sorry. I don't know what to say.

She smiled. I did not mean to have that effect.

It was unexpected.

For me too.

She was looking up at me. I kissed her and she held the kiss, suddenly jumping backward.

Blood, she said. My God. You're bleeding. Then she looked at her hands. It's me. I am bleeding.

Two small lines trickled from her nose, and everything else was lost in the fumble of tissues moistened with cold water from a tap by the gate.

We walked past the undertakers selling *cimetière* plots. Aware of the silence, I turned towards her and she smiled. I looked at the ground. She was wearing brown leather ankle boots, well polished, with a motif stitched into the toe. She took my arm.

You okay?

A little better.

Good.

And you?

I'm fine.

Well, that's good too. And it's nice to see you again.

There was only the wind and the skeletal trees and the threat of rain, clouds giving relief from the sky, as though the storm was in the air and hadn't reached the ground.

Last night, after the concert, she said, and stopped. I don't know how to tell you. Brahms always makes me cry. The pitch of her voice had altered slightly. When I got home I wondered if you would think it was the passion of the music, the beauty and majesty of the performance, or perhaps it reminded me of someone or something, a broken love affair or a place. I don't know what it is, but whatever it is works every time. I cried last night because it was the Brahms Piano Quintet, which always makes me cry. Simple. Now; I thought I could take you to a café, perhaps even a restaurant. We could eat something more than a sandwich, drink a bottle of wine and talk.

She blinked in the Métro light. I have trouble with my lenses, she said, brushing her finger along the bottom eyelash.

We sat opposite each other. I tried not to stare. She wore a wide skirt, polo-necked sweater and a patterned scarf. She drew the raincoat round her, tightened the belt and smiled.

I was reading the reserved seat sign, *mutilés de guerre, aveugles civiles*, and so on, when a busker strung a curtain between the poles at the end of the carriage and with a tape-recorded sound-track began his puppet show. It lasted for one station. He dismantled the apparatus, then slowly went around the carriage, offering the inverted puppet as a collection bag.

We're here, she said.

Where's this?

A secret. Is that word correct, *secret*?

It's fine.

The café was smoky, dark and perfect; lace curtains, chipped terrazzo floors, a smell of polish. We ate a little stew and salad, bread and cheese, and drank a bottle of *vin ordinaire*, a pale red, slightly weak and pleasant drink. She smoked nervously and talked. She had a degree in literature, but was not considered good

133

enough to research or teach, so she had recently started another degree, in computing, to give herself a better chance of a job. She worked part-time in a shop most mornings and sometimes in the afternoon. She had difficulty fitting in the classes and had come to my lecture because of the weather.

Tell me about the shop.

What do you want to know?

What's it called?

Par Essence.

And what does it sell?

Guess.

Can't.

Go on. I am sure you know. *Par Essence.* Do you know what it means?

Bien sûr.

Then what does the shop sell?

Essential oils?

And?

Tarot cards?

And?

Crystals, books on self-awareness, scented soaps, joss sticks, seashells, body creams, dried flowers.

You have such places in Glasgow?

Do you sell relaxation tapes?

She laughed.

Then we have such places.

And I wear a flowered smock.

How did you get the job?

The shop is owned by a friend, she said, lighting a cigarette. She was a literature student who could not find work, but was daring, more enterprising.

It's easy to be enterprising if you have the money.

No. Not at all. If you have money you are more careful.

What I meant was that some people I know couldn't get the money to be enterprising even if they found something to be enterprising about. It's called recession.

Here as well. It's everywhere.

Same as everything else. No longer a national recession. We have international recessions. Same as the news.

Isn't it a good thing? Don't you want to know what's happening in other countries?

Of course, but it has its disadvantages.

Such as?

They depend on whether or not you trust politicians to tell the truth or to act in your best interests. Tell me about your friend. Does she object to your smoking?

I cannot smoke in front of the customers. Hélène went to business school at night, prepared a plan, took it to her bank and they gave her the money.

All of it?

Je ne sais pas.

Did she buy an existing business?

There was another occupant in the shop, and I think she must have bought his business.

What did he sell?

Old clothes.

How did she graft a New Age boutique onto a second-hand clothes shop?

Second-hand: I love that expression. It's funny. The shop sold clothes that were unwanted rather than old.

We have that sort of shop as well, the sort of place where genteel ladies need not feel ashamed.

The area was being restored, I think, when Gare d'Orsay became a gallery. The houses were improved, new tenants moved in. Hélène decided a shop selling soaps and joss sticks would be okay and the bank agreed.

It's the consumer religion. Instant spirituality.

I think that is very cynical. But it may also be true. It is a good shop to work in. It smells nice, there is pleasant music playing and the customers are friendly. More coffee?

I think so.

And wine?

Are you having some?

A Renoir poster on the wall, where a woman is drying herself, with blue and mauve highlights on her body. The painting is in the Musée d'Orsay with the other poster on the opposite wall: Degas, *The Orchestra of the Opera*; oddly arranged, with the bassoon in front and a flute to his left, a double bass in front and a cello behind, then nothing but violins. The faces are wonderful. Tension; again, the performance. The players are mostly bored, though they could be engrossed. The stage is brightly lit with dancers' legs.

What are you looking at?

She was back with the wine; white this time.

The Degas.

Do you like it?

I think so.

I have seen it so often I don't know whether I like it or not. The coffee is coming.

That poster is much bigger than the actual painting. I love the way he compresses so much into a small space, yet manages to keep the tension and proportion.

Yes, I like all that, and the sad faces. I think I have seen it too many times.

The wine's delicious.

It's dry. It is also cheaper. I can never tell whether wine is good or bad, not after the first couple of glasses.

What literature did you study?

Mostly Rilke. There is a slight family connection – she lit another cigarette – and I liked his work.

I know very little about him, other than that he was born in Prague, brought up in Vienna and came here to write a book about Rodin. I think he stayed until the First World War.

Say that again.

Why?

It sounds as if you know nothing about Rilke.

I said that before I started.

Did I insult you?

Not at all.

I must have.

No. You were quite right. I was being silly, pretentious even.

You are funny. I insult you and you apologise. Wonderful. Anyway, Rilke is unique, I think, impossible to imitate. I am sure anyone trying to copy Rilke would be frustrated in a very short time. They could copy his integrity, his passion for perfection, the way he always remained a beginner; they could copy these things if they were brave enough, but they could never copy the work. I like him because he is a great poet who has had little or no effect on other poets.

Excuse me.

In the lavatory I washed my face with cold water. In the past, I had simply left; once walking beyond the table where she was waiting. What's wrong? she had asked outside. What did I say? It doesn't matter, I answered, walking on. She later apologised. My family say I've always had a quick tongue, have never needed assertiveness classes. I didn't mean to hurt you. It's not your fault, I said, and meant it. I'll need to toughen up, or maybe learn to shut up. There's nothing wrong with being sensitive, Rhona said. Women like sensitivity in a man. This is more than sensitivity, I said, not at all sure of what I meant.

AnnA said, They've brought the coffee. Are you all right?

Fine. You were talking about Rilke. What's the connection?

My great-grandmother met him. There was a story. I've forgotten. He did something. I don't know what. I'll ask; I'll ask my great-grandmother and tell you what she says. When will you know if you're staying?

I told her about Bernard and the Casanova papers, my Mackintosh piece and conversations with the editor. She was very still. There was a drift of smoke a yard above our heads. It was like being told of an illness, like giving bad news; having started I was condemned to continue.

I have to go now, she said.

What's the matter?

She folded the cigarette into the ashtray, gathered her

138

belongings from around the table, examining each item as though checking it belonged to her. Goodbye, she said.

In the street, I grabbed her arm.

Leave me. Do not touch me. Let go. Please, leave me.

What is it? What have I done?

It has nothing to do with me, she said. It is none of my business. If you know anything about Bernard you must know what he's like. It can either be ignorance or you agree with him. I have heard things, everybody hears things about him all the time, about his war record. Of course he supports Le Pen, thinks Pétain was a national hero and so on. I don't know. I have even heard he is a satanist. I have heard he is a lecher and is horrible to his wife. None of the students go near him unless they have to. You do what you like. I am going this way. You can find your way back to the hotel?

Look, AnnA. I—

Don't touch me.

We walked in silence to the Métro station, where she told me my first French joke. What is fifty metres long and has an IQ of 40?

A National Front demo.

I wakened with her smell, honey and Miss Dior, as though it were on the pillow. I thought I saw someone like her after breakfast. When I looked up, a flock of starlings turned right, into the Jardin des Invalides.

All day I felt an ache, like a blind horse sniffing for water. I worked in the small room, reading what I could, sorting the papers into compact bundles. It was late when I got back to the hotel. The room was warm. I slept as though I had fever.

I established a pattern that carried me through the next three or four days, working as long as I could, walking back to the hotel and eating alone in the evenings. I wanted to leave, but could not go, especially now. I was compelled to continue.

Saturday, and I went strolling round the Mouffetard. I found the room and took it on impulse. I told the hotel proprietor I was leaving. He lit a cigarette.

On the Sunday evening, after a walk round the Alpine Garden in the Jardin des Plantes and up towards the Arènes de Lutèce, I walked down the rue Monge, where a man and wife were arguing. The streets were almost deserted. I heard their voices before I saw the couple, alternately walking away from each other. One would stand still, staring after the other, who would then turn and shout. The argument came in bursts, one forward, one back.

I thought of sitting in a café on the place de la Contrescarpe – the white buildings dark above the café lights, the small Suzukis round the fountain, the cigarettes and conversation, the sense of theatre and the cobbles – then I thought of AnnA. I was becoming used to a loss I did not understand, feeling bad because I was unworthy of the moment. I was at the dusty Censier-Daubenton Métro station, crossed to the room and smells of dampness and polish.

A note was waiting, written on two sides of a page torn from a Clairefontaine jotter, the envelope pushed beneath the door.

It was in 1918 and I had just returned to Hamburg from Russia. My sister, Annie Mewes, was acting with the Zeigel Theatre and had obtained work for me. Henceforth, I became kapellmeister, pursuing a musical vocation which had obtained my occasional employment as piano accompanist in a small cinema during the last days of the silent movie.

The cinema was in a little provincial town in Russia. I lived on the country estate of the Baroness von R—, whose services I entered shortly before the start of the Great War. The community was parochial, remote and beautiful. Rumours of war did not reach us till 1915. Then came the revolution. The family fled as they could and I was deported back to Germany.

One day Annie, who was a confidante of Rilke, said to me: 'This afternoon Rilke is coming to take tea with me. You must meet him.'

He came to the house dressed in a uniform which gave him an incongruous air, and carrying a small basket of violets. These he placed on our aged lace tablecloth with a gracious flourish, and there they stood breathing a faint sweet scent into the late afternoon, into the smells of furniture polish and dying aspidistra. Eh bien. We talked of people we knew and places we had visited when suddenly I noticed a thin trickle of wetness spreading from under the basket and widening gradually into a large dark patch. At that moment Rilke noticed it too. Oh, my violets, he exclaimed, pulling his *handkerchief from his pocket. 'I am sorry. You must forgive them. They are still so young.'*

I rolled the envelope into a ball and felt the extra fold. Her note was inside: *This is my great-grandmother's story. She is 95 years old, born in 1898. AnnA. PS: The hotel proprietor gave me your address.* Her phone number was scrawled along the bottom.

I've had my eye on a small Art Deco vase with San Toi pattern from the Britannia Pottery. It was in an over-priced antique shop whose owner refused to haggle. Today, he relented. I told him it would complete a collection. Turnover's been a bit slack, he said. I now have examples of every Britannia design.

Carrying my prize down Buchanan Street, I was approached by two bronzed lads with shorts, rucksacks and a map. The taller pointed to the Mackintosh house, now part of the Hunterian Museum, a reconstructed piece of hokum. I thought they should take the subway to Hillhead and ask again from there.

When I said this, he smiled and shrugged.

Do you speak English?

He smiled and shook his head.

Français? Italiano?

Again he shook his head: *Deutsch*, he said.

I fumbled around a language I thought I knew. Eventually I was forced to point to the subway station and write Hillhead on a piece of paper.

I bought a bottle of wine, came back here and stared out the window. Even that which I depended on, that which was certain, appears to be going. Language now seems to be a written thing.

The problem is that I am not certain where The Pages are leading, or even why I am doing this. Is a picture emerging? I have already gone beyond my usual distance. I go for the short sprint; 1000 words is a long piece for me. I tell folk what someone said and what I think they meant. This is more or less the same, but has turned into a monster.

Do I edit these documents?

Of course. If edit means omit, then certainly. I do not reconstruct, neither do I invent, nor do I add. I remove the obsequiousness and irrelevancies, though God alone knows what they might be, and I have to translate everything to find out what's irrelevant.

Which brings me to the matter in hand, a document, written in English by an unknown writer, which bears the seal of the Venetian State Archives.

DOCTORS SAY SHE WILL RECOVER

God has delivered me from the plague. For seven days I have offered a mass of thanksgiving at the Church of Santa Maria del Giglio, built by the Zobenigos and rebuilt by the Barbaro family, who have mingled their exploits with God's upon the façade.

Venice herself sits at the top, crowned between Justice and Temperance. Stone boats are blown across the Campo Santa Maria Zobenigo, with the doorway in between.

My son has died and my daughter is feeble. Doctors

say she will recover. They said the same of my son. I pray every hour upon the hour for the repose of my son's soul and for the healing mercy of God's Mother to visit my daughter and lift her to health. I have prayed each day at the holy shrine beneath Titian's depiction of the Descent of the Holy Spirit in Santa Maria della Salute, prayed at the Salute for my daughter's health.

I have offered my services to the state in order to meet the doctors' bills. They bleed my daughter daily. She grows no better. Two nights ago her mother applied a poultice of herbs which brought sleep to her body and, I pray, to her mind.

I believed God had blessed me when she was born. Now I constantly try to thank Him for what He has given rather than what I fear will be taken away.

I believe fish are immortal. They are our souls. We become them when we die, when we inhabit another world. I have searched the waters from the Rio di Santa Maria Zobenigo to the Canale di San Marco, to the seas and the oceans themselves, fancying I see my son swimming with a shoal as he played with his friends. I did not weep for my son. He was as beautiful in death as he was in life.

Days are no longer hour by hour. The sun moves pain by pain. My comfort is in the behaviour of souls. They become unbodied here on earth, rising to heaven. When do they become fish? This is a subject of great controversy. Debates have taken place, without agreement.

What else can fish be but our souls? They drown in air, inhabitants of another world, a world we can never know. Agreement on this has been reached. Fish are souls in purgatory. By harvesting them from water we may be saving them from further torment. God may take these souls to heaven, or they may be forced to return as fish, swimming so we can know they are with us, a reminder of what will come to us all.

At certain points upon this earth, the souls rise to heaven to return to the sea. There are times of the year and, with a conjunction of equinoxes, magnetic lines, cardinal points, stellar observatories, there are places where the pull of the moon on the water can be studied more clearly, places where we can feel this force, can see its power for ourselves.

How then are thunderstorms explained? When we feel the death of a child, when we sense a murder or a bad death, we know that God our Creator expresses His wrath, sends the rains to warn us, and at these places, where cardinal points and magnetism meet, we know the souls of children dwell, who have not yet been able to understand sin, though they have been taught by diligent parents that they are human and born in sin, conceived in sin, and whatever they may do on this earth should be mindful of ensuring their later salvation.

Who has not known of children who are born deformed, difficult births where children did not want to enter the world, or children so unwilling they have died in the womb or soon after birth, being born too thin and unable to breathe?

This is the point of dispute. For is man so sure of himself, so self-centred he now believes he can create a soul? Man can barely save his soul, far less create life.

Souls were created in the Garden of Eden and God has ordained one for us all. There is a shelf upon the perch of heaven where souls reside. When we are made we are given a soul, in much the same way as we are given other gifts we do not understand: speech and movement, thought and hearing. These are components of the soul, rather than individual entities, existing themselves in a single body.

Think of a boat. It is composed of a sail and a rudder, a hull and a mast. We place this boat upon the water and expect it to float. It is immobile unless there is wind, which we can neither see nor explain. God's breath. Without wind the earth would be uninhabitable. We hoisted sails before we saddled a horse. Boats and wind are the source of all trade, and trade has built the richness of Venice. Our souls are to our bodies as wind to a sail.

Little souls descend to earth like rain or particles of matter. They find a child about to be born and give it life. When the soul arrives the child can be born, can make the journey from nothing to now, as a boat leaves Venice for Constantinople.

When they descend, the souls often do not know they must come to a child. They may find themselves inside a goat or a sheep, a dog or a hen. There they must stay until the animal is killed, when once again they must rise to heaven and wait in a box on the shelf for an angel to send them downwards, let them fall to earth like gossamer.

Does my son await on the perch of heaven or does he swim as a fish in the sea? I ask, but will never be told, any more than I know where my mother waits or my father swims.

I have taken this time to explain to Your Excellency the urgency of my petition. I have done the work you

146

requested and desire that I should be paid in full. Your Excellency has been kind enough to make certain arrangements concerning the doctors' bills, for which I am grateful. My daughter is ill. Doctors say she will recover. I have worked quickly, and I hope worked well. I am sure Your Excellency will be satisfied. Please now let my daughter be treated.

You asked and I will tell what I know.

Sgr. Casanova presently lives with Senator Bragadin in the district of San Marco, near to where they say Marco Polo was born. I do not wish to insult Your Excellency; he, like most Venetians, will know the Bragadin mansion. On the other hand, I have, as Your Excellency already discovered, known Casanova since we were students at Padua University, and though I have always known of his humble origins, I have never known him to be poor. He was never impoverished, as I am now impoverished. He has always had a patron. There were many rumours and considerable gossip surrounding this and other aspects of Casanova's life, especially since there was no other Paduan student from a similar background receiving such obvious help. It is true, as Your Excellency suggested when we met, he has always attracted interest and has done little to avert attention. I can only remark that the difficulty with our system of patronage is that ability is not always recognised. He was not entirely happy when I renewed our acquaintance.

In Padua he studied music, having learned to play the violin. He studied mathematics and logic with his bosom friend, Padre Rodolfo, who kept the library and looked after the injured. I know Giacomo helped him mend a coachman's leg and I believe he was also involved in the amputation and castration of a boy soprano whose lower body had been crushed by a horse. Rumours were widely circulated.

He had drops of alchemic devising which he would openly insert in a woman's wine. Should they agree to the initial insertion, he would tell them subsequent insertions were imminent. These drops were known to be successful and were very popular. I myself can vouch for their effectiveness.

A company of players came to Padua with a foolish play, where an older man is enraged with passion for a younger woman, who loves no one or nothing more than herself. She owes everything to the older gentleman, yet has forgotten his goodness, believing goodness itself to be transitory, dependent on what could be bartered in return. She said she was unable to surrender to goodness lest it devour her, like passion.

Giacomo Casanova, whose background I later learned was theatrical – his mother, I believe – had seen this piece, implied he might at one time have even performed in it, and was mightily moved by a theatrical device.

Early in the play, the old man, with a grey beard, bent back and strong stick, declares his love for the girl, who laughs at him before running off. Her laughter hurts him.

'See my heart,' he says, inviting the audience to thrust their hands into his chest, having thrown his cloak aside to where his heart was visible. He invited the audience to clasp their hand around his heart.

'Is it warm?' he asked. 'Is it beating? Is it full of life?'

Inside his chest was what I presumed to be a phial of hot water, which the audience clasped and smiled.

Later, when his feelings have been continually violated, the old man asks the same people to feel his heart. He throws aside his cloak. They plunge their hands into his body, feel for the heart – and find a stone.

Casanova thought this was very powerful. Theatre by stealth, he said. Even the great Goldoni could not have devised such a way of showing, he said.

I remember this because he usually condemned what we had seen. I remember we had seen a piece by, I think, Beaumarchais. 'Awful,' he said. 'Worse than awful. Contrived, pretentious and without substance. It depended upon the ignorance of the audience. One wondered what one was applauding, the actors' ability to fool or our own stupidity. Do you know the work of the great Goldoni? He would refuse to piss on such a script. This is a travesty. The legal documents he wrote in the tavern while pretending to be a lawyer are better than this. Anything he wrote, his laundry lists, gambling bills, letters to his creditors are better than this.'

And when the company appeared, he left us standing: 'Brilliant. Absolutely stupendous. A work of magnificence, masterfully interpreted,' he said with grandiloquent gestures. 'Worthy of the name Goldoni. I can praise nothing more highly.'

I understand he obtained a law degree in Padua. Who bought it for him, I do not know, though I understand his father, Sgr. Grimani of the San Samuele Theatre, may know something of his unacknowledged son's graduation. If Casanova is not Grimani's son, why did

Grimani pay his way through university, effect letters of introduction and cover his expenses? Why has he subsequently introduced him to society? Why bother to clear the way for the son of one of his actresses?

I have, as you instructed, sought to ascertain what happened between then and now, and will relate only what I have heard from more than one source.

He claims to have been seduced by two women simultaneously, the sisters Nanetta and Marta Savorgnan, who were between fourteen and sixteen years old at the time. They are also related to Grimani.

The grandmother had been living by Palazzo Grassi, opposite Rio della Toiletta near the San Samuele Theatre. How could her daughter, an actress, get a house like that? When granny died, the grandson sold her furniture.

More can be learned from Razzetta the bailiff, who was sent by Grimani after Casanova had taken a suit against them.

He was lodged with a lady who has also worked at San Samuele, a lady who does not wish her name recorded, but is readily available. The mother wrote from Warsaw, I have seen the letter, urging Sgr. Grimani's brother, the Abbé Grimani, to remove her son from such a place. I think she feared for his physical and spiritual safety. He was removed to Murano; but returned at night to thrash Razzetta and participate in other forms of entertainment. I do not suppose Razzetta would speak for nothing, but his information could be cheaply obtained. He has a debt of honour to settle.

These activities were discovered. There were considerable problems for all involved, resulting in a hasty tour, when everyone, especially the Abbé Grimani, thought their incubus had gone for good. Where he went or what befell is not at all certain. He seems to have been in Rome and Naples, visiting clerical acquaintances of the Abbé, who had effected a number of introductions.

I would be at pains to insist no hint of scandal has brushed against the Abbé Grimani. The same cannot be said for those of his friends and colleagues for whom I understand Casanova was an enthusiastic, willing and capable servant, especially where their mistresses were involved. Prelates, as you know, often need some assistance in these matters. No one is sure whether the periods when they are absorbed in ecclesiastical business are as frequent, necessary or prolonged as they often appear. Neither do I believe the time spent in prayer is as absorbing as it would seem, nor as lengthy.

I have heard a rumour from a single, impeccable ecclesiastical source who was there at the time. All did not go well in Rome. Through connections within the church, Casanova became the protégé of Cardinal Aquaviva, who some say is more powerful than the Pontiff. He is certainly one of the wealthiest men in Rome. Again, we feel the hand of Grimani. Who but he could effect such an introduction?

Aquaviva introduced his protégé to the Pontiff, and he is reputed to have composed the love poems Cardinal Sciarra Colonna sent to the Marchesa Catrina Gabrielli to such effect. I believe the Marchesa recognised their true author – who wouldn't against such competition? – and rewarded him cardinally.

Never less than dedicated to self-improvement, he

used his time in Rome to learn French. The teacher found his daughter and her lover abed. She was pregnant and they were about to elope. The intended bridegroom is said to have borrowed money from Casanova.

The couple were caught in the act of elopement. The bride escaped to Casanova's apartments, where he convinced her to throw herself on Aquaviva's mercy. Aquaviva let her escape with her lover, but dismissed Casanova, because, it is said, the cardinal's superior and Roman propriety demanded a sacrifice. I believe, and others have suggested, that Aquaviva saw an opportunity to rid himself of an impediment.

Casanova was dismissed with money, introductions and a passage to Constantinople.

Having concluded that a life of honesty, poverty, prayer and devotion was not for him, there next befell a curious incident, of which again I am compelled to relate what I know. Before beginning, I would trust your worships will realise that the information I have gathered and have so far disclosed was obtained in costly circumstances. I have paid dearly for these understandings and have used more than a single source. I need only tell where I gathered this talk and your worships will know how my time and money has been spent in their service. I would ask you to remember me and my daughter in our time of need. My daughter has sold some teeth and most of her hair to pay for the doctor's visits. I have sold all my teeth.

I have been forced upon the kindness of others, especially in matters concerning the subject. Here I was fortunate, for many are willing to talk. I approached him directly. Were we not together at Padua? Did we not have exploits, play games and take chances together? Did we not share our youth?

He looked at me. His eyes were so clear one could almost see him calculating the good I could do him.

'Padua?' he asked, as though he had barely heard of the place.

'Indeed. We were students together.'

'I do not remember you,' he said.

I think he remembered me all too well. He remembered the money I gave him for gambling and the fact that I rescued him from a delicate situation which could have cost him his university career, a situation from which his connections could not possibly have saved him. I know he remembered. There was memory in his eyes.

Next time we met was not in such company. I was crossing the Ponte dei Barcaroli o del Choridoro. He was alone, sheltering in a doorway. He pulled me in towards him.

'How do your investigations proceed?' he asked. I told him I wished I had a better subject. He pushed me into the rain again.

Since then, I have feared for my life and the life of my daughter. Again, I plead for her protection. He obviously has a lot to hide. I know he can be very vindictive. Nor is my subject known for his tact. He cannot retain his own counsel, which has made my task a little easier, my information fuller, more rounded, related with greater detail and veracity. There is a continuous drawback. What I hear from one source I have to check with another. I do not scour bordellos nor give parlourmaids a satin purse or chicken wing.

I have mingled with the scribes who shelter in the arches around the Piazza San Marco. For days I have lingered by the Porta della Carta, hovered in the Cortile, bribed and cajoled *gondolieri*, even those who are paid to remove the bodies of the cats, dogs and people stinking the canals. I have spent more time in churches, with drunken priests and anxious prelates, than at any time since I was christened or confirmed. This has taken a considerable effort, especially while ensuring my daughter's needs are met, though she is as blessed with a caring mother as I am with a dutiful wife. Needless to say, I can vouch for everything I say. I am in no position to mislead Your Excellency.

There is a priest who served at San Giorgio Maggiore, but who seems to have spent more time in the nunneries of Murano – her name was Violetta, an orphan, now in the service of Galuppi's orchestra, an interesting connection I will develop later. Had I time and unlimited expense, I would have investigated Baldassare Galuppi's association with Grimani's San Samuele Theatre, where operas he has written to libretti by Goldoni are frequently performed.

Fr. Thomasso travelled from Rome with Casanova. This story was related in the sanctity of the confessional.

Our subject fell for a singer he found posing as a *castrato*. He told Fr. Thomasso her name was Bellino, a stage name presumably. He knew she was not a dismembered male at the start of his courtship, but reached a point where he did not care.

He abandoned the priest and went with the *castrato*, no further than Sinigaglia. Her name, he discovered , was Angela Calori. She was born in Milan in 1732. They were to be married in Venice, but she had to fulfil a contract in Rimini.

Casanova lost his passport and was imprisoned at Pesaro while Aquaviva had another document prepared. He escaped by stealing a horse.

Fr. Thomasso met him in Bologna, where he heard the confession. I do not know how distraught he was at losing his lover, but can confirm that when he returned to Venice disguised as a soldier, Abbé Grimani greeted him with open arms. I understand Angela Calori is now prima ballerina at the Duke of Castropignano's theatre in Naples. A talented lady.

He has travelled to Corfu and Constantinople. All I know is that during these expeditions he established, nurtured and developed his love for faro and there was talk of other liaisons, Turkish delights of the bearded variety. I am told all Corfu knew of a woman who gave him the pox after he had her hair ground into sweetmeats and lost money at cards.

If I discovered these facts, they are open to anyone who may interpret them as they wish and do with them whatever they like. A citizen in Senator Bragadin's position ought to be warned of his actions and of the problems that may arise. If he liaises with someone who is open to blackmail, is he not open to blackmail himself? Does Senator Bragadin care? And what of Senators Dandolo and Barbaro? I fear they are also implicated.

Difficulties multiply nightly. He leaves the Bragadin

Palace, moving along the Rio di Santa Marina, turning into the Rio dei Mendicanti for assignations at the Cimitero on San Michele or in the nunneries at Murano.

The other day, I heard someone say, 'Bragadin, who will neither leave heirs nor be troubled with finding husbands for his daughters, has taken another catamite on board the good ship *Bravaducci*.' The gossip went on to relate: 'This one is a violinist, a second fiddler – where else but in the San Samuele Theatre?'

Let me remind Your Excellency, Fr. Thomasso's Violetta is also a violinist in Baldassare Galuppi's orchestra. I know Casanova has carried messages, for the priest has told me. He does not fear for Violetta's safety. 'I know too much about Casanova,' he said. Of course, Casanova is no longer employed at the San Samuele Theatre.

There is a romantic tale. He met Senator Bragadin at the opera house. The senator was taken ill and Sgr. Casanova, the poor violinist, came to his aid. I ask Your Excellency, knowing them as you do, does that seem in any way likely? Who but a fool would believe such a story, especially from one who has been known to indulge in midnight pranks of which I mention one all Venice knows and which I am sure the rulers will never forget.

With his brother Francesco, who is even more of a *castrato* than the 'damoiselle Bellino, and other blades, including Balbi and Androlino, pretending to be, amongst other things, representatives of the Council of Ten, they have taken women to San Giorgio and abandoned them after their desires were sated.

Can you forget the weaver's wife who did not support her husband's complaint, though we all knew better?

Senator Bragadin met Casanova while the violinist was playing at a wedding ball at the Palazzo Soranzo. Senator Bragadin insisted on giving him a ride in his gondola, where the senator was suddenly taken ill and Casanova found a doctor, I believe it was Grimaldi from San Benedetto, who bled him. The violinist's shirt was used as a bandage.

Upon arriving at the Palazzo Bragadin, the fiddler claims to have been surprised when he discovered he had saved the life of Matteo Giovanni Bragadin, whose best friends, the Marcos, Dandolo and Barbaro, came to offer succour and comfort. Everyone agreed Casanova should move in, to keep abreast of the situation and be of service should anyone fall ill.

I understand Your Excellency has commissioned other reports concerning the surgeon-barber who attended Senator Bragadin. I do not wish to interfere with another inquiry that may be continuing, except to say the senator believes Casanova saved his life. This assertion is well supported by his friends, which may account for the barber's later misfortunes.

My understanding is he applied a mercury poultice to the patient's chest, which aggravated and inflamed the skin and heart, which was in no state to put up much resistance. Casanova removed the poultice and the senator slept peacefully. Consider the consequences had the senator died. That has to be said, especially when the subsequent developments are considered.

Senator Bragadin is 57. Dandolo is the youngest of

the trio, being aged 42, and Barbaro is the eldest, aged 58. Casanova is 21.

They hailed him as a genius, an assertion he did nothing to discourage. Rather he felt free to discourse upon anything in the absolute certainty of having an audience.

Again, I know Your Excellency is well acquainted with Senator Bragadin's beliefs on sinning and repentance. I will later be relating a visit the quartet made to San Marco, where the sermon was on the stars and fortune-telling, on crystals and their power, on sorcery, alchemy, black art and *diablerie*, on water cures and fables, on the Philosopher's Stone, oils, plants and palmistry, cards, birds' eggs, rocks and fire. Easy ways to spiritual fulfilment, the archbishop said. Tools of the devil. Pretence.

Your Excellency has, I know, investigated these matters many times and has, I believe, been unsuccessful. I have gathered firm evidence, recorded in the Turkish bath which is part of Senator Bragadin's home. I knew it would take place because we had intelligence of what the elderly trio were contemplating. This conversation will, I am certain, make absolutely clear that the Cabala is behind their deliberations.

We know *De la Caballa intellective, art majeur* is possessed by all three. By constructing the magic pyramid of letters, they believe it is possible to actually create the Almighty's presence.

It is suggested that Casanova studied this art in Corfu and Bologna, where the church of San Petriono is supported by eight columns. The dimensions of the building demand twice that number, especially since it is made of brick. The lower part of the façade has been faced with marble, to hide the scale.

San Petriono is a miracle of mass and space. There are holes in the ceiling where circles of light descend to a brass rail which runs at an acute angle down the left side of the cathedral. I do not know the purpose of this, but have heard it attracts many visitors. Fr. Thomasso told me these things himself. What disturbed him was the precision. The rail runs from an exact point in the wall beside the door, down to another in the adjoining wall, which has a Latin inscription he has forgotten. There are numbers, months and letters beside the rail, which supposes it to be a calendar. It is, according to Fr. Thomasso, proof of universal wisdom, communication with the Hidden Ones.

Senator Bragadin was convinced that his protégé's wisdom meant he was not as young as he seemed, that he had cryptic communication with the Hidden Ones. Casanova knew what this meant. Dandolo was the inquisitor. Barbaro was elsewhere, but party to the discussions nonetheless.

I need hardly remind Your Excellency of the difficulties in obtaining such a transcription. Secrecy has been ensured. Venice is cruel to those who serve her. Paoli Rainier and his son were blinded when they made the Torre dell'Orologia, preventing another city from having such a clock. Bodies of the scribes have been recovered from the Rio de San Polo, for the good of our beloved Mother and the protection of her citizens, those who love her.

I have lodged copies of everything, along with Your

Excellency's letters on this subject, with an official who is employed in a building of plain wooden doors, ornate walls, ceilings and surrounds, of giant stairs and golden stairs, a building Casanova entered recently on the arm of his protector.

Your Excellency knows this building well. We have sat in a working room decorated with maps of the known world, from the Mediterranean to Asia Minor, northwards to the land of the Scotch and the island of ice, with both American continents in the west. This room has a plain ceiling, not to distract from the business of trade. Other ceilings are so sumptuous they would disturb a woman on her back, especially if she was interested in geometry or floral design.

Casanova has said he learned geometry at the San Marco floor. 'I wondered at the tiles,' he told Dandolo, 'how they were placed in that order.' This building is not San Marco, but it also has uneven floors.

Neither Your Excellency nor I have been welcomed in the halls beneath the paintings at the top of the golden stairway. But Your Excellency has walked the plainly mottled floor, between wooden walls, and raised his eyes to the glory of Venice on the ceiling, framed and surrounded in ornate gold. Your Excellency also sits in the sumptuous council chamber with hard wooden seats; as do the other recipients of these papers.

My daughter does not improve. The surgeon bleeds her. We have no money for medicine, nor for any other treatment. Were this Your Excellency's child, I do not thinks he would be treated this way. I do not know what will become of this material should my daughter die.

Please at least send confirmation that you have this material, that it has not fallen into other hands.

We are not finished. Was it then or shortly afterwards that we saw them in San Marco?

Consider: it is impossible to meet in the Piazza San Marco. The smaller streets where barely two can pass, the streets with continual dark corners are more likely meeting-places. Look down the piazza from the San Marco doorway and what do you see? Some see the pigeons. Others can count the columns and figures on top of the columns, the windows and decoration on top of the Procuratie Nuove.

Others are there to be seen. Need I remind Your Excellency: a mosaic of Christ with his Cross and Saints, whose very border is entwined red, blue and green, and sculpted faces and figures of Venetian trades, with Christ again at the centre of the world, angel graces above him, dominate the central doorway through which everyone must enter San Marco. How many saw the quartet whose costumes rivalled the mosaics? As many as the marbles in San Marco, or as many as the colours and mottles within the marbles.

They fopped and giggled, paraded and flirted. Even pigeons enter the cathedral, swoop around the saint's sarcophagus through the bronze gate, desecrate the tomb of he who wrote the gospel of Our Lord. My daughter used to be entranced by the birds that swooped through our own poor chapel, gliding among candlelight and incense.

Creeping round the galleries at the top of San Marco, where hawks and doves are imprisoned in the stone-latticed pillars, near the windows where we can see the gold and smiling horses of San Marco, their right or left foreleg lifted and three spaces in each of the golden manes. I intend to show Your Excellency I have been there and will relate what I saw beside the places where the workmen have drawn on the walls, where we can examine the mosaics in the minutest detail, the small figures, birds, a child among corn, a kneeling mother or an old man. What I saw on the wooden platform I will explain when we meet.

They laughed at the sermon. Two masses were celebrated in San Marco that day, one whose music rose with incense from the altar over the saint's body; the other in the gallery, where the glamourie of Satan renounced the works below.

I have felt my son's soul hovering for the past four days. And now he has a companion. My daughter died with nothing left to sell, with nothing anyone wanted, with neither hair nor teeth, while I was working on this report, begging Your Excellency to provide. She died singing: My head is filled with angels, she told my wife, who curses you as thoroughly as I do myself.

The last of my money has gone on having these pages copied by public copier. A version is being prepared for Senator Bragadin. This will go to you as agreed and another to my anonymous party to whom I will testify. I have nothing left to lose.

'The harvest is past, the summer is ended, and we are not saved. For the hurt of the daughter of my people am I hurt; I am black; astonishment hath taken hold on me. Is there no balm in Gilead; is there no physician there? Why then is not the health of the daughter of my people recovered?' *Jeremiah 8:20–22.*

FIVE

Tell me what you want
and I will tell you who you are.

A Boring Story,
Anton Chekhov

Mathilde brought coffee three times a day, sometimes with a sandwich. She opened the door and put the tray on the table. She never addressed me directly, but answered politely, only when Mme. Bernard was not at home.

Mathilde told me, Monsieur is ill and Madame is worried. He should not have spoken at the conference. He should not have gone out so soon after his illness.

What's wrong?

No one tells me. He is now in hospital. I have to stay here some nights to prepare breakfast and help Madame with lunch if there are guests. At night I am used to the professor coughing. He had no peace. One hour before lunch, he was up and dressed. He seemed in excellent form during lunch. The company would leave at two o'clock, perhaps half past, and when the door closed I have seen him collapse on the floor. I have helped carry him into his bedroom and have watched Madame give him oxygen from the cylinder by the bed.

She'd smile and leave. You have papers to attend to, she'd say. I am certain she thought I was a clerk or a government official. She sewed patches on the elbows of my threadbare jacket. One day she brought a silk dressing gown, which I wore while she washed and ironed my shirt.

One Wednesday, maybe two or three weeks after

AnnA's note, I did not go to the flat. I wondered how to tell Mme. Bernard I had failed. I did not know where or how to begin. All I had were bundles, divided into separate languages, and a list of what was in each bundle. Nothing else. There were no sources. The papers would have to be authenticated and dated; only then could they be properly studied. It was a massive commitment which would clearly need to involve other people.

I rang the doorbell on Thursday morning at half past nine. There was no reply. I telephoned every hour until 6.00 p.m. Mathilde answered. *Monsieur est mort*, she said.

I went back to the room and packed, thinking I would leave sometime on Friday. On impulse, I called the number at the bottom of AnnA's page.

I got your grandmother's story, I said.

You got my grandmother's story some time ago. Are you really living in that horrible room?

Bernard died this morning. I'm going home tomorrow. I phoned to say goodbye.

Can I see you before you go?

We ate from the 75F menu at Le Trumilou on the quai de l'Hôtel de Ville. The main restaurant was busy, so we sat at a table beside the bar, with smoke from the restaurant and *le zinc*. It was a noisy meal. When anyone raised their hand the waitress shouted, *J'attends*, and carried on with what she was doing.

We walked across the Pont d'Arcole, where contemporary dress seems out of place, the city like a stage set. The Seine divides at the Ile St-Louis, like the prow of a cruiser coming upstream.

It seems a shame with your work half done.

It's hardly started.

What do you have to do?

Everything. I don't know what I am doing. All but a few documents need translation into English. I don't even know what many documents are; some are very lengthy, others a few pages. There are bills and statements in with documents, diaries, letters and notebooks. It's a mess. Initially it seemed interesting, but none of it makes sense. There seems to have been an attempt, perhaps more than one, to catalogue what was in there. Perhaps it was the basis for something Bernard meant to write. I don't know. Maybe he did write it. The whole thing is a mess.

Then take it away and work on it.

I can't do that.

Why?

The papers don't belong to me.

They certainly don't belong to Bernard.

How do you know that?

Tell me how you think a man like him, an academic, managed to acquire such an apartment? And how did he gather this collection?

I've no idea. Perhaps his wife had money.

As a matter of fact, she was not poor. Neither was she rich, but she was well connected.

That hardly explains anything.

Precisely.

So what's your explanation?

I don't know for certain; what I mean is I can prove nothing. Bernard, as you know, was a well-known Nazi sympathiser.

AnnA, for God's sake. France was full of Nazi sympathisers during the war.

Hear me out. Or have you already decided it's too stupid?

She shouted this. We walked in silence and after a while she spoke in quiet, measured tones.

Are you an only child?

I am one of three. I have a brother and a sister who married an American airman and lives in California.

Do you see her?

Three times since she left. She came to Scotland twice and four years ago, maybe five, I can't remember, Irene and I went to Long Beach, had dinner on the *Queen Mary* and saw Howard Hughes's *Spruce Goose*. It's a wooden aircraft which Hughes actually flew and they play a recording of the flight to prove it. The rest of the time we were taken round a circuit of bridge and dinner parties. I was socially inadequate because I do not play golf. We left early, lied about our flight, hired a car and drove from Los Angeles to San Francisco along the coast by San Simeon and through Salinas. Cannery Row was a big disappointment. They have a Bear Flag Restaurant and all that. It's like Dublin, where there are brass plaques on the pavements telling you where Leopold Bloom stood.

I understood about half of that.

What didn't you understand?

Never mind; tell me about your brother.

He plays golf every morning and visits my sister every second year. He sleeps in the afternoon, watches television at night and reads the *Scotsman* to prevent him vegetating. He lives in a place called Carnoustie, on the east coast of Scotland, above Dundee. He has a small, two-bedroomed bungalow and a tiny garden which he has stuffed with roses because he says they don't need much attention. Do you know what a bungalow is?

Of course.

He bought the place in Carnoustie because property was cheaper there than anywhere else, he said.

And it obviously has a golf course?

Very much so.

Is your brother mean?

Do you know that in all my life I have never seen him spend any money? I used to take him to the pub, buy the first couple of rounds, then he would ask what I wanted. If I wanted a drink, he bought one for me alone. If not, he said, Right then, let's get going.

Do he and his wife have any children?

A girl called Andrea, who occasionally comes to Glasgow, say about twice a year. I buy her lunch and she gets the train back to Edinburgh, where she works as a solicitor. Her parents are proud. They think she's done terribly well. My sister has two children, a boy and a girl. I have no idea what they are doing. I did know one time, but I've now forgotten.

And what about your own children?

What about them?

Tell me about them?

I'd rather you told me about Bernard.

Why? Aren't you proud of your family?

Not especially. I sometimes find it painful to talk about them, especially to a stranger who simply seems inquisitive.

I am trying to get to know you better.

We were walking by the river, across the cast-iron Pont des Arts and past the square-faced Mint, through a pattern of incongruities, the Louvre coldly lit and naked in the night, the prow of the Ile de la Cité and the wings of the Pont Neuf, the continual buzz of traffic and the clatter of the *bateaux mouches*, two storeys high, the top decks empty, floodlighting the banks, so Paris appeared flared on its own screen, its images rising and falling, the substance having become an illusion. When they passed, the boats left a trail of water lapping the bank, and a squawk of seagulls. The trees were bare and fankled. AnnA took my arm.

You sounded angry, she said.

I didn't mean to.

You're not angry?

Not really.

Sure?

Certain.

Good, though I hope what I have to say will make you angry.

An old couple passed. He stepped in front of us, making us stop while his wife and dog passed. They were identical, wrapped in woollen coats with scarves and hats, he in dark blue, she in brown, the dog in a knitted jacket.

Merci, he said, raising his hat.

Bernard moved around during the war, said AnnA. Some say he was doing one thing, some another. What is certain is that during this time he gathered an immense fortune. It has been proven that documents from university libraries, from public records offices or the Bibliothèque National, documents we knew were there before the war, manuscripts, letters, diaries, some maps and drawings, in some cases key documents, not so in others but always rare or unusual things, always of interest to the discerning collector – these documents have landed up in private collections or in the many huge American university libraries. Research has been done, going to owners and asking questions such as: Who did you buy this from? How much did you pay? – not these questions alone, of course; a far more complicated and extensive survey has been carried out involving libraries and the like here, in this country, and at other centres.

Who's done it?

The government.

And how do you know the results?

Everyone knows these things. They are a matter of public record, available for anyone to see. Bernard seems to have been at the head of a massive fraud, swindling the country, taking what in many cases was our birthright and lining his pockets. I believe it was how he became respectable, but obviously can't prove it. How do you think a second-rate French academic, with no published papers, no real research to his credit, how could he gain a prestigious position at an American university, stay there for twenty or twenty-five years, returning only after the students' revolt of 1968, in time to denounce Sartre as a traitor? How could that happen? I can prove nothing. Nor, I believe, can anyone else; but there are some things you never forget. My great-grandmother, as you know, was born in what is now Germany. My great-grandfather was French, a chemist, working at the University of Clermont-

Ferrand. They were Jewish. He was transported during the Vichy regime. First of all they came to Paris, then he was moved to a camp. I don't know what happened or how she survived after that; she'll talk about Rilke but not about the war. My father said there was something to do with Bernard. His brother, my uncle, was killed in the 1968 riots. He went missing. Many did. The snatch squads. They would go into a crowd and remove someone who was never seen again. He was demonstrating against Bernard after the Sartre denunciation. Bernard said the country needed a period of stability, a return to normality. Things, he said, should be allowed to settle. Sartre was a troublemaker. Great-grandmother saw it all on television. That man is shadowing us, she said. He is haunting my family. My father told me. It happened the year I was born.

And stealing his papers would make it all right?

They aren't his papers. Nor are they all French papers. Someone in Bernard's position, a privileged academic, could travel across Europe. Again, nothing can be proven, but I have heard he has pieces from the Venetian State Archives, from the National Library in Vienna, from Berlin, the Lukács Library in Budapest, from Warsaw, Prague, God alone knows where.

How do you know?

I've told you, I don't know. But I know about him. And even you with your English sense of fair play must say it seems unlikely the papers are his.

I'm not English, nor do I have a sense of fair play. Neither do I think it's right to steal. Just because he might have stolen for his ends doesn't make it right for me to steal for mine. The papers should be returned to their proper owners.

Then do it. Photocopy what you want and send the originals to the Bibliothèque National with an accompanying letter.

It was not immediately obvious. Perhaps I would never have noticed had it not been for the first time, in Montmartre, the delicate walk and nervous fragility that settled like the moon on water. Again, she caught me staring. I thought she might be crying, but she wiped her eye and quickly smiled. I held her arm and we stopped. She turned towards me and I pulled her collar up to save her from the Paris night.

She tried a smile. It isn't you, she said. It's this and everything else.

Is there much else?

She shrugged.

Anything you want to tell me?

She shook her head. It isn't you, she said, it's me. I know that. I don't seem able to shake off the past.

Your past?

Not only mine, but yes, that too.

A star is a star because we see it. Our knowledge goes as far as we know. She was fine within her boundaries, she managed to survive while Vesuvius rumbled in the bathroom cupboard, the breakfast bowl or morning paper.

Again, the glancing smile and gesture, to take the subject away from herself. She moved on.

About the papers and assuming you are serious; it's not that simple.

What isn't?

I'd have to take the documents out of the house and I doubt very much if I'd get permission.

Then do it without permission.

I couldn't do that. Mme. Bernard has been very kind. She has trusted me.

Why? Did she even ask for, let alone check, your credentials?

No. I could have been anybody. As I said, she trusted me; do you think this trust is part of a subversive plot?

I suppose you accept it as simple human kindness, the great professor sharing his knowledge. Do you think she would have let you in during the Sartre business? I bet she doesn't even remember you.

That makes no sense. Who am I? She'll never see me again. Who can I tell? A couple of friends in Glasgow: Say what you like about the fascist Bernard, but his wife was good to me.

How good was she? She let you use a room to catalogue stolen papers. She let you work for nothing.

Maybe, but that's not the whole story. I'm sorry, AnnA, I'm not convinced.

I am not trying to convince you. I am telling you what I think. After all, I have said and, again, I repeat, I can prove nothing. The very least, you must agree, is that you have been compromised, but then we have all compromised ourselves one way or another and you are certainly no worse than the bastards who vote for them. All of this avoids the central issue of what are you going to do about fascism?

Are you serious?

Yes.

Leaving apart the colossal imaginative leap, first question: Why me?

Why not you? This is the second coming. It's been here before. And this time it's just as respectable, maybe even a little chic to believe in them. It is difficult to go against the flow, to oppose something that is fashionable. It takes heroism. Everyone is wise and heroic after the event. Think about what happened last time and tell me what you are going to do this time. Complain? Say it isn't right? Try to make them see sense? Hope they'll go away, that people will see reason and not vote for them? Look at you, trying to be reasonable about people who are unreasonable, offering democratic freedoms to those who would remove them, arguing the finer points of morality and ethics while they dictate the election agenda. Armchair socialism. Let someone else take up the struggle; or confine it to domestic issues, complain about the Poll Tax but let fascism rise in Europe. I think you're right. I think you are getting old. You're too comfortable.

What do you know about the Poll Tax?

That's right. Change the subject.

It's a straight black and white issue for you, isn't it?

Not just for me. Reverse the roles and see how nice they would be about things. Everything's black and white for them.

No pun intended?

Again, you're being flippant.

The only way I can support or oppose any cause or issue is by writing about it. I'm no good at anything else.

I know. Thank you for the meal.

175

The city changes after rain, melts before thunder and shines in the light. Stone buildings shadow themselves, create a pattern of reality and the beginning of dream. There is the ledge and the shadow of the ledge in sunlight; both will be transformed while undergoing transformation.

I grew up in a Glasgow where buildings were black. Those of us who thought they had always been that way were dazzled by the red and yellow sandstone, the shadows on the buildings, rain and sunlight on Ballachulish slate.

Now we live in an outpost. The housing schemes we built on the edge of the city are being redecorated. I stare out the window, watch the planes come and go, live my life apart. This is me saying hello. This is me getting in touch.

Regeneration is now in the churches, warehouses, schools and offices where the first-time buyers and the elderly live, the single parents separated from their children, the second and third marriages in one-, two- and three-bedroomed houses where commerce flourished.

There are two Glasgows, this and the other one. This is the silent, residential Glasgow. There are noisier Glasgows around the fringe, apolitical and depoliticised, where they don't give a fuck.

The buildings remain. In this autumn light they are mellow and dying, the sandstone and the leaves, the greens and russets, red and gold merging with the charcoal streets and the grey skies like a Whistler painting.

I am looking at a blonde sandstone building, whose eaves and aprons, even the little cartouche, are tinged with green mould, I suppose from stone-cleaning chemicals, leaking pipes and weather.

They cleaned the building. Now it needs to be cleaned again. First they removed the black smoke. Now they need to remove the remnants of the stuff that removed the black smoke. It's a big job, especially since folk don't think it needs to be done.

It's fine as it is. No one will notice. You only see it if you stare. Glance and you miss it.

Irene's mother telephoned last night. She was in Glasgow, she said, to stay with a friend.

She phoned around four o'clock. I was working, staring out the window, rearranging paper clips.

I was wondering, can I come to see you? she said.

She came out the taxi brimming with shopping. We had a cup of tea, and as casually as possible I mentioned would she like to eat, go for dinner, stay the night perhaps? That's the problem, she said. I need you to take me back to Edinburgh. I was thinking you could drive me back and stay with me.

I can't possibly stay, I said. I have work in the morning. Which was more or less true.

She had come through by train. A drunk man was annoying the passengers: So I thought it would be safer if you took me back, she said. And I'll get a refund on my train ticket.

Every time I drive along the M8 I think of the time Irene's mother asked why they piled the stones like that. Irene laughed.

They're not stones, she said. They're neeps.

Pardon.

Turnips, to feed the sheep.

It's not my fault, the mother said. They look like stones.

We drove back in the new car. I told her the salesman had asked to see three months' bank statements in case I had been laundering drug money. There's a lot of funny people about and they have peculiar money, he said.

Fancy that.

Coming into Edinburgh I remembered Jenners. Lovely, she said.

She had a discussion with a woman whose son was a lawyer and whose daughter was married with two children, living, for the time being, in Loanhead. She was a member of the Edinburgh Toastmistresses' Guild.

I was introduced as the son-in-law who had driven from Glasgow. You should get a newspaper, the woman said. Men like to read the paper.

Within five minutes it was obvious no one was listening, but they enjoyed the conversation. The minister had said charity begins at home and she had agreed. Our minister said his cat had kittens.

There were too many beggars. They should get them off the streets. There was no need for it, especially since so many of them were on the dole, collecting money from the state for doing nothing.

I'll get a taxi, said Irene's mother. I'm sure you'll need to get back to your work.

I love what Stevenson loved, the Jekyll and Hyde of Edinburgh, James Craig's New Town and the Old Town shambles, genteel and restive, seeking preservation, the bourgeois centre and the crumbling schemes, old ladies and traffic.

I found a bookshop that was a delicatessen last time I passed, but now looked as if it had always been a bookshop, shelves to the ceiling down either wall, ladders and a table in the middle, Radio 3. There were a couple of Edinburgh etchings: Jessie King, D.Y. Cameron and Muirhead Bone.

The man at the table by the fire at the far end of the room put down the *Scotsman* and smiled when I came in. Take your time, he said.

When do you close?

He shrugged.

I called on Sunday morning, when I figured Mme. Bernard would be at church. I told Mathilde I had misplaced my notes and could only have left them with the papers in the box.

I've brought a letter for Mme. Bernard, I said. I am leaving today. I suppose the notes are with the documents.

Would you recognise the box? she asked, opening what I thought was a bedroom door. Madame would never allow anyone into this room, she said, closing the door again.

Please, Mathilde. My train leaves at two o'clock. She need never know I was here.

She opened the door and walked away. *Cinq minutes*, she said.

There were cardboard boxes, maybe thirty or more down either side of the room. Six said *Joker Jus de Pamplemousse*. It was the third box I opened. I removed the documents, put them in my bag, replacing them with the newspapers I had brought. I put the box back in place, and, with two pages of notes in my hand, called Mathilde from the hall.

That's them, I said, showing her the notes.

Au revoir et bonne journée.

Please give Mme. Bernard my letter.

She nodded and shooed me out of the house.

The letter thanked Madame for her hospitality, sympathising on the death of her husband. I said I was sorry not to have seen her before leaving, that I did not want to intrude upon her grief, was sure this was a family time when there were many things to do and I was certain she would not want to be bothered by strangers.

Walking by the Café Voltaire. I changed the bag to a different hand, twinged with a sharp and sudden pain, as though I had stolen from Mathilde.

I phoned.

I am going to work, she said.

I have something important to tell you.

What is it?

I don't want to tell you over the phone.

She giggled. Is it a surprise?

Yes.

I hate surprises.

What time do you finish?

I don't know. When I finish I am going to study.

Where?

I have classes and won't be home till late.

How late?

Why don't you meet me at the shop?

Because I don't know where it is.

Rue du Bac.

Oh God.

What's wrong?

Have you any idea how near Bernard's house that is?

So what?

It's just that—

I thought Bernard lived in Jean Nicot?

He does.

Rue du Bac is nowhere near Jean Nicot.

I think they're very close.

Rue du Bac is by the Pont Royal. Jean Nicot is much further down river than that, by Alexander III, I think. Anyway, I have to go.

I thought of taking the papers back to the room, but elaborately tried to cover my tracks, asking the way to Charles de Gaulle Airport, walking to the RER station at Châtelet Les Halles. Line 1 (La Défense) to Concorde, then Line 12 (Mairie d'Issy) to rue du Bac, where I sat on the platform.

It was now impossible to take the papers back to Mathilde, but I thought of throwing them into a bin, or returning them by post. Something that simple could set up a reaction I could not control, the domino theory, knock one down and others follow.

I put a piece up for sale today, one of the first I bought, something that came under false pretences.

It's the white pigeon whose body is spotted in gold. She is resting on a clump of brown and green foliage, protecting the three eggs in her nest, each with the golden spot of an embryo. The claws, beak and eye are exaggerated in black. The nest is mottled, black and yellow. It has a small chip at the bottom of the first clump of foliage.

Janie loved it. She used to turn the piece over in her hand and kiss it. The foliage got chipped playing house, with the pigeon as an ornament. It fell while she was dusting.

Irene gave you such a row. You cried and told me you did not mean to hurt the bird.

I've seen two others like it, both larger. The first is in the Kelvingrove Art Galleries and is horrible, painted yellow, red and blue. The other is marked like mine, in Kellie Castle on the East Neuk of Fife. I saw it when your Uncle Tom was playing golf with a friend at Elie. I asked about the piece, but knew more than the curator.

It was made by the Prestonpans Pottery in a style known as Portobello Dabbity, though that may not be correct. There were a couple of famous potteries at Portobello. Buchan, for example, made brown stone whisky jars, probably for export, and their two remaining kilns are all that's left of what was once a thriving industry. Maybe they've been demolished. It's years since I've been there. I'm sorry. I know I can go on about pottery. I also know you're not interested. I thought I'd mention the pigeon because Janie used to like it.

I bought it when your mother and I were first married, from the only obviously gay man I knew. His name was Angus Atholl Robertson and he wore the kilt; the Murray of Atholl was blue and the Robertson was red. Call me Gussie, dear, he told me. He had a furry animal-headed sporran and was known to ask your mother, How do you like my beaver, Rene?

We met him and his partner Derek late one night.

Having been to dinner somewhere in the West End, we were driving along Bath Street, back to Giffnock at two in the morning. We saw them coming out a close, holding hands and wearing make-up.

He died of a wasting disease, just took ill. His hair fell out. The last time we went to see him he wouldn't let us into the bedroom until he was fully shaved, made-up, wearing a wig and obviously clean pyjamas. He coughed up blood. Three weeks later he was dead. If it was now, we'd say it was AIDS.

But what about the pigeon? asks Janie.

Gussie had a shop in a street whose name I've forgotten. The shop now sells second-hand TVs.

I had a flat near there. It was handy for the university. I was very happy and lived there with your mother until we moved to suburbia.

I did not know Gussie's shop existed. Only opened, dear, he said. You're not exactly the first, but you are quite early. Look around, tell me what you want and I'm sure we can come to an arrangement.

He was wearing a scarf, tied in a kerchief around his neck. He smoked from a cigarette holder and put on a tape of Maria Callas. He sat in a wide armchair at the end of the shop and read the *Guardian* by the light of what I later discovered was a Lalique lamp, which I thought was hideous.

Lovely piece, he said, when I picked up the pigeon. It's Staffordshire, dear. And I don't think I've seen one quite like it before. You can get them bigger, but size isn't everything, is it?

How much?

What does it say on the bottom?

Seven pounds.

That's far too much. A fiver.

Very pretty, said Irene. How much was it?

Which is how she and Gussie met and we had our first row. Five pounds, she said. Five pounds. I cannot believe you spent money we do not have on something like this. Take it back.

Next morning we walked to Gussie's shop. My dear, he said. Do you know what happened? A man asked if you wanted to sell. Where's the dove? he said. An expert. He'd give anything, ten, fifteen pounds were mentioned, simply to make up a collection. It appears, you see, that I was wrong. And he told the Portobello Dabbity story.

Irene said, Let's buy a bottle of wine to celebrate.

Silly how objects have affections and associations; the piece held too many memories. I tried to keep it, but had to let go.

My darling children. Do you know how much I love you? Did I ever say? Where are you now? Tell me how you are. Can you possibly imagine what this is about?

Wrong, Colin.

I am trying to let you see your father. Your mother is dead. She was also my wife. I tried to love her and believe she also tried to love me. I am now trying to tell you how difficult that was for both of us and how ultimately unsatisfactory our lives became, not through any fault but our own. I never stayed for your sakes, nor did she. There was no choice, really. I am writing this to reach you, because I need you just now, but you are busy with your own lives and probably feel things are best left alone, that I'll make contact if I need you.

I have Robert's number and could give him a ring.

Dad, he'd say, loudly, letting David know who was on the phone. Or else I'd get the answermachine. Dad, he'd say. Great to hear from you. How's things?

I'd say, Fine; and he'd say, Great. Within five minutes he'd be telling me how much the call was costing and how I couldn't afford it. Lovely to hear your voice, he'd say. Listen, I'll call next time. Two months later I would ask myself if I was being precipitate in wanting to call again.

No use calling Colin, and I am sorry about that. Colin was our first child. I remember the pregnancy, the kicks and tumbles as thrilling as electricity. I remember his first steps, arms in the air, running down the garden. I remember him standing in the hallway, cap in hand for his first day at school. I remember Robert resolutely stayed in the kitchen to eat his breakfast. He's only going because he has to go, he said.

I do not believe I bullied my children in the name of discipline, character formation or any other benefit I felt they needed. And even if I did, we lived in an area where such things were invisible.

Why then does my son present a polished, toughened front to the world, when he has none of the reasons but all of the pain? I know he is pained, can hear it in his voice and see it in his eyes. He cannot go but does not want to stay.

I wondered what was wrong, wondered why he was always so curt and sometimes impolite on the phone, why he never let me speak to the children or why Marjorie was always busy in the kitchen, even after answering the phone.

It is difficult to say when I became certain, when I knew what was wrong and why. I mentioned it to Colin, tried to discuss it, but he said he didn't know what I was talking about. He hummed and hawed, asked about Bobby, any word of Janie, that sort of thing. I want to know about you, I said.

I'm fine.

And are things with you and Marjorie fine?

Great, actually. Better than ever.

He either hasn't seen it, doesn't recognise his position, or has allowed it to happen. Perhaps the pain of changing is too severe.

I know nothing about Marjorie or her background, but I know she kept herself distant. I know Colin has been isolated from his family and friends and now seems a stranger. The move to England, the continual striving, the school fees, new cars, clothes accounts and a golf club membership are indicative of a life to which my son has never aspired.

You must be proud, an old lady said. We were having tea after her husband's funeral. Mrs Lawson, who lived across the way, held my hand as I was leaving. Your family have all done well, she said. Robert's in America, Colin's in London and Janie is at university.

I beg your pardon?

Janie is at university, she said.

I don't know what I said or did. I suppose my face betrayed me. Janie turned up and told Mrs Lawson her grant had not come through and borrowed fifty quid. I'll get my dad to pay you, she said.

No, said Mrs Lawson. I don't want it. She's a student and I know how tough it is for them.

I said I'd get Janie to visit. I thought she might have come today, said Mrs Lawson. She always was a cute wee thing. In and out of here all the time. I remember her well. Jack used to laugh. She'll be a dancer, that one, he'd say. You mark my words. She'll be a dancer. Every time there was music she could hardly keep still. She'll be at her studies though.

Janie. Do that again and I will fucken well kill you.

I am not trying to make you feel guilty or ashamed. I am trying to make you face the truth.

I am trying to hug you, all of you. I am trying to let you see my life, which has obviously become some sort of yardstick. I am trying to say no one has failed me. The concept simply does not exist. I may have failed you, but none of you ever failed me. I loved you too much for that.

And I have chosen this way because I know no other. Colin doesn't speak, Robert is on the other side of the world and at the time of writing, no one knows where Janie is, not even Janie.

It's two days later. This is a new jotter and the pen's a Papermate Flexigrip.

But what about the bloody pigeon? I bought it back. Stupid, isn't it?

In the move from Giffnock to Glasgow, I packed the pottery items myself, wrapped them in newspaper and cardboard, lined them into a tea chest stuffed with newspaper and carried these tea chests here myself, in my car, humping them up the stairs to the lift.

With the carpets laid and the books on the walls, the pictures up and the kitchen finished, with everywhere finished but here, this room with its view of planes and spires, unchanged since I got here, a junk room. When the women from the soft furnishings shop had hung their curtains and arranged the cushions, when I had bought myself a few bunches of flowers to put in the Bells and Buchan jugs, I unpacked the tea-chests, brought the pieces into the light.

The bookcase where they stay was gleaming. A solution of turpentine and linseed oil was one of Gussie's better suggestions. Preserves the wood, he said. It's better than any kind of polish because it gives the wood a lovely coat and a real shine.

This is you coming to visit.

Open the door. The Willie Rodger linocuts are in the more-or-less hexagonal hall with the Ferguson drawing and the small Eardley oil, a table and flowers, the Albert Irvin print and the Victorian altar-piece, two angels, one red, the other blue, one with a trumpet, the other with a lute, sounding out on Judgment Day, smiling, their hair glistening with oil and light from the haloes. The bookcase is the first thing you see if the sitting-room door is open, which it always is, never closed, because of the position of the hall lamp and the fact that I have a real Victorian Vaseline glass lampshade in the hall, which is simultaneously green and blue and yellow and brilliant, but not very bright.

So I unpacked the tea-chests: all my figures, William Wallace and Bonnie Prince Charlie, William Charles Macready as Rob Roy Macgregor and Sir Walter Scott with Maida, the dog, at his feet, the shepherd and his lass, the kilted, blind musician with his daughter who takes him by the hand, the Newhaven wifies with their basket of herring, Burns and Highland Mary, in bowers and among the corn, and the small pastille burners and fairings of castles and cottages, the small Crimean pieces, the kilted dancer with the begging dog.

I unpacked the pigeon, but it would not let go. I sold it in the end because it upset me to look at it, especially the chip, which was the only bit I saw. A whole bookcase, four shelves of bristling colour and dignity, I walk in the room and see the chip, the bit that's missing, that which once was here, but is now broken off.

I took the pigeon to a dealer who said he would send it to auction, where a similar piece recently fetched £750. What would I do with the money? Because he knows me, he let me take the bird back. I gave him a tenner for a small Bell plate and a fiver for a drink. The plate's a knock-down, he said. Trade prices. I knew he was lying. He knew I knew, but he is an antique dealer and therefore compelled to say what he said.

The house is fine, but this room needs some order. Things should be arranged. Mrs Shaw comes twice a week. She does my cleaning, washing and ironing. I have told her to stay clear of this room. There's a sign on the door: Keep Out. You ought to do something with that place there, she said.

I cannot help but wonder if its present condition is some sort of embodiment of myself.

The flat is in a genteel area, quiet and refined, cluttered with cars and a spectacular view across the city, looking outwards to the hills beyond, the Campsies and the braes around Balmaha. I may have mentioned, on a clear day I can see Ben Lomond.

This place is a converted church, with a glass door

and entryphone, secularised in every degree. I have more rooms than I need and have furnished the place tastefully, taking little or nothing from my former existence, but using my new-found wealth, redundancy money and an insurance payout on the death of my wife, to surround myself with objects of desire which will crowd around my declining years, will take away the ghosts that remind me I haven't got a life.

I have paintings on the walls, carpets on the floor, rugs, books and pottery. I have joined the lemmings in their rush towards oblivion by buying a CD player, despite the fact that I have more records and tapes than I play and am aware that the need for a market (so perfectly and eminently defined by Marx) will render the CD player redundant in less than ten years. The final indignity is that I can't tell the difference: vinyl or CD, it's all the same to me.

I have learned to enjoy my own company, see folk as and when I choose. I have no women friends, whatever they may be.

I spoke to Rhona the other night. She tells me she is getting married. I asked where she got my number. The office, of course.

Channel 4 News was starting. I had deconstructed Elizabeth David's recipe for Seafood Risotto, dressed the salad and poured the Vernaccia di San Gimignano, a Thresher Wine With Food Club recommendation, when the phone rang.

She said, How are you?

Rhona?

Of course.

I was stuck. What could I do but answer her question? Nice to hear from you, I said.

And how are you?

Fine.

I phoned because I don't want you to hear from anyone else. I'm getting married.

Congratulations.

Thank you.

When's the happy day?

We haven't fixed anything yet. We only agreed the other night. I haven't even told my parents.

Is there a problem?

Not at all. I wanted you to know and didn't want you to hear it from anyone else.

I'd like to send a wedding present, so maybe you can get back in touch when you've named the day.

Of course.

Is it anyone we know?

He knows you. I'm not sure you'd know him. Eric Morrison. He was on my course.

I remember, red hair.

That's him. We've lived together for about six months.

Didn't you move in with him when you went to Edinburgh?

Not move in move in. I shared a flat with him. He works for a PR firm.

That's right, I remember now. He does hand-outs for whisky sponsors, fireworks and the like.

Among other things.

And how's the job?

It's okay. It isn't wonderful, but it's good experience. What are you up to?

Nothing much. They paid me off with a specially prepared redundancy package.

I heard.

And I was in Paris for a while.

I heard that too. Was it nice?

It was partly research, but something came out of it, so I'm working on whatever keeps me occupied. I've started translating again.

Good. Is the research finished?

More or less.

I wondered if you ever come to Edinburgh?

I was there not so long ago, but only for a couple of hours.

Next time you're here, let me know. We could have a drink. It would be nice to see you again. I'd like to catch up, see how things are doing.

I'll phone.

When will you be through?

I'm pretty busy this week; say some time next week?

That's fine. I might be in Glasgow before then.

Well, you have my number.

Okay, then. That's great. I'm glad I called.

It's nice to hear from you.

Tell me something.

What?

Were you about to eat?

How did you know?

I have a good memory. I hope it isn't cold.

I'll manage.

What am I to make of that conversation? I wonder if Eric knows he's engaged to be married.

Needless to say I dumped the risotto, ate the salad and drank the wine. I was about to draw this elaborate parallel between myself and my home, that the place where I stay is a reflection of myself: attractive, elegant, cultured with pretensions, well dressed, but with a dark corner where all the work gets done, a small untidy place I use more than all the other amenities put together, except the lavatory, and that may also be significant.

Rhona will phone, and if she phones from Glasgow I'll probably see her. If I see her there will be recriminations and name-calling, tears and remorse. I think she has tried to tell me something I could neither accept nor believe: I am certain Rhona was trying to say she loved me. I am not sure how she feels now. I think she thinks she'll be all right, having decided the agenda if she sees me. I think she's wrong. What I don't know is my own reaction.

There is a fine irony in the fact that I am writing this because I am scared you will never know how much I love you, while simultaneously excusing myself, justifying, if you prefer, for loving or being loved by someone else.

How can you possibly justify this? asked Marjorie.

Control your wife, Colin, I said. Tell her to mind her own business. Just because she has isolated you and now can get you to do what she wants, doesn't mean it'll work with me.

She was thinking of a previous conversation. She was talking about my reading habits. I don't read a lot, she said, but looking at your books I'd say you were more interested in sex than reading.

Unfair, I told her. Unfair and superficial.

I don't know why I should have such a conversation with my daughter-in-law, or how often these conversations take place in other families. For Marjorie and me, it was as though I had witnessed her secrets.

She is a stiff little woman who appears to be continually enrolled in self-improvement. When she met Colin it was Italian. They honeymooned in Florence and complained about the crowds on the Ponte Vecchio. I told Marjorie about the Florentine journalist who came to Glasgow. I took him to the Horse Shoe, where he ordered two whiskies, came back and said, I ordered in Italian and he charged me the same as if I had ordered in English. That would never happen in Florence. If I ordered in English, they'd charge me double.

Then came flower arranging, creative writing and aromatherapy. I discovered these secrets from my grandchildren.

Would you like to hear a poem my mummy wrote? asked six-year-old Tracy-Ann after a visit to *Snow White*.

It was a list: Love and warmth, joy and fear / Fill my heart when you come near, were the first two lines.

Is it about your daddy? I asked.

It was about her feelings.

How do you know?

I heard her tell Jenny on the phone. But it was about somebody too.

She does aerobics, sings in the local operatic society chorus and plays Tammy Wynette on her Walkman.

I asked how the writing classes were going. She laughed. I don't think I am a poet.

Nor are most people.

I would like to write a decent poem.

So would most people.

Colin was working late, a budget meeting, he said. Marjorie got drunk enough to burn the lasagne and shout at the kids, who threw their eyes towards the ceiling. I guess Daddy's not coming home, said Robin, who is eight.

I don't know when I'll see him, she said, after I had bathed the weans, read them a story and listened to Tracy-Ann's tape of *Puff the Magic Dragon*.

I expect a phone call, said Marjorie. He'll tell me he's missed the train or the meeting will be continued over breakfast tomorrow morning, that everyone has had to put up in a crummy hotel and are the kids okay. I'll ask him for the number and he'll say, Don't phone. I'm going to bed. I'll call again in the morning, and guess what I think is going on.

Colin phoned. I was doing the dishes.

Bastard, she said.

At one o'clock in the morning in her Marks and Spencer's housecoat, a glass of white wine in her hand, her hair round her shoulders, she lit a cigarette and asked if it was true I had a big prick.

Her eyes never left my face. She held the cigarette in front of her mouth.

Who told you that?

Colin mentioned it soon after we met. I was admiring his proportions. He said, It runs in the family. I asked what he meant. He said his brother was well hung, but that was a waste and neither of them were as lucky as you. I asked how he knew and he said you walked around naked when they were kids, but never in front of Janie. He said your cock hung down your thigh. Right or wrong?

I don't think we should be having this conversation.

I have seen men's pricks before now. I'm curious, that's all. Curious.

And I'm not going to satisfy your curiosity.

Don't you think such things are proper?

I think you'll regret this conversation in the morning.

Come on, she said. We're adults.

She passed out with a cigarette in her hand. I carried her upstairs and put her to bed. I cleared the kitchen, got up in the morning, gave the kids their breakfast, sent them to school with a packed lunch, gave Marjorie a cup of tea in bed, phoned a taxi and left.

I'd like to exchange notes with Colin sometime. I don't know what he's been told, if anything. No doubt about it, that was the start. My daughter-in-law had revealed her sins. Seeing me would remind her of what I knew. Better banish me altogether.

I later discovered she was far more skilled than I expected, never directly confronting the issue, but dropping barbed little slivers; never criticising directly, but alluding in a way that is as difficult to describe as it is to locate. It was in the voice and the tone of voice, in both the subject and the object.

What have you done to Marjorie? asked Robert.

I shrugged.

We noticed, didn't we? And David nodded. We noticed she didn't actually say anything nasty, but she didn't say anything nice either. All in all she gave the impression not so much that you were a creep, but that she found it creepy being round you.

They were over for the Artscape Arts and the Environment Conference. David was representing a group called Buddies in Bad Times and attended a Resourcing the Library session while Robert visited his grandmother in Edinburgh. I think he took her to tea.

They were flying back on Sunday. This was the Saturday and we were daidling through the woods at the side of Loch Katrine, having climbed Ben A'an, descended down the west side of the shoulder, crossed the glen and climbed the hill to the farm, where we dropped along the forestry road. It was cool and dampish, with cinnamon bracken and fallen leaves of red and yellow, the loch in a mist.

Any word from Janie? asked Robert.

I shook my head.

So he returned to his favourite topic. Marjorie had said I was obsessively tidy, that she was frightened to even so much as put a cup out of place in her own home for fear I'd pick it up and either wash it or put it in its proper place, or both. I suppose it was meant as an insult. I think tidiness is a compliment, a trait I never knew I had, which was developed in small and crowded student digs in Edinburgh.

Three of us shared a basement flat in Scotland Street, round the corner from Drummond Place.

It was damp and rebarbative. I replied to an advert: *Apply P.L.G.P. Symington*, it said, giving the phone number of a call box in the pub where Symington worked.

He told us he carried the names of four Popes, Peter Leo Gregory Paul. I saw his birth certificate when he was taken to hospital. The snake he bought one Festival bit him. The name on his birth certificate said Thomas Peter Symington, born Patna, Ayreshire; father a coal miner, mother a spinster.

Help yourself, he said. Look around. Bedroom's here, kitchen through there and this is the sitting room. Facilities are in the corridor between here and the kitchen. He was wearing a dark green velvet smoking jacket and cravat, smoking Balkan Sobranie.

Thought we might organise it this way: living area's here, spick and span in case of visitors, no need to remove smelly socks and the like. Kitchen's where we eat and drink and generally congregate, mattress there for overnight guests, ladies and so on. Bedroom's the place where we sleep, three single beds, airless and fetid, I shouldn't wonder, bit like boarding school. Bit of a shagger, are you? Leg man? Very good. All perfectly acceptable here. Thing is I might do a spot of that sort of thing myself; except, and this is a rule from which I rarely stray, the woman I entertain will, I do assure you, be not at all to your liking, but I also assure you, I will be using the kitchen mattress more than you or anyone else. Any questions?

You said three single beds?

Thought there might be three of us sharing. One chap's moving in tomorrow, skinny bloke from Aberdeenshire. He seems to find the house rules acceptable. Think he's doing science.

Bobby Meldrum mixed ethyl alcohol with fruit juice and served it in a tall glass. He smoked his horsehair mattress and disappeared for days at a time, leaving a note which said, I'm not here. He had two of everything, except a raincoat. Wear one, wash one, he advised me. Same as the monks. Every week he wrote a letter to the *Scotsman* and caused a controversy by suggesting the McEwan Hall be turned into an ice rink.

For six months I slept between two mattresses. The sheets and blankets my mother had given me were stolen when the flat was burgled by Lindy Macintosh's boy friend. Lindy's parents lived in Kenya. Pete Symington brought her home one night. They stayed in the kitchen for a month. She cooked lasagne and chips, every night. Don't you like lasagne? she asked when Bobby complained.

She was five feet four inches tall, with black hair and a pale complexion. She smoked cigars, could open beer bottles with her teeth and weighed just under ten stone naked. She could recite *The Pied Piper of Hamelin* from memory, repair a tractor, shear sheep and from the top of Calton Hill named me the stars in the sky. She told me she lost her virginity one Christmas afternoon while her parents were watching the Queen's broadcast.

She turned up one Friday: Is the mattress being used? she asked. Her boy friend's name was Davie. They were still there when we came home around five o'clock. Lindy told us Davie was a butcher; thirty bob each and we could have sausages, steak, liver, chops and mince. We gave him the money. I'll be back in an hour, he said.

He took three shirts, a sweater and the bedclothes from me. He'll wear the clothes and pawn the bed stuff, said Lindy. He took Bobby's watch, a radio and a pair of shoes. He took Peter's Daks jacket, his Scrabble, backgammon and the money he'd hidden in the cistern. Sorry, said Lindy when he didn't come back.

Lindy introduced us to Maxwell Morrison, who had one Durex, which he rented for a shilling, half a crown if you were desperate. His friend Tommy Simpson was arrested climbing Edinburgh Castle rock for a bet. Tommy's girl friend Susan cried for the first year and carried a rabbit around in second year. She cried in her third year when she lost the rabbit. Popular opinion reckoned it was eaten by the brothers Clark from Elgin, who claimed to live off seagulls and pigeons. They made us a casserole one Saturday night. Seagull, said one, I can't remember who. Delicious, don't you think? Harry Robinson got scurvy from a baked-bean diet and four people whose names I have forgotten had their hair come out in handfuls before each exam.

Barry Low put on a short play during one of the Festivals. I think the only folk who came were like ourselves. It was what he called a sponsored reading. The sponsors were a local brewery.

It began, Enter Man Juan kicking a Bible. Enter Man Two kicking Man Juan.

And there was an operatic exchange at the end of the First Act. A group of workers come on singing: Rub-a-dub-dub, We want a sub. While the boss stands resolutely replying, Titty-fal-all, You'll get fuck all.

There was a nude nuns' chorus and Lindy had a simulated sex scene with a dog.

Bastards, said Barry. I've done everything I can to have them bar it and the fuckers never even showed up. That's the press for you. Bastards. They've landed me in trouble with the brewery. I promised I'd get banned.

Edinburgh's precipitous image, the Old Town representing the Scots' struggle against nature, the weather and themselves, and the New Town representing their idealism, aestheticism and sense of order, means fuck all. There is scarcely a city that stands so fiercely in defiance of the elements, a place that responds so well to winter or simultaneously encourages romantics to overwhelm rationalism. I have never thought of Edinburgh as complacent, douce, respectable or even beautiful; far less as the European capital which comes alive for three weeks in the year then closes down. It has always been the place where I was young, where I learned everything I have carried with me since, where I learned my extremities.

Rhona rang.

What you need to know is that I cared for her and still do. AnnA showed me this was possible. She showed me none of these things had gone.

I watched a girl do something similar. She forced the gull's beak open, and dripped the fluid into its mouth, holding the neck and the back of its head so it had to swallow. Then she scraped the oil off with a spoon, restoring mended birds to an empty sky.

I met Rhona at work. She was doing a post-graduate journalism course. Part of their placement was with us and the students were circulated pretty well around the departments. They were asked where they would like to go for a month, what was their special interest? Politics, she said. No one had ever chosen me before. I was flattered.

I have no idea how long it lasted, but know it ended

when I did not return her calls, when she left messages to which I did not respond. You have used me, she wrote, and I feel cheapened.

I sat in the garden of my empty house, read the letter and thought of her by the dashboard light. The image returned when I heard her voice. Hi, she said. I'm in Glasgow.

We met at five in Café Gandolfi. She called me a bastard at the end of the meal. You hurt me very badly, she said.

I apologised and told her this was partly why I was seeing her, why I thought we needed to talk.

You're right, she said. But you could have told me sooner.

I paid the bill and walked her back towards Queen Street Station, along Ingram Street, past George Square.

What are you going to do now? she asked.

I could go home, but there's a film at the GFT I'd like to see.

What is it?

The Magic Flute.

Eh?

The opera. By Mozart. The Bergman film of the opera is on at the GFT.

We sat at the back. She kissed my cheek when the place went dark.

Sorry, she said.

What for?

I was grumpy.

We held hands. After *Das klinget so herrlich*, she said, I want to kiss you properly.

It had been warm all day. Leaving the cinema, the air

was cool. We ran up the hill, past the kids' park with the extravagant lighting, past St Aloysius and part of the Art School, till, going downhill towards the synogogue, she asked, Is there a phone?

Where?

Here.

I suppose so. Tell the truth, I've no idea. What do you want a phone for anyway?

I need to phone Edinburgh to say I'm staying with my mother.

We didn't go far. There was a lane. She leaned against the wall at the side of the building, the gable end of the tenement, at the start of the lane, before the entrance to the back court with the drying green and middens; she leaned against the wall and I was beside her, never more than three or four inches away since we knew we were going into the lane at eleven o'clock on a summer's night with the television sets from the ground-floor and first-floor houses speaking loudly, the sound of water running down the waste pipe and a woman's voice singing somewhere up above with the window open, singing softly to herself as she washed some clothes at the sink.

She leaned against the wall. I touched her waist. She turned towards me.

There is a time when you walk through the centre of Glasgow, say round about five at night, though it can also happen late on, especially in the summer with the combination of heat and dust, the sky is visible and the traffic low, when anything seems possible and the city again becomes a village where everybody knows everybody else. This is when the game stops; when the place is open, undisguised, when the elusiveness and aura are suspended, when it takes off its clothes and snuggles in beside you, naked. It is no longer scary. It is gentle and kind, very loving, and it whispers, no longer trying to deceive or outwit you, it puts its tongue in your ear and you sigh because you love it very much.

Ann McPherson tried to be good but was never good enough. Her daddy was okay when he was sober, nice and quiet most of the time.

What's the matter wi her? he asked when he was drunk.

Nothing, said her mother. Lea her alane.

Is she too good for us? Is that it? Does she think she's too good for us noo she's supposed tae be stayin on at school?

Ann knew it was best to be quiet. She spoke to her mother, who said there was nothing she could do. Ann knew what it was like, had lived with it all her life in the house with the neighbours who revved their cars at three in the morning.

Her father wasn't working. Her mother had three part-time jobs.

She spoke to a teacher, Miss MacPherson. Same name as myself, she said. What can I do for you, Ann?

Miss MacPherson was getting married. Ann looked at her engagement ring when she spoke.

Miss MacPherson said, I think you should be careful. You know what can happen with unprotected sex. Is your boy friend working?

He wasn't her boy friend. It might as well be him as anyone else, she thought. Might as well be him.

You're like a lump o meat, he said. Just lyin there. I like somethin wi a bit o life.

She didn't say it was her first time. She thought he would know. He had nice eyes and she thought he'd be kind.

Miss MacPherson gave her a packet of condoms. Tell your boy friend to use them, she said, and smiled.

Her father found them when he was looking for money for drink. What the fuck is this? he shouted. Is that you carrying they things aroon in case ye meet some cunt that fancies a go?

Ann slept on the stair. She went to school and fell asleep at dinnertime. When she came home at four her dad was drunk: Where the fuck were you last night, he said, and hit her, hard again across the face.

She did not know what to do or where to go. She walked into town and thought she'd wait with the crowds in the railway station where she wouldn't be noticed, where folk would think she was waiting for a train.

He had dark hair, was six feet tall and wore Air Max trainers. Not a problem, he said. There you go.

He gave her fifty pounds to spend on clothes, bought her burgers, fries and shakes and took her to the pictures twice a week. Sometimes he was busy, but she didn't mind. She stayed at home and watched television, videos of all the soaps she'd missed, *Neighbours* and *Home and Away*, the ones she watched when she came home from school.

How much to you reckon you owe me? he said.

I'll pay you back. Every penny.

How?

I'll get a job.

Doing what?

I'll pay you back.

He slapped her hard across the face. You'll pay me and pay me now, he said, with a knife at her throat. I need fifty by twelve o'clock.

Sandra told her what to wear. A wee skirt and a skimpy top, high-heeled shoes, a bag for the fags and condoms, a coat and umbrella in case it rains.

They'll mostly want gams. Do you know what that is?

Ann shook her head.

You'll learn. If they like you, charge them extra. Always smile when you tell them the prices and always tell them other lassies are dearer but you're daein it cheap cause you like the look o them. And you'll need a dummy name. Call yoursel Diane. There's naeb'dy doon here wi that name and tell nae cunt your second name. Watch the junkies and gie naeb'dy money.

She made eighty pounds within an hour. That's cause you're new. They like new meat, said Sandra.

One of the junkies took her up a lane, pulled her hair and kicked her, took her money while Sandra was with a punter.

I cannae protect you aa the time, said Sandra. I'll dae it this time, but you'll need tae come doon wi a dug's lead the morra night and dae tae her what she did tae you. An if she beats you you'll need tae keep daein it till you beat her and she stops daein it. Here. Try this. She gave her four Temazepam tablets.

I can no more describe my love for you than make a ladder of light. I am hopeless at impossibilities.

Sometimes I see my life take place on a distant shore, as though I am in the middle of a river, being driven downstream, unable to influence myself or what I do. I watch myself and would love to change creeping particulars which stunt my growth, but I'm condemned to be me, watching my parallel life pass by.

This thing here has served its purpose. I am happy and sad and filled with the knowledge that I am trying to be honest and impress you, so which is the truth, my honesty or the bits I put in to impress you, what Jelly Roll Morton called the fancy left hand?

In the meantime, a testament from Father Marin Balbi, who was imprisoned in The Leads with Casanova. A note in green ink, signed Lisa, says, This statement is believed to have been taken in 1761, following the publication of Casanova's *Story of My Escape From The Leads*. The Venetian Inquisitors appear to have been anxious to satisfy themselves that Casanova's account was fiction and spoke to as many of the parties as possible to confirm their suspicion. Balbi's account is by far the best and most practical, since he is directly implicated by Casanova, who claims Balbi not only aided his escape, but also left us with him.

Lisa does not tell us how she knows this.

THE CITY SPREAD BELOW

I am scared, sir. God bless you, sir, and keep you well; the family, your children, wife and father. May your mother never see you hanged.

God bless me too, for I am frightened. If I tell you

what you want and if you write it down on paper, then anyone with eyesight and ability can read it and I'm a doomed man, for he told me so himself.

One word of this and you are hanged, he said.

Who, sir?

He whose name I dare not speak.

I have been foolish, have abused my position and betrayed the trust of others. For this I have both paid dearly and repented. I daily ask for God's forgiveness.

I have never been numbered with this world's gifted. I was a slow child who became a dull adult. But I have learned from my mistakes, paid for my transgressions and daily repent with the birch and thong. My back bleeds and my cries fill the courtyard. I would have damned myself to the eternal flames were it not for my wife, who is my comfort and my torturer, administering strokes when my own strength fails me, washing my scars with salted water.

I repeat these indignities for the souls of those who have borne my children. I was jailed in The Leads, sir, and paid for my transgressions here on earth, jailed for committing that most venial of sins.

But now I am free and thank the Lord for my deliverance.

My life is spent in service. I am a blacksmith and a farrier who has had no contact with my former ways for fear of God's right hand. I also fear the ways of man and know what has been written in a book of magic. I once learned how to decode such symbols, but have long forgotten. When I was released I left my former ways, my habit and my sandals, my missal and my sins.

I have served the Lord by serving others, and am hoping to earn my way into heaven.

My strength was my weakness. As a child they called me Ox. I knew I could overpower anyone who would not do my bidding. There was little I could not achieve through force. I therefore made myself an exhibit, used my strength for entertainments, lifting great weights, balancing others upon my shoulders, hands and body, drawing carts and combating horses.

I was tempted more than once by those who knew my history and desired to see a strong man grounded, weakened by the flesh that strengthened him. It was then I remembered the lessons I had been taught as a child. I could see Father Mendini, with his red hair and single tooth, shake with fury as he told us how Samson was destroyed by the temple and the barber.

When I met my wife, I knew we would marry. I also knew we would marry in church, leave Venice, and that I would work till I died. I know how I will die, but do not know when. I dreamed it in a powerful dream. I will die by water and work with fire. I therefore avoid water.

I see you pause; how do I know these things? Because I am more animal than human, more dog than man. I can sense disaster before it happens, can smell food, see things from another world made visible at night, ghosts and shadows, wraiths and spectres. I knew my brother would be drowned when he saw the woman sing in the lagoon. I knew my sister would leave home and return with a child when she met the smiling *gondoliere* who ferries the dead to San Michele. I knew my other sister would lose her babe with fright if she

walked through the Aparchia by moonlight and I knew
my mother would die when she cursed the church for
taking her child, even though the child was me. She
cursed them because I was her Ox, twelve years old
and could work like a man. The church would rather I
worked for them than for my mother.

My wife has cured me. She has replaced the
wickedness with a sense of duty to her and our
children. She has told me to tell everything, has helped
me remember and reminds me of my transgressions
with the birch and thong.

I am fearful of a man with powerful friends, who are
used to their way and paying to get it, then paying for
protection and the protection of their secrets. Need I say
more?

I seek assurances against harm. I know there are
bodies in the canals every morning. I know these bodies
are disfigured, that faces and often heads are removed. I
cannot enter heaven without a head.

Whether a man has done what he says hardly
matters; if he believes he has done it, it is the same
thing. I learned that when I was with him.

Most of all I remember the rats. The Leads is full of
rats. Does he mention them in his book? There are
men there who hunt the rats and eat them. I have seen a
crazy man tear the flesh from a rat and eat it raw. He
died two nights later, screaming in agony.

He never had to do such things. He was always well
attended. He washed in warm water. Need I say more?

That time has no place in the memory of a man who
earns his living heating metal and shoeing horses. It is
from another time, when I was different from who I am

today, when I was a poor and penitent servant of God, an office I shamefully abused by committing the crimes which took me to The Leads.

This was punishment for any man, but for a man who had devoted himself to God and to saving souls for God's grace, it was a severe and bitter recrimination, which no matter how hard I try, no matter what tortures I endure, I cannot erase from my memory.

I have told you I cannot mention his name. Though the tongue be ripped from me, though tortured and damned I would never mention his name. Be assured, I know who you mean. And though I have not heard or read what he has committed to print, I am certain it would not be true. Truth is ignominious. He sought glory.

This I do know. He was born on 5 April, the worst day of the month. With a birthday like that, no one need whisper a curse by his cradle.

He was a dreamer, and was anxious to impress even me. At first he wanted my company for the same reason everyone sought me, but what use was strength in a jail from which no one escaped? The jailer Lorenzo became a prisoner. Other jailers had been prisoners. They knew what we were up to, knew the tricks and how to avoid them. He was no cleverer than they. He had nothing new to offer, other than stories.

He told me of his travels. How he had been to Paris, where he fought a duel over a restaurant bill and a lady's honour. From there he and his brother went to Dresden, where he had a play performed. He said his play was rewarded by the king.

He also went to Prague, Vienna and Pressburg, where

the chevalier with whom he had fought the Parisian duel beat a bishop at faro, removing a considerable fortune on the turn of a card. He who cannot be named borrowed 100 ducats.

I do not believe I have earned 100 ducats. I have worked all my days and never earned such an amount. Imagine my wrath when he told me he got that money because he had earned it; had worked for it, he said. Work, he said, should be rewarded. I agree, sir. I do, truly, agree. Work ought to be rewarded. But what are we to make of such a reward, or of such a man, who can earn more with the turn of a card than I, who am stronger, have earned from a lifetime's work? I told him what I thought and we fell out.

But he needed my protection. He needed my help. There were others in The Leads who would have robbed and abused him. He could hardly be saved from their attentions. I was his friend because he needed me. He paid for my protection.

He was used to being liked, expected he would be the centre of attraction and did not know how to survive where he was despised. He was anxious to please, wanted others to like him. He also washed his hair in urine. Imagine how that was treated by his fellow prisoners.

He saw The Leads as an end to his dreams and the finish of his hopes. His dreams, he said, began in childhood, but their practical beginning was in the Palazzo Soranzo, where he was one of the hired fiddlers at a three-day ball and helped the sick senator who adopted him as his son, making him a nobleman instead of a fiddler. The old man dropped his handkerchief and the young man picked it up.

What did he tell? He told me everything. I do not know why he was imprisoned. But I am aware of how he was released. Senator Bragadin paid for his release. I know because he told me. He promised that if I would help him, the senator would pay for my release. I believed him because I had no alternative. He also taught me how to dream, to hope for things that will never happen.

I am aware of the fact that he has written a book detailing his escape from The Leads. What can I say? Senator Bragadin paid for his release. I served my sentence.

He kept me entertained with a great many stories. He could paint a wonderful picture, draw character through his voices and mimic almost anyone. He made us laugh by imitating Senator Bragadin when he was sick. Not tonight, he would say. Not tonight, *mio caro Giacomo*. I am too tired and too ill. Perhaps another night, but not tonight. He covered everything with that phrase. Not tonight, he told the guards. Not tonight.

I am in the book? Surely not. If it is true – and I do not doubt Your Excellency's word – then I am flattered to think he has remembered me. I am honoured to believe my name will live, that he has given me a kind of immortality. Would that I had earned it. Perhaps Your Excellency will tell me how I am mentioned?

Of course. I will tell you what I know, beginning with the fact that Senator Bragadin did not want to witness the marriage of the city to the sea and left Venice seven days before Ascension Day.

An actress, Maria Coldona, was known to my jailmate. He told stories which I am certain were untrue – if they were true they are far in excess of anything I have ever imagined, far less witnessed, and I have been jailed on charges of which Your Excellency is well aware. Piero Capretta and the actress Coldona performed an unmentionable deed, sir. I am sure Your Excellency is aware of the deed to which I am referring.

Please, sir, do not make fun of me. The four of them – Capretta, an officer in the light cavalry, and his sister, whom Capretta thought would make a match for my companion, the actress Coldona and my cellmate – were at a box in the theatre when the actress and Capretta indulged in an embarrassing display of intimacy. He pulled her astride him and did the business in front of his sister and her companion.

Needless to say, it did not take my companion long to puncture Capretta's sister, which did not please her father, who sent her to, I think, the Santa Maria degli Angeli convent on Murano, where she fell victim, I believe, to the Venetian disease, having been converted when she shared a room with a woman of this persuasion.

He continued with the delusion. I do not know why. I believe her father was wealthy. No. I cannot think of any other reason.

For weeks he attended her church in Murano. He told me he received a letter from one of the nuns. Vanity, sir. Why else? His vanity would have forced him to swim to Murano.

Of course, he met the nun. He could not have done

otherwise. I have forgotten to say Capretta's sister lost the baby, which caused alarm for her life. I doubt if her father was pleased.

As for the nun. Sir, it becomes tedious, but in jail there is little or nothing to pass the time and such tales are a wonderful source of entertainment. I was fortunate in this respect, my cellmate had many such stories.

They met on Murano, in a private room. It became obvious to my informant that she desired him, but that her pleasure came from the fact that they were being observed.

He told me who he thought had observed him. He had no proof, of course, but he had reason to suspect the French ambassador. It was well known that the nun was his mistress. Yes, sir, the ambassador, the Abbé François Joachim Pierre de Bernis. The English ambassador, Sir John Murray, also participated in such adventures, though I believe money changed hands on these occasions since his mistress was the well-known harridan Ancilla, whom even I had heard of, a woman my associate would certainly not have found as attractive as a nun who rearranged the furniture to ensure the Frenchman's view was unobstructed.

No, sir. I do not believe this was why he was arrested. I do not know why he was arrested. Nor, I believe, did he. He made dark references to what he knew and that he feared he had overstepped the mark in his relations with Venice's nobility, but was never specific. He said they wanted to get rid of him, but that Senator Bragadin would save him. He will never desert me, he said. He will protect me.

Of course, he spoke of Messer Grande.

No, sir. He was not complimentary.

He told me he believed it was Messer Grande who put the spy Manucci onto him before breaking into his lodgings for the salt.

Salt.

Giovanni Manucci was a jeweller who flattered my cellmate with inquiries about the lodges and the Cabala. My friend even loaned him books, which the jeweller took to his masters. I do not mean to be impertinent, but I suggest it would be a simple matter for Your Excellency to discover the truth of this matter.

I beg your pardon. His lodgings were burgled. They told the landlady they were looking for contraband salt. Needless to say, the gentleman was furious, but Senator Bragadin was far more circumspect. He said it was a warning and pleaded with him to leave Venice for the time being and return later, when things had died down.

He stayed because he believed he was invincible. He believed he could do anything and get away with it, that they could not touch him, that he was smarter than anyone and better protected. He wished he had heeded the senator's advice, wished he had gone.

I believe that when he referred to them, he was referring to Your Excellency and his colleagues.

As far as I know the senator told him the Inquisitors would never send anyone as important as the chief of police to a young man's lodgings over a matter of salt. They had deliberately fired wide. He should leave immediately.

He stayed and was arrested at dawn on 26 July, 1755. I remember because we arrived at The Leads at the same time. I was arrested at dawn and taken from the Dorsoduro. He stayed at Messer Grande's house while I was in a cell.

He, who could tell me the view from the state apartments – the Campanile and the domes of San Marco, the figures praying and posing in the doorway, the place where all can be seen to perfection, where the plain brick façade gives as little competition as possible.

He was placed before the stern dark wood in the Salle del Consiglio and led through the door beneath Justice with her golden sword and scales. I have never seen these, sir. He told me, as he told me about the box for secret denunciations and the seats gilded in red and gold leaf painted onto a dark green background, a place where footsteps echo with more hard wooden seats – this was where he wondered if the justices had to squeeze in or if they got stuck.

He was taken past three closed rooms on the left, to a passage where the ceiling changes to plain wood and into the Hall of the Grand Council of Venice, where patricians are assembled back to back.

From there he went downwards, down a slope, through a dark, damp and smelling place, barely lit by torches, through a heavy bolted door, past cells with half-round ceilings, stone floors and crossed iron bars, past two half doors, grilles and crude oil lamps, a guard on every corner, smiling and saying, Goodbye. Another door, and this time he was dragged through a series of cells where guards were eating, playing cards, spitting and saying, Goodbye Forever.

Down across the Ponte dei Sospiri with the canal below and no more than a glimpse of the Ponte della Paglia and San Giorgio Maggiore, a smidgeon of green water, with, he said, a gondolier's shout coming from behind, from another place, and only downwards through the filth and into The Leads, where I was waiting in a cell whose window bars went straight into stone. There are eight frowning lions on the keystone of the arch of The Leads, one facing the palace across the canal.

Escape, sir? There was no escape. He was kept alone for a month. He said he tried to escape then, but reached the same conclusions as everyone else: escape was impossible. Bribery was possible. He came to me at the end of August; by the end of October he was gone.

As I have said, sir. I remained in The Leads. I did not escape. I have not read his book, sir. I cannot read. I have told you what happened. Read me the statement. I will mark it as correct.

SIX

For I say, this is death and the sole death,
When a man's loss comes to him from his gain,
Darkness from light, from knowledge ignorance,
And lack of love from love made manifest.

A Death in the Desert,
   Robert Browning

She was arranging flowers on a table in the middle of the shop. There was music playing, a string of sound that demanded no attention. She looked up and smiled: Now that you've found us, are you going to buy something? she said.

I tried a smile that didn't work.

You sounded awful on the phone. What's wrong?

I can't tell you here.

There's a café on the corner, just down a bit. Over there. In you go, have a Ricard and I'll see you in about half an hour.

I did not want to sit in a café, but couldn't go far because of the bags. I walked up one side of rue du Bac looking in shop windows. It started to rain when I crossed the road. I bought a couple of the small, orange-covered Rhodia notepads with squared paper, 10F each. She was outside the café, on tiptoe, looking in the opposite direction.

Where have you been?

I couldn't sit.

What's wrong?

Nothing's wrong. I've got the papers.

What papers?

The stuff we talked about last time.

From Bernard?

Yes.

The papers you've been working on?

Yes.

She shrieked and tilted her head to the air. My God, she said. Why? What on earth are we going to do with them? What possible good can they be?

I thought you wanted me to take them.

I said Bernard had probably stolen them, that they should be returned. But I did not know what they were, nor where they had come from. I was trying to convince you of Bernard's past rather than have you steal them.

Sorry. My mistake. I'll take them back and say I found them in an envelope on the street. Don't ask me what I was thinking; maybe I thought you meant what you said.

About what?

It doesn't matter. I've been here too long. I need to go home. I need to be in an environment where I can understand the nuances of language, where I can actually understand what's being said.

Are you angry with me?

No. Not with you. I'm angry at myself. Yet again, I am amazed at my own stupidity. Not stupidity so much as gullibility. My problem is that I believe what people say. Must stop doing that, must learn to treat everyone like a liar.

Where are you going?

I don't know.

Why are you carrying your bags?

You'll be glad to hear I've left that miserable little room.

She giggled. Sorry. I am not laughing at you.

You always say that.

I can just see you trying to cover your tracks. I realise something I have never realised before: you meant it, didn't you? You really do take people at their word.

Take this stuff and do what you want. Burn it if you like. I am past caring. I'm off to rewrite this entire incident, to turn it into something else, to assume it is you rather than me who is acting from a lack of information. That way I can be the good guy, misunderstood. It's a normal process. I do it every time I am humiliated.

She reached up and kissed my cheek. Come on.

Where?

Home.

What about your class?

Too late now.

She picked up a bag and we walked to the Métro, where we continued on the line I'd abandoned. She held my hand, and did not speak until Notre Dame des Champs. This is where I live, she said. This is at the other end of my street, but it is quicker to come off at the next one and walk along. Then she held my hand between her hands and rubbed.

Are you feeling better?

I nodded. I still feel silly.

She kissed my hand. This is where we get off, she said.

We walked down boulevard du Montparnasse in silence, each with a bag. Here, she said. This way. I had been watching the reactions of the men who passed us. They noticed her, looked away, suddenly looking again as they drew near. She seemed oblivious. We turned down a dark street, with cars on either side, crossed the road and walked along the narrow street behind

223

boulevard du Montparnasse, rue Notre Dame des Champs. I live here, she said.

We were almost at the end of the street. The facings on the right seemed starker, as though they were at the back of one street rather than the front of another. I was about to say this when she stopped, inserted a brown plastic key card into a glass door, pushed the handle down with her elbow and held the door open for me to enter a terrazzo hall. Floor, walls, desk and cornice were dark cream and yellow terrazzo. The plaster ceiling, lit from the side with a small chandelier in the centre, was white. There was what looked like an Afghan rug in the middle of the floor, a low wooden table and four chairs by one wall. The terrazzo desk was empty, though the small lamp, with a dark yellow shade, was lit. A man stuck his head round the corner and smiled. *Bonjour*, he said to AnnA, looking at me.

The lift was cramped. The third floor reflected the Art Deco design of the foyer, yellow and orange wall lights, rugs and terrazzo, pale yellow wooden doors with adequately spaced metal numbers. Before we go any further, she said, the key in the lock. This is my parents' flat.

Where are they?

Mother is living with an emigré Russian and teaching in Montpellier. My father is in Ireland, breeding horses, so he says, and living with a wife who is younger than me and the second since my mother. And that's your bed, she said, pointing to the leather sofa in the sitting room.

Being English – pardon, *écossais*, she said. *Voulez-vous du thé?*

Tea's fine. With milk, but neither sugar nor racial stereotypes, please.

It's odd speaking English here, she shouted from the kitchen. I looked round; then, as always in a strange room, went towards what I knew, what I hoped would be familiar.

Are you warm enough? she shouted.

The furniture was low, metal-framed chairs and lots of patterned rugs on a dark blue carpet. She had classical CDs in racks up the wall by the window, with a small jazz selection: Jelly Roll Morton, Louis Armstrong, Sidney Bechet, the Hot Club of Paris, Dizzy, Miles. There were books and magazines, on shelves and tables, or lying on the floor beside a chair. The books were mostly expensive, pictorial accounts of exotic places, hard-covered presentations of informative thought, or the beautifully produced, inexpensive French paperback novels. There were a number of art books covering such subjects as Impressionism, Post-Impressionism, Fauve Masterpieces, primitive paintings, icon treasures, *Les Très Riches Heures du Duc de Berry*, or individual painters: Giotto, Rubens, Rembrandt, Dix. There were a number of poetry collections: Aimé Césaire, Mandelstam, Neruda, Catullus. There was Reznikoff, Brodsky and Rilke. There was Robert Burns. I was moving towards the bright and delicate water-colour paintings on the walls when she came in with a tray, which she put on a low table in front of the sofa, the slice of tree trunk, darkly varnished, with an ashtray filled with stubs in the centre.

I saw you looking at the books, she said.

I'm sorry. It's the first thing I do.

I'm the same. Let me read you something. She lit a cigarette and let it hang from the corner of her mouth while she flashed through the Mandelstam *Selected Poems*.

This was written in 1923, she said. It's called *The Slate Ode*.

> *Two stars coming together – a great meeting,*
> *a flint path from an old song,*
> *the speech of flint and air,*
> *flint and water, a ring with a horseshoe;*
> *on the layered rock of the clouds*
> *a milky sketch in slate –*
> *not the schooldays of worlds*
> *but the woolly visions of light sleep.*

Then what did she do with her hair? She was on the sofa, sitting on her feet with her skirt pulled round her legs. It was a brightly patterned thing, mostly dark red with primary-coloured embroidered overlays, and she wore a chenille cardigan on top of what I remember as a silk shirt, all dark red; neither maroon nor any of the darker crimsons, but a distinctly darkened red. She wore yellow beads of unpolished amber and turned a couple while she was reading, forward and back as though winding a watch. But it was her hair. It almost seemed to reflect the light, then fell from either side like a curtain across her face which she had to adjust with her middle finger, pushing it back behind her ear, where it lingered till the other side tumbled back to drape her view.

I was on a low, uncomfortable chair, legs crossed, both hands round my darkish tea. Her voice was softer than in conversation. She was slightly unsure of the text in English; I doubt if she had read it aloud before. She was hesitant, evenly paced, giving the words no emphasis, not bothering with the rhythm, how the lines ended or that one idea was carried on to the line below. I was unaware of her accent, though I remember it when she talked.

> *We sleep upright in the thick night*
> > *under the fleece hat.*
> *The spring runs back whispering into the*
> > *timbers*
> *like a little chain, little warbler,*
> > *speech.*

She snapped the book shut. No wonder they killed him, she said. And I'm sitting on your bed.

She showed me the bathroom, the spare bedroom, which was a workroom, and the door of her bedroom, then left flannel sheets and a duvet on the sofa. I had brushed my teeth when she shouted from the bedroom, Do you want a pillow?

She was wearing what could have been a man's pyjama jacket, and took a pillow from the pile at her back.

I have a heater that sometimes works, she said.

I should be warm enough.

My mother hated the sound of her voice. Throughout her schooldays she had been told to speak properly. She hated Scots accents, especially her own.

Speak properly, she told us. The word is butter. And milk. Say milk, not mulk. It's awful. Sounds so common.

I heard the language my mother did not want me to speak when my father came home from work, I heard it on the streets and I heard it in the playground, but not at school.

At school I was belted for having a character in an essay say Aye in answer to a question. I was belted for calling a mantelpiece a brace, trousers breeks and for saying didgie instead of midden. A nyaff was always a nyaff. Geggie, faunty, stoon, cundie, glaur, sleekit, dreich, bealin, slosh, bellosis and eachie-ochie; dreep, moocher, nyuck, boggin, pixie, shirrackin, sannies and wulk were similarly frowned upon, though the teacher who belted me for using Aye, said, I'll take command o that, when he caught us with a ball at playtime. I thought everyone played on the streets.

Voice was not the worst of it. Worse was the shame. Rising on a winter morning, cold linoleum, tea, toast and porridge for breakfast, the continual cold, the coughs and running noses, huddling round the fire at night, hand-me-downs. I won a bursary for £25.00 to redd me up with a badge and blazer, scarf and tie, a couple of shirts, trousers, a good pair of shoes. I ordered my clothes from Paisleys in Jamaica Street. Edinburgh University, sir, the assistant said. On a bursary.

At least he'll no end up workin in a shop, my mother said.

Jean made what my parents thought was a good marriage. Initially, Tom was a disappointment, not going to university, but he married into a good family who had a nice business.

Education was the only known way out of Partick. Teachers told my parents I could go to university. My course was set. My mother said she took comfort from the fact that her other children had done well. She told my father, He'll get the education that nane o us or the other yins evir got.

No matter how much my mother tried to refine her voice, she never got round to changing the way she constructed her sentences, and when she spoke the way she thought she ought to speak she sounded ridiculous.

She hated waste. When we offered to take her to a tea-room she would tighten her lips and shake her head. No, she would say. It's too dear. A wee café'll dae me fine, though we could wait till we get hame.

And she'd clutch her handbag, smile at the waitress and leave a tip. This is a nice hotel, she said when we took her to the hospital from which she did not return, trusting us completely. Are we having a wee run in the car? she asked Irene on the way there.

I think I look like her. We have the same colour of eyes. Jean and Tom have my father's eyes, but I have my mother's eyes and complexion. I have my father's shape and temper. I have his hair and chin, but I have my mother's eyes. I also have her will power.

What she taught has stayed. All my life I have believed in betterment in everything, have strived towards it, believed it would bring its own rewards. I have wanted to do well and thought it was an end in itself, that it would be recognised and credited.

Wrong.

A glass exploded in my hand today. I was emptying the dishwasher, picked up an ordinary, medium-sized Duralex tumbler and it shattered in my hand. That which was there, a substance, is no longer there, yet nothing obvious has happened to change it; the destruction came from something else, perhaps a fault within the object.

I fumble down old streets in search of a half-forgotten smell, rummage around bookshops, junk shops and stores that stink of cats in the corridors. Flowers or soup, cabbage cooking can raise the dead. I can capture landscapes by closing my eyes, cross oceans and climb mountains as easily as I can frill a stone across a perfectly still water, calm at midnight with a sheet of its light reflected on the surface of the moon. The lines on my hand and face are map readings. I have lost a hair with every missed opportunity and brushed my teeth with hope. I hurl rooftops at the sky and leave sunsets on their deathbed. I love the weeds that thrust through tarmac or that part of Perthshire, looking across Glen Truim to the Monadhlaith Mountains, that has a solitary deer fence which is piled till June with winter snows.

These are the times when I turn to The Pages. When I feel the cornfields breathe in at night, when a thorny light fankles in the drizzle of my mind, I find the simple deliberation of fitting one language into another is enough to make me believe something else is happening.

A note attached by pink paper-clip to the front of these Pages tells me Paris was the summit of Casanova's fortunes, but I remember the phrase from the Masters biography, which tells us something about Bernard's researchers.

Every once in a while I come across AnnA's handwriting. I remember her working at the kitchen table, biting her pencil and lifting the strand of hair when it fell from behind her ear. She seemed as though she wanted to explain everything, gathering references and quotations, deciphering, leaving notes and clues, traces for others to follow. This was the first time I saw her write her name: AnnA.

Why do you write your name like that?

Like what?

AnnA.

So that it's seamless, never ending, like a circle, she said. So that it goes on forever, like this, and she wrote her name on the back of an envelope. AnnAnnAnnAnnAnnAnnAnnA. The beginning is also the end, she said.

These two documents are together, and they appear to be connected. The first is a letter from the Comte de la Tour d'Auvergne introducing Casanova to his aunt, Jeanne Camus de Pontcarré, the Marquise d'Urfé. AnnA's note tells us Mme. d'Urfé was mad. She had been the mistress of the Duke of Orleans, Regent of France while Louis XV was a child, and was almost fifty when Casanova met her. She was anxious to be reborn as a boy; was convinced this was not only possible, but that Casanova alone could help her. Since he had reached the highest levels of enlightenment, in both the Cabala and the Rosy Cross, nothing was beyond him. An early problem may have been cost, but Mme. d'Urfé had plenty of money.

NOTABLE, IN EVERY WAY TRUSTWORTHY

I understand you no longer wish to fly to the moon. So be it. I was recently approached by Lascaris, who leaves for the heavens in four days' time. Should you change your mind, I am certain he would take you with him. However, I hope you will remember our last conversation on the subject of M. Lascaris and the decision you reached then.

In the meantime, I wish to introduce a Venetian, who is very well known in Parisian society, M. Giacomo Casanova. I believe he is notable, in every way trustworthy.

You have, dear aunt, often bemoaned that occult law prevents the ultimate secrets being revealed to a woman, and that, with this in mind, I should turn my intentions to finding a suitable guide and companion, a fellow questor who is knowledgeable enough to instruct you. I feel I have found such a man in M. Casanova, knowledgeable in his own right and yet humble enough to learn from you. Furthermore, he comes with a secure fortune. M. Casanova has no need of your wealth.

Already his powers have freed me from quackery. As you will remember, I have long suffered pains in both my legs and back. I have consulted widely, been given powders and liniments, herbs and incantations, many of which were accompanied by a loosening of the bowels, spewing and retching, as well as bleeding, headaches and sweating. I mentioned this fakery to M. Casanova, who told me the condition was caused by evil humours. In the end I could stand unaided, walk free of pain.

There is no doubt the cure was affected by the great Cabala, in which M. Casanova is an expert. My knowledge is, as you have often reminded me, painfully slight, but M. Casanova not only effected a brilliant introduction, he convinced me of its efficacy. I have asked him to instruct me in its uses and he has agreed to guide me for as far as I wish to go into its mysteries.

Though I have met him only recently, M. Casanova came to the attention of the court long ago. His opinions and counsel have been constantly sought and his good advice has benefited the state. It was he, for example, who established the state lottery, which has been of great benefit to us all.

Much has been whispered. He was here previously, for two years, as part of a tour. During this time he was noticed in Versailles because of his insistence on laughing every time he saw one of the ladies at court wearing the raised heels which were popular at that time.

He met La Pompadour and Richelieu, saw Louis XV and his Queen. I mention this because it is possible you may have met him then. He was in attendance around the time you were at court with the Duke of Orléans, though as an honoured guest rather than as his companion.

It is rumoured he and Lebel quarrelled over who introduced the Irish strumpet O'Murphy into His Majesty's harem. St Quentin, His Divine Majesty's earthly administrator, says the child's name is Marie-Louise Murphy and that she was delivered to him by Lebel, but the Venetian swears Lebel acted on his behalf since he did not know St Quentin.

Casanova claims to have paid three francs to watch the child undress. He could not afford the twenty-five guineas her sister demanded to deflower the child. Instead he had her portrait painted, gave it to Lebel, who passed it to St Quentin, knowing His Divine Majesty's preferences in that area. Everyone was delighted, including the sister. Lebel, on the other hand, says Casanova ordered a miniature from the Dutch rascal Johann Peters, who copied the Boucher original, which so enthralled His Divine Majesty. I am certain neither are telling the truth, not that it matters. Such a story would only be told by someone who was anxious to retain favour in court, and M. Casanova has little need of such recommendation. He does not advertise himself.

It was in the court at Versailles that his great capacity for healing first became known. He cured the Duchess of Chartres, daughter of the whore you knew, but still with her mother's appetite. She was also president of the female Masonic Lodges of France, and in this connection may have been known to you.

She sought his advice from the Cabala. Her skin was a mass of suppurating sores, a terrible sight. Men approached her masked and by dark. He firstly ordered regular sleep and that she sleep alone, no matter how difficult. He then ordered a number of purges, which were followed by a fruit diet, and that her skin be washed in cold water into which the plantain herb had been soaked. His instructions were followed. She was cured and sings his praises to this day.

His financial status can be vouched for by Cardinal François de Bernis, who had made Casanova's acquaintance while serving as our ambassador in Venice.

Pompadour's devotion to her military cadet school, and its superintendent Joseph de Paris-Duverney's

devotion to his job, are matched by our wily
Comptroller-General Jean de Boulogne's devotion to
royalty for their grace and favour in the difficult
position he adroitly maintains, finding the millions
needed to run such an establishment without raising
taxes. They said hundreds of others like them thank
M. Casanova, whose idea it was to have a state lottery.
This device, which he has established and maintained,
has not only kept these men in their position, but has
ensured his fortune. Many have cause to be grateful,
including those you may already know, such as Gluck's
itchy librettist, Ranieri di Calzabigi. I mention this in
hopes of making you smile at the prospect of *der grosse*
Gluck and his scrofulous hack pondering their lost
loves.

I do hope I have not seemed over-zealous. I know you
do not like mention of court, but I felt you had to know
M. Casanova's credentials. I have taken this time and
mentioned such people, circumstances and conditions as
I am aware will impress you because I am sure it will be
to your advantage. I have urged him to leave this
letter, then call. I await your instructions and remind
you always that your best service is my intention, your
desires my command.

More staples, paper-clips and a researcher's note saying
this is part of a report in English, believed to have been
composed for the British government, who were per-
petually concerned about what was happening in
France. This report appears to have been written by a
British spy and it is possible that either the author or the

note's recipient considered using Casanova in a similar capacity. His ability to move around society would have made him perfect for a job he often did for other employers.

SHE WAS ALONE

Versailles is filled with every crank and ne'er-do-well, sycophant and trickster, with cures for everything from baldness to gout, though most of the cures are concerned with the middle. Splints have been mentioned, with ropes and pulleys to aid the infirm. I cannot believe what I have heard and seen, from demonstrations on the removal of warts and unsightly hairs to journeys around the globe by night and afternoon trips to the bottom of the sea. I have seen animals and birds I never thought existed. This is the place where water flows uphill. Nature has been harnessed, the river diverted for entertainment, fountains and pools.

Lapdogs are as popular here as they are in England. I saw a feathered bird so big it could not fly but ran along the ground, its neck like a rubber pole bouncing before it, the head smaller than the eggs it lays. I watched an ugly creature bathe in mud, blowing air from its nose as the only indication of life, though when it opened wide its large and hideous, foul-smelling jaws, small birds picked their food from its teeth.

I understand these things will amaze you. Yet, there are monkeys who can read and write, in French only,

236

and small rodents that have been trained to pick a gentleman's pocket or lift a lady's skirt.

Bare arses abound. The Paris mob are restless. They are too stupid and too ugly, too useless to do anything other than complain. I mention this fact because I have not forgotten that the threat of sedition is feared in England more than the pox or a pregnant daughter.

I have told the French they should take their worst and decapitate them publicly. They should take the complainers and string them up, after a fair trial, of course. If they cannot trust the judiciary to provide the necessary verdicts, who can they trust? The rogues should be tried by those who know upon which side their bread is buttered.

I have told them not to rely on us for help. They laugh, but I simply remind them we are surrounded by water and there is nothing better than a cold soaking for a hot head.

There are beggars on the streets, more than before. This should not trouble us. Beggars are too concerned with their own welfare to be anything other than compliant. It is their own fault they have chosen to sit around all day waiting for money to fall from a rich man's hand. Damn all, I tell you, falls from mine.

They remain because they are encouraged. If we made a few disappear, then told the others to get off the streets, they would leave. We should tax those who offer money or support, then sweep them away.

There appear to be more deaths by misadventure than ever before. If they want to kill themselves, I say we let them. Let their bodies rot for the world to see what

237

damn fools they were and when the dogs have eaten the flesh we should throw away the bones.

Now to other matters. The Venetian Jew Casanova is not at all like M. le Comte de Saint-Germain. I understand your concern and praise the depth of your information. There are a number of differences, I believe in our favour.

M. le Comte de Saint-Germain claims to know everything, to have lived for hundreds of years and never to have eaten. There are fools who believe him, including His Divine Majesty King Louis XV. His Majesty gave him money and a castle to pursue his researches into starvation.

Casanova has so far only managed to ingratiate himself with the old fool d'Urfé, who wishes, it seems, to be born as a boy. He has promised to help her achieve such a state. The whole nonsense seems to have little to do with money, though during her time as Orléans' mistress she acquired a considerable fortune, as well as what she got from the husband she cuckolded and whose death surprised no one. She now seems intent upon dispersing this fortune in Casanova's direction.

In the beginning he went as far as procuring a Dutch boy, whom it appears Mme. d'Urfé believed she was to become. This child was at least as unscrupulous as Casanova and lost no time in getting himself into the old fool's bed. The sage convinced her it was folly to corrupt herself this way, that she should give herself a proper start in life, so the lad was packed off to school, with a name he chose, Count d'Aranda. Need I remind you, there is another Count d'Aranda, Prime Minister and Chancellor of Spain, Grand Master of Spanish Freemasonry and a First Class Grandee.

After a time in jail, the wealth and entire assets of a silk printing company he founded having mysteriously evaporated, Casanova was released to find his love wandering about Paris with a magnet round her neck, a device she believed would attract lightning which, in turn, would make her soar to the sun.

All things, he told her, emanate from God; and we may well anticipate that similar pronouncements were made concerning Wisdom, Love and Endurance, which are said to be male, while Understanding, Power and Majesty are female. In this case more than most, the central unifying pillar is neither male nor female.

One feels the central pillar was frequently called into service. He has borrowed heavily to support his gambling losses and is considerably in our debt. Every time he came to borrow, we got another instalment in the d'Urfé swindle.

These events took place over years rather than months and were well established by the time I arrived. He had made a fortune with the lottery, which he charmed the French authorities into running, mainly with the support of the Abbé de Bernis, a thoroughly disreputable pervert whom Casanova met in Venice. The government allowed him to establish six ticket offices in Paris. He sold five, kept the best for himself and made more money than the King, though no one complained. Pompadour's interests were preserved, money was distributed and there are people wandering round Paris whose wealth had been increased by Casanova's lottery.

His popularity waned when respectable society could not tolerate his presence. He tried to terminate his mistress's pregnancy. Her father is known to us. Other documents concerning this will reach you.

When I came to Paris, he had settled into d'Urfé's apartments on the rue du Bac, staying to convince her that his sole intention was her conversion, and to make proper devotions to the seven planets.

It seems he told her he would impregnate a virgin who would give birth to a boy who would not at first know who he was, thus preventing the scandal of having a two-year-old discuss his affair with the Regent of France forty years previously. After the age of three the boy would gradually become aware that he was Mr d'Urfé who used to be Mrs d'Urfé. He would also be its guardian until the child was twelve.

He chose a virgin of divine origin, mistress of a count in Prague; she was a dancer and an actress. Mme. d'Urfé watched the deed being done beneath an April full moon at her estate in Pontcarré. The Cabala informed her that conception did not take place. And during the May full moon the virgin writhed so much, Casanova never having paid her, that insertion did not take place, so the Cabala this time instructed Mme. d'Urfé to write to the moon for instruction.

The virgin told Mme. d'Urfé what Casanova was up to, but the old fool did not believe her. While she was writing to the moon, he composed the reply, silver ink on green paper. At new moon they stripped themselves and entered a bath, where her letter was burned. As she watched the ashes float upwards, the moon's reply appeared on the surface of the water.

It told her to get rid of the previous virgin, who went to Turin and published the story. Casanova found another whore, who became a celestial virgin and Mr d'Urfé's mother. After more money troubles, he convinced her that seven salamanders had transported the real virgins to the Milky Way, leaving *doppelgängers*.

Nothing for it but to impregnate d'Urfé himself, though he needed a young assistant to help them both. Next day, d'Urfé tackled the girl herself.

The only problem was that when she gave birth to herself he would be a bastard, so Casanova would have to marry her. The pack closed in and, as you know, he has fled to England. The old fool is dead, leaving her money to herself when she is reborn. Her family seems to be contesting the will.

I fail to understand what he could possibly have gained, apart from her money. Everything I know about him tells me he is not the kind of man to do something without benefit to himself. Gain and comfort are his sole motivation.

With someone else, I would say it was money, but originally he had more than enough. He gambles, and gamblers never have enough money, but when this nonsense started he must have been one of the richest men in Paris, if not France.

However, when he went to Holland on behalf of the French, she gave him sixty thousand francs' worth of shares to trade. She had not collected dividends for a number of years. He sold them for 72,000 francs and, again acting on information which came from the

Cabala, he made a profit of several million guilders for a Dutch merchant.

It is important to realise that during this time, and for all the time he was in Paris, there was a child, a virgin when he met her, who trusted him as the friend of her brother. She was alone, waiting for him to return to rue du Petit-Lion-St-Saveur. She wrote endless letters, some of which we intercepted, for at one time we believed they were transactions of another variety. They were simply the pleadings of an innocent girl, hopelessly in love with a man who did not care in the least for her.

In sleep, the essence of a person seeps into their surroundings. A woman in love or a dog can catch this smell. This child wandered round the bordellos of Paris, through d'Urfé's bedroom as well as the rooms of the poxed and the great, disguised sometimes as a chambermaid, at other times as a laundress, taking the clothes he slept in, removing the shirts and bedclothes that covered him and his whores; she wrapped herself in them, in order to be near him. She has stopped and sniffed these garments in the street to catch the scent of her love, to be as near as he will allow.

But Manon Balletti seems a sensible girl. When her mother died and she was left to mourn alone, she came to her senses, having sent him her diamond earrings while he was in prison following the great silk fraud. This followed the sale of his share in the lottery. He claims to have lost money printing silk. It was gambling. He put the company up as credit, though already it was over-committed. Mme. d'Urfé got him out of prison, Manon Balletti lost her earrings and

Casanova went to Amsterdam. She wrote breaking off their engagement. He does not seem to have pined.

This is a man of no feeling for anything other than himself. To focus on his misdeeds, conquests and adventures is to miss the point. He cares for nothing and no one at all. The chase, the conquest, is everything. When his victims have fallen, they have no further use. He will continue as long as there is something for him: pleasure, perhaps, though I doubt if he derives pleasure from anything.

We know because we have been told. Happiness in humanity is extended by making humanity happy. Everyone wishes they'd had more love. I mention these things because this man has confused the two. He is restless and relentless, can find no happiness in himself and therefore seeks his happiness in others. He is remorseless. I recommend we use him.

Forgive the doting parent. You hate it when I talk of your childhood, but it was a time of discovery for me as well. If this embarrasses you, please move on.

Janie was born at 9.25 p.m. on 1 June, 1972. I think she was conceived in an autumn holiday.

I don't remember much until Irene told me Janie sobbed herself to sleep after midnight, repeating over and over again, I want my daddy.

I did things I never imagined, watched Christmas ice shows, pantomimes, adaptations of fairy tales and children's novels, along with every appalling children's film, Christmas and summer. I wandered round clothes shops and toy stores, discussed doll's dresses, ribbons, houses and a pram.

Irene said, I think that child doesn't need a mother. Then she said, I think you're too soft on her. She gets everything she wants.

Janie knew how to get around me. I adamantly did not reject the boys. In fact, I probably spent more time with them than they wanted to spend with me.

Everything was a delight. I loved the way she spoke. A crayon was a bothum, milk was sauce and a biscuit was kathorwandy.

What do you want, Janie?

A kathorwandy, please.

What's that? I asked at Edinburgh Zoo.

It's a giraffitysnake, she said.

Who's that?

Father Crispies.

And where are you going?

I'm away for a kip.

She'll go on the stage, said Irene's mother.

I will not, said Janie. I'll stay at home and look after my daddy.

She was ticklish. As a baby she smiled when I rubbed her feet and she loved being chased. It was enough to run after her clapping my hands.

She loved balloons going off, bangs and pops of any description, especially when she thought they sounded like a rude noise or were accompanied by Peekaboo.

She loved word games. From the earliest puns and silly rhymes to palindromes and crossword puzzles, laughing at the silliest rhymes as much as when she refused to do something she'd been told. Janie, don't do that. She'd do it and laugh.

On her first day at school, she danced around the kitchen singing: I'm a big girl now. I'm a big girl now.

Primary school was always exciting. Birthdays and Christmas came and went. Eight years old in the school nativity play, when Joseph said, There's no room at the inn, she told him, You can stay at our house.

She cried every night for a month when her Labrador pup was run over by a lorry on the Fenwick Road. Later, she asked, Is Towser in heaven?

I'm sure he is. How do you know about heaven?

We got told it in school. Miss McAlpine says we go there when we die if we're good.

And what happens if you're bad?

You go to the other place.

What other place?

Miss McAlpine wouldn't tell us.

I feel it my duty to raise these children in the ways of the Lord, Miss McAlpine told me.

You can do that with your own children, but not with mine.

I am *in loco parentis* when you're not there.

Will I be punished when I die? Janie asked one night, still awake after three chapters of *The Lion, the Witch and the Wardrobe*.

Between then and Miss McAlpine's removal, she asked, Who was I called after?

My mother. Why?

Miss McAlpine says I have a silly name.

Saturdays were busiest. Art classes in the morning, a football match with Colin in the afternoon, then I'd collect Janie and Robert from their drama class at half past five. We strolled around art shows and watched adaptations of *Romeo and Juliet* into Glaswegian as well as scenes and stories of the group's devising.

I told you she'd end up on the stage, said her grandmother, who was always too busy to attend a performance.

She was upset because life was unfair, with hunger, starving babies, pollution and animal testing. Others liked her ability to laugh at herself, and they liked her kindness. She often took neighbours' dogs for a walk or visited the elderly and sick. She fed a string of stray cats and always helped with sales of work, daffodil teas, bring-and-buy and jumble sales.

Friends were important. I wondered whose nature she inherited when she distributed her sweets, put money she'd been given into charity cans in the street. Boys came to her sixth birthday party, then no more. I was surprised how even at eleven or twelve the girls still played circle games, enjoyed pass the parcel and blind man's buff. Boy friends sent them into fits of giggles.

Janie was teased by her brothers and me. Do you know a guy called Jack?

Yes.

He phoned here.

He did not.

He did.

What did he want?

To speak to you.

He's a pig.

Her period caught her unawares. She wakened one morning and the bed was soaked. I was confused, a

246

child having to deal with adult things, taking it all in her stride, changing her towel then going out to play, bloody clothing on her bedroom floor, basins of pants in pink water and packets of towels in the bathroom.

I don't think she had started school, was maybe four or five when she found out I was ticklish. Of course, I pretended and tickled her back. Say, by first year of secondary school, we had developed a routine, play-fights and tickling.

Don't you think she's maybe a bit big for that? said Irene.

A week later we were rolling about on the upstairs landing, I stretched up to tickle under her arm and accidentally put my hand on her breast.

What's wrong, Dad? she asked. Are you all right?

Fine. I think I must have caught something in my throat.

Irene smiled.

It was awful.

Maybe she's not your wee girl any more.

She doesn't know that. It was me that pulled away.

That summer she went on a school trip to Chamonix and came back chewing gum and lying around, cuddling up with me in front of the television, stopping for a cuddle in the hall, putting her arms round my waist in the kitchen.

It is easy now to move to the mood swings and tantrums, boredom and fashion, excessive energy, dress and make-up, Saturday afternoon trips into town, pocket money, phone calls, clothes allowance and the continual stream of pop music from the bedroom. It is easy to step from there to the subsequent disasters. But during these times Janie was happy, playful and studious. She worked hard, got good reports, and the scrape of her cello practising the *Lieutenant Kije* Troika for the school's Christmas Concert was almost as frequent as Radio One.

She left school at seventeen. We agreed she should not go to university straight away. Janie fancied working for a year then maybe travelling with friends, taking time to decide what she wanted to do and where she should do it.

Wonderful, said Irene. Of course you must. It's so much easier now than in my day.

Most of the jobs were voluntary, working in a theatre box office, sick visiting and environmental clean-up; but she did a bit of waitressing, worked for Mr Patel, and eventually got a job in a nightclub cloakroom. I think this was where she met Steve.

We could hardly have been more naïve. He came to the house and we thought, So what, leave it alone, it can hardly last.

You don't like him, do you?

We don't know him.

You won't let yourselves get to know him.

Do you think it's entirely our fault? asked Irene. Janie said she was moving in with him, left that night and we did not see her for a week.

When she came back it was to collect clothes, tapes, and the like. Steve waited in a Y registration Ford Escort. I went out to talk with him. It's her life, man, he said.

When I came home from work about ten days later, Irene was sitting in the dark in the downstairs sitting room, staring at the wall, watching the patterns made by passing headlights. Eventually she said she had visited Janie, called unexpectedly.

I thought she might want some things for the house. I thought we might be able to go shopping.

She lived in a room in Keir Street, Pollokshaws. Irene called at the back of twelve. Janie was still in bed. Steve was shouting, Get her to fuck out of here. Now.

Janie walked Irene round the block. Give us a score, she said. Irene told me it meant £20.00.

We both went down next day. You don't understand, said Janie. He's sick. He needs help but the doctors won't treat him. He wants to go in, wants to go off it. He's trying to get on a methadone script, but they won't give it to him because he's a known addict.

Don't leave me, Janie, he shouted. Don't go.

I'm staying, she said. Then she smiled at me. Give us a score, Dad? She had sold her clothes and jewellery; even the tapes were gone.

And so it started and continued for more than a year. Any time we saw her she wanted money. Steve was in and out of detox units, from the shores of Argyll to Maryhill, from Rutherglen to the Borders. We gave up after three.

It sounds daft, but we never thought Janie could be addicted. I thought of Irene when I met her and after we were married. I thought of her in Germany and thought Janie maybe was like her mother. I also felt she was being manipulated. I knew she would believe what he said, would try to support him.

Her visits were infrequent. She telephoned and always wanted money. I refused. Irene told me she also refused, but I know that was not always the case. Janie turned up, but never stayed long.

You only come here for money, I told her. When she arrived, I asked, How much is it this time? But she ignored me.

Irene said, This has to stop. You are going to have to be civil with her. Try to talk.

Then she told me she bought clothes from Janie. Nothing much at first, underwear and tights, but now it was silk shirts and skirts, jumpers, cardigans and jeans.

Where do you think she gets that stuff?

She says she gets it from a friend.

She steals it.

I'm sure that's not right.

It's called reset, Irene. You are buying stolen goods.

That was a huge row. I confronted Janie. She denied everything. I persisted, made sure she was in no doubt that Irene was buying no more clothes, that we would be giving her no more money for whatever reason.

I suppose I could have gone on indefinitely. I had been to a drug counselling support group and though I found their methods and message a bit stark, I could see it made sense. The problem was one for which I had been prepared. Janie was no longer my daughter. I did not know her any more.

One Sunday she said she was literally passing, had been visiting friends in Ayr and was on her way home. She was pale, looked tired, but had obviously tried to make an effort. She had tea and left within an hour. Next morning Irene told me £50.00 had been taken from her purse.

I went straight to Janie. Do you think, she said, do

you actually think I would steal from my own mother? Do you think that's why I turned up there, so that I could steal? Next you'll be telling me I wasn't at Prestwick.

You said Ayr.

Prestwick. Prestwick. I was at fucking Prestwick. What difference does it make? You don't believe me anyway.

Every time she came to see us, money went missing. We could not leave her alone, even watched when she went to the lavatory. You think I'm here to steal, don't you? she said. And Irene said, Yes.

Right, that's it, said Janie.

What's it?

I'm leaving.

You are my own daughter and I want to kill you. Look at you. Look at the state you are in. Look at your hair and your clothes. You are skin and bone and might as well be dead. Let us help you. Please. Come back home and let us help you.

I can't.

Why not?

Because there's no point.

No point to what?

Anything. What's the point, Dad? What's the fucken point, eh? I suppose you'll want me to go to university? Well, I'm not going, because there's no point. What do you say to an arts graduate? A Big Mac and a portion of fries. Get it?

Nobody said anything about university.

You don't know what it's like. You don't understand. Where can I get a job? What can I do?

The government are—

Don't hassle me with the government. You're supposed to work in a newspaper, so you tell me what's happening. Tell me what jobs there are for folk like me, tell me how much benefit or training I get. I'm not talking about what they say; I'm talking about going to a Social office and asking for that stuff. I'm talking about dealing with the system. You need a hit when you come out because you're there all day. As far as I know we don't grow heroin in this country. So how does it get here? Who lets it in and why? They could stop this if they wanted to. They could hit the big guys, hit the dealers and the suppliers. Have you ever asked why they don't? I'll tell you why, because as long as the likes of me are looking for a hit, we're not bothering them. The lost generation. They don't want us and we don't want them. Give us a score, Dad. That'll help. I don't need advice. Especially not about the government. I need a score.

Then the police came. Janie had been arrested for shoplifting and was in Stewart Street Police Station. She would be in court in the morning. They expected she'd be remanded for background reports, transferring her to Corton Vale, where she'd be detoxed and examined. Did we know she was pregnant?

We saw her in prison. This is it, she said. I'm clean. I've been clean since I got here. I'll need to get off it for the baby.

Where's Steve?

I think he's in Keir Street. Can I come home? If they ask will you say I can come home?

She stayed two nights. It's a problem, said the social worker. It always happens. I don't know where she'll be.

That was the worst time. The phone would ring. The receiver was replaced when we picked it up. Steve had left Keir Street. If you find him, let me know, the landlord said. They owe me money.

I drove around town, round Glasgow Green and the Anderston Centre, spoke to prostitutes and dealers, addicts, anyone who would look at her school photograph. I was passed from the Beggar's Rail by the police station at Gorbals Shopping Centre to houses in Killearn Street, Possilpark, from Maryhill Shopping Centre to the high flats at Cranhill.

I got to know most of the prostitutes. I just need another wan, they'd say. I need a score, then I'm done. You don't fancy it, dae ye?

She definately doesnae work here, but she doesnae need tae. She'll be shoplifting. I don't know. There's ways and means, you know yoursel.

If I see her I'll get her tae contact ye. Definately. Okay. Thanks very much.

One night I drove round Anderston, between St Vincent Street and Argyle Street, for three hours. A red Escort pulled in front of me as I turned into Cadogan Street. They showed their warrant cards and told me to get out the car.

We're fucken fed up wi you.

Have I committed an offence?

I don't give a fuck if you've committed an offence or no. We want you out o here. And don't come back.

I'm looking for my daughter.

Does she work here?

253

I don't think so.

Then why're ye looking here?

She's a drug addict.

Look. This was the other one, thin, with dark hair. He lit a cigarette and sneered. You've been seen wi lassies in your motor. We asked, an they said you gave them money.

That's right.

Did you have sex wi them?

No.

Then what'd you gie them money for?

Information.

Fuck sake. A private detective. He walked round the car.

Is this your vehicle, sir? asked the other one. Do you have your driving documents?

They gave me a ticket to present my driving documents to the local police station within three days. We don't want to see your daughter's picture, sir. We want you to get out of here and never come back. If we see your car here again we'll charge you.

What with?

Wasting police time.

The editor was sympathetic. I don't think we can report what you've told us, but it would make a good series, get the aid agencies involved, set up a helpline, that sort of thing. There's public interest in the drug problem. I'd like you to look at the politics of regeneration, Lanarkshire, places like that. Have a word with the people, fish out the prospects for employment, redevelopment, whatever. It might even make a three-part series, run it at the start of the week. By the way, somebody mentioned. None of my business, of course, but what's the score with that student?

Irene and I held on tight. She visited the hospital and tried to do some voluntary work, but gave up when she could not remember where to go nor to put the dates in the calendar.

I'd like to think there was a point to all this, she said.

Janie phoned. I've been in London. I'm at the bus station. Come and get me.

I told her about Irene in the car. Fuck this, she said. I need to split.

Janie. You need to see your mother.

Give me fifty quid, take me to Possil and then I'll see her.

She stayed for less than an hour.

I'll need to go, she said when Irene opened the door.

Where's the baby?

Gone.

Did you have it adopted?

Lost it.

What happened?

Don't hassle me with that. Right. Just don't hassle me with that right now. I've got a lot to do. Things are really heavy. Steve died. Right. O.D.

Last time I saw her, Irene was in hospital. She turned up some time after one in the morning. I heard a shuffling by the front door. She hid her face when I put on the light. She was dirty, thinner than ever. Her face was bruised. Her eyes like ice. She was wearing dirty jeans and worn trainers, a black leather jacket three sizes too big.

Daddy, she said. I want to come off. I can't take it,

can't go on. I want to come off. She was crying, trembling, pathetic.

She drank two cups of tea and slept in her room.

In the morning the room was empty. Television, video, radios, telephones, the money in the house and my credit cards were gone.

Rhona phoned.

I've got a job in Glasgow, she said.

There's an old folks' home across the way. On summer mornings from the back of nine, the residents come out for a read at the paper and a seat in the sun. Sometimes the nurses bring out tea. They sit in groups of three or four, smile and talk to passers-by.

Some have got to know me. They say it's a fine day and ask how I'm doing. They tell me about their families and visitors, relations in England, Canada, Australia, New Zealand.

Lately they've been worried. Rumour says the home is to close. It's on a good site and could easily be sold as a hotel development. No one has denied this possibility. Everyone says they do not know what will happen, which worries the residents, who wonder where they'll go. They like the home and staff, would like to think they have settled, but there's consultations going on at present. Men in suits come and go, smile and ask how everybody's doing. Ask them a question and they tell you to talk to someone else.

The residents have organised a petition, but don't think it'll do much good. We're like pensioners everywhere, said one. They do what they like and expect us to be grateful.

Annie needs a hip operation. She's been on a waiting list for nearly three years, was in the next batch when the first hospital closed, then her second lot ran out of money, so she is on another list and waiting. She is crippled and in constant pain. The doctor gives her painkillers. She is 74.

They recently installed a bottle bank in the supermarket car park at the foot of the hill. Twice a week Annie makes her way downhill, almost bent double, in her blue coat, leaning on a metal stick, a Safeway carrier bag with two empty bottles in her left hand. She stops to hold on to the railings, to catch her breath. She waits until someone tall enough to put the bottles in the skip comes along, has tea in the café and walks back uphill, which takes more than twice the time to go down. She covers a distance of just over half a mile. It takes more than three hours. I like the fresh air, she says.

A note from AnnA says this comes from the same source as before and was probably written by the same author. It was written in English.

THEMSELVES TO BLAME

My health improves. Some days are better than others, though I have to say the last month has been an improvement on anything I imagined. I can now use my stick and there are small, significant improvements in my general abilities. With a new will, and a new direction, knowing how important it is for you to have someone healthy and active, I have launched myself back into society.

Every night tumbrils of bones and rotting corpses cross this city, resurrected by those with a family to feed. Every night I tell them I am not yet ready.

Everything in Paris is below the surface. I am certain what exists above ground is an illusion.

Stone from beneath the ground has raised the city towards heaven and country fields are scattered with fertiliser brought to the surface by men who are known as the noonday ghosts. The quarries whose stone was reincarnated in St. Germain and St. Séverin are being filled with bones from the Cemetery of the Innocents.

This is the harvest of Les Halles, where the dead from twenty parishes were tipped into a pit, covered in quicklime and left to rot. The stench has become too much even for the French, so the remains are being carted by torchlight to fill the quarry. The job nears completion, but still they arrive. The bones are piled from floor to ceiling, patterned into hearts and stars, daisy-chains and crucifixes.

It is the latest venue, more fashionable than a salon, more respectable than Versailles. I have lost count of the courtiers I have seen prowling the Catacombs in search of pleasure.

At last I am able to move my right hand for extended periods of time. I can grasp and lift some fairly heavy objects and hope to be able to hold lighter objects for longer periods.

I fear my spirits are not yet lifted. It takes time to mobilise me in the mornings. My Scotch servant

Morrison feeds me. Every day I dread the prospect that this will continue or even extend. My time is divided. I wake at six and rise before eight. Morrison brings me coffee, warmed milk and gruel, which he spoons to my mouth. I can hold the coffee cup. He also helps me bathe and dress; I am usually ready to receive the first of my visitors by midday. I rest in the afternoon, dine in the evening and circulate at night.

As you know, I have taken some younger and fitter, though scarcely more able, men into my employ. I have also secured the services of a number of women, from all ranks, and have found this beneficial. I have, as you advised, been very circumspect as to whom I use and the purposes for which I use them. We cover the city from dawn to dusk. They bring their snippets the following day.

One young man delivered a fable of the Catacombs. As always in cases of this nature, I ask others to do precisely what was originally done and report their findings to me immediately. All the women knew of this place; the ladies because they heard it was scandalous, the whores because of their employ. Another man knew its reputation. Everyone confirmed the egregious findings, which were sent to you by separate mail. When all was considered, the stage set and ready, I descended into something I had never imagined.

Morrison was with me, under strict instruction to utter not a single word. You would have admired the way he smiled and tilted his head to one side, as though retarded, then ran to help with some other matter. Everyone felt sorry for me, having such a fool of a servant, and offered to loan me something better till I was repaired. They admired my fortitude.

The evening began well, with the youngish Mlle. Alexandra Walderstein, whom I have mentioned many times. Her information has been admirable in the past, so much so that Versailles have planted renegade whores inside the establishment. Nothing comes of it. Mlle. Walderstein knows who they are and feeds them nonsense about English shipping off Cadiz, Italian uniforms marching at the border and Spanish manoeuvres in the Pyrenees.

I know nothing of her origins, but everyone talks of her great abilities, the least of which is not patience. So stellarly is she imbued with this virtue that, on top of everything else, she regularly manages to help the aged relive their youth.

Your Excellency would have enjoyed the bath she gave me, filled with salts of blue and yellow which turned the water green and smelled of flowers, mainly, I think, the rose, though I also detect a hint of lavender. She had me lie in this water for some time, continually refilling my tub.

A child was playing draughts with a Dutchman who filled the place with smoke. Her eyes were glazed and distant. She was more self-contained than anyone I have ever seen in this type of work.

No matter how young, a woman seldom settles. There is a continual mechanism about her movements and though she may capture or recollect the memory of a love, she is always detached enough to remember her role. Pity the poor man fooled by that nonsense. It is as near to the real thing as opera is to life.

This child was skilled and practised. My belief remains that she was preoccupied, distracted rather than detached. She performed her duties well enough to allow me to suggest to the estimable Mlle. Walderstein that this child be considered for our work in the future.

'Why wait?' asked Mlle. Walderstein. 'I gave her to you to allow you to gauge her for yourself.'

I mentioned the child's preoccupation.

'She thinks she is in love. No matter. It will come to nothing. He does not even know she exists.'

'Why then love him?'

'She loves the dream. She knows he is older, believes he is popular, gallant and rich. He is, of course, nothing of the sort.'

'Do I know him?'

'Certainly.'

'I take it the girl is not infatuated with me?'

'I regret to inform Your Excellency that her choice was not so wise.'

I later saw the child cross the room during an opera performance to give M. Casanova a rough bouquet, presumably purchased from the flower sellers who occasionally linger near Mlle. Walderstein's establishment. Gentlemen do not like to arrive empty-handed. The flowers are returned to the seller when the bearer leaves, a simple arrangement from which everyone benefits. She gave the Venetian the flowers because, it was said, he had written the libretto. Everyone was applauding the composer, of whom I am certain we shall never hear again, and, of course, the performers. She gave the flowers to Casanova, whose libretto was undistinguished:

261

Apollo's bright rays shall cover the land;
We are his servants, all at his command;
Triumphant and happy, together we sing,
Long life to all lovers and happiness bring.

The last line is repeated.

As for me, she washed me well and gave me a robe, silken and the length of my body, red and yellow patterned with stars and diamonds. I asked her to help me to another room and she did so, allowing me to lean as though she was, quite literally, a walking stick. We entered a warm room with a clairvoyant air, white and full of whispers, yellow shafts from the chandeliers, colours reflected from the crystals, turned to white in the mirror. Girls of a similar age, dress and demeanour moved like reeds below water. There seemed to be one child per person. I asked for nothing, nor did my girl speak directly to me. She fetched coffee, held my hand while a colleague sang and another played the spinet. She brought a platter of fishes, reached for some small piece, removed the skin, bared the pink flesh and fed me this morsel on the end of a small piece of bread.

After an hour or so, the child fetched a wheelchair. I was taken to a room covered in satin layers of pink, laid on a couch and told to wait.

Mlle. Walderstein is a handsome woman, sternly dressed in black with her hair pulled tightly behind her head, which tends to exaggerate her rather stark features. She gave me some advice, which I will now relate to you, should anyone suffer from my condition.

She learned her skills from the Cabala and her teacher was, of course, the Venetian Casanova. She claims to ease all afflictions and has also been known to effect some cures. They seem fanciful. She gives her patients nothing for a day, keeps them locked in and entertained, then, when she feels they are desperate to be treated, she tells them what to do with the donkey hair, herbs or the unguents she provides.

For me, she was insistent. I needed the Breath of Youth. I should first sweat out all the impurities from my body. A purge and a bleeding, the cups on certain places, a leech to my afflicted arm and the Breath of Youth. My disease, she said, was caused by an imbalance between the four humours – blood, phlegm, yellow bile and black bile. Fever was needed to burn off the bad humours. She prescribed sudorific herbs, steam and hot baths, after which I should have a long rest. Fever, she said, would also purify the blood. She claimed I would not only feel better, but would look younger and be more vital after my treatment.

'You will be all right,' she said. 'Stay with me and return restored. Then, the Catacombs await you.'

The child was my companion, slept in my room by the fire, sang me to sleep with lullabies, songs she said she learned from her father, a shepherd, whom she had never seen, but she knew he wanted her to learn these songs and the other things he sent to her in a dream. Neither has she known her mother.

She is boned like a boy, small-breasted, with skinny legs and knees. She has short hair and the name Marie tattooed on her right arm.

I asked about the Catacombs and she laughed, claiming to have been raised in the Paris underground. Mlle. Walderstein says this is correct.

The glazed look was caused by the fact that her eyes have never become accustomed to sunlight. Her face has never felt the rain. She does not know the word breeze. She sleeps by day and rises by night.

'Ask about Marie,' said Mlle. Walderstein.

The child raised her arm and kissed the name.

I was by now completely repaired and still with Mlle. Walderstein, because of comfort and child. 'Why are you here?' she had asked in the morning.

'To repay you for my health.'

'I have been paid.'

'I could pay you handsomely, enough to raise you out of here.'

'I have no need to leave.'

'We will talk of it later. Tell me about Marie.'

Her father became a coachman, and turned to idiocy when he was kicked in the head by a horse. The family were thrown from their house.

The father died on the road to Paris. His body was left by the roadside and the two elder children were sold. The mother was heavily pregnant when she and her younger son arrived in Paris. They found employment digging the Catacombs and lived there when the work was finished.

The child said she was born into darkness. She played in the underground, her brother surfaced for food or errands.

When the mother died her bones were mingled with the others. The brother abandoned the child, having shown her how to pick pockets, lure drunken gentlemen to places where they could be robbed, to cheat at cards, especially faro. These were the only gifts he gave her. She was raised by Marie.

Marie came to the Catacombs by choice. Her life seems to have involved the fringes of society. She came as a socialite attending a party at the Empire of Death.

I understand Marie introduced the Venetian Casanova, who continues to gather intelligence and is, I believe, coming to England; Marie introduced him to Charles Edward Stewart. This pair were firm in their debauchery.

The Jacobite wept for his Highlanders, after beating his Scotch mistress. I have not yet learned if they discussed the approach to him by the Americans to become their monarch. He has been known to say he favoured the move because it would both restore the old and rightful throne and give the new nation legitimacy. He has also been known to say that since travelling to North Britain and back he fears sea journeys.

'I would be dead were it not for Marie,' the child told me. She had not eaten for days when Marie gave her food and introduced her to Mlle. Walderstein.

The child's main advantage is her background. She has been raised in a society where survival is all. She will therefore not return to poverty or penury for anything. She will want to eat and keep her finery around her.

She has agreed to spy upon Mlle. Walderstein. I have also asked Mlle. Walderstein to keep us informed of the child's movements. She has one weakness, and will respond to anyone who treats her kindly.

She believes herself to be in love with the Venetian

Casanova, who gave her chocolate violets, strawberries and cream. Mlle. Walderstein has provided additional information on Marie; both she and the child have agreed to inform on Casanova.

He has a brain like a silver thaler, a brass real or a golden doubloon and goes wherever money goes. He is a gambler and tells us he is necessary to the functioning of society, that everything, commerce, trade and all, would collapse without him and others like him. It is the men, he says, those who are despised, who work in private, who keep money circulating, who encourage others to come from abroad and to invest in Parisian life. I believe he knows every coin in Europe and can tell their worth, one to the other.

'I bring foreign money into Paris,' he told the child. 'Sometimes when I move my head I hear my neck creak. It is nothing more than the bones moving, adjusting to a new position like cogs, like machinery. I sometimes think it is memory returning, working, inventing or elaborating. I sometimes think it is time; the crick of a neck, the tick of a clock.'

The child says he carries a town in his head. It is always with him, he is always there, usually visiting the palace, though he sometimes finds himself in the gutter. Some things never change: the climate and his home, his servants and opinions. There are stars in the gutter, excrement on the landing, candlegrease and satin.

I am told his manservant has been seeking employment, though he firstly sought money for his master to gamble, then food for them both. The child has confirmed most of these stories. Mlle. Walderstein has confirmed the others. He has tried to borrow money, though no one will give him an advance. His debts exceed 100,000 francs.

He is said to have refuged in a Benedictine monastery, though he emerged as soon as everyone thought he was inside, asking his daughter's hand in marriage. She turned him down.

He is here because he cannot return to Venice. Should he go back everyone will know he was released from the prison known as The Leads. Venetian authorities could hardly survive the shame.

His servant has a letter of recommendation from the old fool Voltaire. Meanwhile his master styles himself de Seingalt, even though La Renaud has removed his clothes and jewels, leaving a pox in their place. He must be the only man in Paris who did not know she'd been riddled for years.

He is compelled, cannot stop gambling and presents a pathetic, shambling picture, haunting the Catacombs day and night since old d'Urfé tired of their nonsense. He is well known among the bones, peering into corners, begging, following every swish of silk, lingering where he hears a moan, a sigh or a whisper, thrusting his light to whatever he can see.

The people here know nothing of care, sorrow or worry. They are perfectly happy, do not have the constraints of society and are therefore outside its influence.

And yet they say, We hate you. Hate what you stand for and hate what you've done.

Casanova takes things apart to see what is missing. For him the Mass is an act of cannibalism.

He is coming to England.

Morrison wants a better horse. He claims French horses are lame, would like a thoroughbred English racehorse and lives for the day when he can mount her back and ride through the shires like the wind.

I am repaired.

SEVEN

. . . the wild regrets, and the bloody sweats,
    None knew so well as I:
For he who lives more lives than one
    More deaths than one must die.

The Ballad of Reading Gaol,
    Oscar Wilde

I was aware of her moving round the house, and lay pretending to sleep, uncertain as to what I should do.

She knocked on the door. Coffee's ready, she said.

The kitchen was small, covered with pale green gloss paint onto bare plaster, topped by an assortment of cuttings from newspapers, magazines, prints and small posters. The table, in an alcove like a bed recess, was set for breakfast: bread and jam, milk and coffee.

What plans do you have?

I'm not doing anything today. I was going to study, then go to the cinema, but I would like to have a look at these papers of yours. What are you doing?

I suppose I'll have to find somewhere to stay, book into a hotel or something.

Stay here for the time being. If you don't mind sleeping on the sofa.

The sofa's fine.

Most people find it comfortable enough. If you're finished we can wash these dishes, then let me see the manuscripts.

I showed her what I'd been doing. She took the manuscripts I could not read and made a brief summary. We settled into a way of working, with the kitchen table covered in paper, eating on the sofa, a tray on our laps.

She left some time in the afternoon. I worked on, ate a little, drank most of a bottle of wine, which made me sleepy and in need of a cigarette. Instead I listened to the Beethoven Mass in C, thrilled by the shout of a Gloria and the final resolution in the dying bars of the Agnus Dei. While the choir sing Dona, dona and the soloists complete the line, beginning the third petition, for peace; as the prayer is about to end, the opening music of the Kyrie Eleison is recapitulated. Long ago, this stroke of genius ended my search, confirmed my belief in man as a spiritual being, rather than in God.

I closed the shutters and tried to sleep, but was awake when AnnA came home in the early hours of morning.

I didn't see much of her over the next couple of days. We communicated by notes on yellow paper stuck to the kitchen table. By Thursday we had read and had divided the documents into bundles with separate headings: *Journeys*, *Society*, *Venice* and so on. I was unsure of the way forward, thinking again about home. She came in around one o'clock. Come on, she said. You've been in here long enough. We're going out.

What's brought this on?

The weather's changed. Spring, or a definite change in the air. Shirt sleeves and dresses. Come on. Hurry.

I washed and shaved while she changed into trousers, still not used to the hard water that produced a grey scum rather than lather. You smell nice, she said.

Leaving the rue Notre Dame des Champs was like walking along a corridor, through the door, up one of the side streets and into the wind, white sky and sun on the boulevard du Montparnasse. Maybe now more than any other time, I wondered about the drab people, the air of respectability which was so unlike the images I loved.

Paris is a city of ghosts. It is still possible to imagine Lautrec and Van Gogh in Montmartre, Joyce off to scrounge some money, or Hemingway scribbling in a café. It is impossible to imagine the Montparnasse of the 1930s in this place. What would Kiki and her cronies have made of this? Where would Conchita, Miss Diamonds or Suzy go? Where are the street fairs, the *bals-musette* or Le Bal Nègre?

I mentioned this to AnnA. She smiled.

What does cronies mean? she asked, adding it to the list she was compiling, and for which she searched every dictionary: thrawn, glaur, fozie, sleekit, gomeril, dram, foozle, nyaff, glaikit.

I think you make them up, she said, taking my arm. What do you think of this? She nodded towards the Tour Montparnasse. It was one of our first regeneration projects, a business centre for a run-down area. I think they learned something and decided not to do it again.

I come from a different country, a city which produced some of the most original architecture in Europe, but which lost its nerve, a place where every building is turned into a hotel or the guts are ripped out and the façades preserved, where new buildings are like anywhere else. They built in that style because others were doing it; they are condemned to continally repeat the mistake because it's the only big idea they've ever had.

You sound bitter.

Someone told me I care too much. It's probably true.

The ash trees on the streets and limes in the cemetery were beginning to bud. The view across Montparnasse

Cemetery is of a fabulous, imagined city, with divisions, streets and crowded apartments. Sartre and de Beauvoir are in the Grand Cimetière, a light tan, simple stone with black lettering; the family Pétain are in the Petit.

We found a white florid cat for Ricardo, no Christian name but 'young, loved and beautiful'. The plastic roses were faded to pink and white at the edges. Henri Langlois had cinematic images sliding down his name, opposite Jean Seberg with her photo in the centre of a white cross and posies. Suzanne and Sam Beckett have grey marble and pink carnations; Serge Gainsbourg has plants, dolls, messages, Snoopy, poems, tickets, cigarette ends, a joint roach, a scrubbing brush, a cabbage and a record. Paulette Mollet has mirrors, lanterns and wind chimes.

We passed Emmanuel Chabrier and a blue figure floating like a cut-out Matisse, but couldn't find Baudelaire until an attendant told us to look for his stepfather, Jacques Aupick. His mother was buried above him almost four years to the day. We never found Tristan Tzara, Guy de Maupassant, Man Ray or *The Kiss* by Brancusi.

Le Veronèse, in Place Picasso, was noisy and smoky. A small, rude waiter, whose broken nose and curious nodding movements, crew-cut and broad shoulders, gave the appearance of a retired boxer, charged more than £8.00 for two teas and two coffees.

We should have gone to La Brioche Dorée, she said.

Where's that?

Along there, by Métro Vavin.

Half an hour later in the basement of *Art et Littérature, librairie et papeterie*, 120 boulevard de Montparnasse, she laughed again, put an arm around my waist and the other hand on a pile of notebooks.

Don't look so shocked, she said. You were engrossed in what you were doing. I simply wanted to remind you I was here and that we ought to be going.

Going where?

Anywhere, she said, and kissed my coat. Upstairs, she was thumbing through a book of Man Ray photographs; I looked up as a shaft of sunlight caught the side of her face, forcing her to squint and turn towards me, to look into my eyes. She stretched up and kissed me.

We wandered past the small patisseries, boulangeries and the Hôtel Novanox along the boulevard, turning at the RER station on avenue de l'Observatoire, where Marshal Ney in full cry tilts his sword on the edge of boulevard St. Michel, remembered alongside Francis Garnier, hero of Indo-China, Mekong, Fleure Rouge.

She went round one side of the Fontaine de l'Observatoire, I tried the other. Copper green goddesses with the world in the centre. There were trimmed horse-chestnuts, classical statues and yellow earth in the Jardin Marco Polo, where turtles skoosh water onto prancing horses.

She sat on an uncomfortable, narrow bench in the Jardin Cavalier de la Salle while I admired the red, brick Institute on the corner of rue Michelet and avenue de l'Observatoire.

Hold these details. Preserve every one.

Well? she said, squinting up at me.

Later, that night, when we started to unravel a kind of rapture, when we began to dig deeper into the mystery of bringing alive those parts of ourselves we had considered stunted, maladjusted, missing or spent, I remembered that look, as though my mind was a machine, recording and fixing the image forever, locking her face in the back of my mind.

In the Jardin du Luxembourg we sat facing the Palais, sharing a double-edged bench while we watched a T'ai Chi group exercise in front of what AnnA called the Luftwaffe's Parisian headquarters. Students on the steps read on, as oblivious to the exertions as to the chatter of the school tours, where girls blethered and held hands, the boys monosyllabic and apart.

By God and that one'll be a right ould ram when he gets started, said the woman behind us.

How do you know he's not started alreadies?

Surely to God. Do you want a napple?

Not till I'm finisht. His sister was goin at it when she was his age and if family traits is anything to go by, I'd say they took it off the mother.

Gracious God. I thought she looked that shy too, just a wee lassie. How did you hear about the sister?

We did not speak till the Medici fountain, with its curtained knags of ivy. Then we simultaneously giggled.

Were they Scottish? she asked.

Irish. I think from the North.

They must have thought you were French.

From the rue de Médicis to boulevard St. Michel, past the maroon settings and yellow formica-topped tables of the Café de Cluny, whose windows were bare.

Café? she said, and we sat inside, staring to the street, her head on my shoulder. Let's go home, she said.

On the way back, we collected some shopping, looked in the windows on rue Bréa. This was where rain came again; sudden and angry, it seeped beneath the awning and created a roadside torrent that moved the carpet fragments from the syvers.

We stared at our reflection in the boulangerie window, smiling at each other, and ran from store to store, shaking the rain from ourselves in the doorways, lifting our shoulders and narrowing our eyes when we emerged. At each successive shop, the assistants smiled and shook their heads. It's a good day to be working, said one, and we laughed.

By the time we reached the corner of Notre Dame des Champs, we knew it was hopeless. We walked home. When she pushed the handle down with her elbow, the man stuck his head round the corner. Oh, he said, and raised his hands in the air, smiling.

In the lift, she breathed on my glasses, then licked the rain from my face. There's lovely warm water, she said.

We abandoned the groceries by the door, to remove the clothes from ourselves and each other, as happened once before in another time with another person. AnnA hopped up the hall, one trouser leg on, pulling at the other, and as I sat by the door peeling off my sodden socks, a scud of steam drifted out from the top of the bathroom door. Quickly, she shouted. Quickly.

She was wearing a vest and her socks, a darker blue round the soles of the feet. It's too warm, she screamed. Far, far too hot. The floor was covered with soaps and bath salts, a variety of balls and essence. I was in the water, running the cold tap and shower simultaneously, hopping from one leg to the other, when she came in with a bundle of pastel-coloured towels, dropped them on the floor, removed the last of her clothes and slid

277

beside me below the soaps, blowing foam onto my hair and giggling.

Just once.

After climbing Carn Gorm and Meall Garbh we descended from Carn Mairg, leaving Creag Mhor for another day. Walking down the stalker path to Invervar, the fading sun somewhere to the right, but high enough to make light fidget through the leaves, above the smell of pine and moss, faintly rippled with woodsmoke, above the noise of wind in the leaves and the rush of water, a bird's voice tinkled. Smoke wavered through the glen, dragonflies sprang from nowhere then disappeared, bees thundered home. The scrape of our boots disturbed the silence. Our heavy arms and shoulders carried unimagined memories that could recall a completeness that would continue being completed again and again.

Wrapped in towels, we cooked an omelette with fried potatoes, tomatoes and mushrooms. I carried the plates into the kitchen, lit a Gitane and poured more wine.

Why are you smoking?

I've no idea. It seemed the right thing to do.

I think I am a bad influence.

I disagree.

Perhaps we should get dressed, or wear something other than wet towels.

Have you any whisky?

There should be some. I'll have a look when I make the coffee.

She came back dressed in a blue and yellow silk

kimono, a white towelling robe beneath one arm, a bottle of Caol Ila, two tumblers and small black coffees on a tray.

Give me those towels, she said.

The robe was enormous. Where did you get this?

It came with the whisky. They both belong to my father. The whisky was a present from a friend. He told me not to drink it and I never have, but I think this is an occasion to break all the rules.

The whisky tasted of home. We smoked and drank in silence, watching a game show.

Do you usually watch this sort of television? she asked.

Not usually, no.

Do you ever watch this kind of programme?

Never.

Never?

Never.

You mean to tell me you have never in your life watched a game show?

Never.

I mean a game show in English.

I know what you mean.

You've never watched one?

Never.

Why not?

I don't know.

You've never watched them, but don't know why?

That's not what I meant. I have never thought about why I never watch game shows, or shows featuring singers of almost any description.

I'm not talking about them.

I know, but I thought I'd mention them.

Don't change the subject.

What is the subject?

Game shows.

Sorry. I thought it also had to do with the television programmes I watched.

No. It has nothing to do with that. Nothing at all.

Then why did you ask if I ever watched game shows?

To make a confession.

On you go.

I can't.

Why not?

Because you'll laugh. Don't say you won't, because I know you will. You will laugh and be terribly self-righteous.

Terribly self-righteous?

I'm afraid so.

I promise not to.

You can't help yourself.

How do you know?

Because I know.

Not an answer.

All the answer you're going to get. What programmes do you watch?

News mostly.

That's right. News and documentaries.

Sometimes.

What about nature programmes?

Yes. I watch them. Everybody does.

And films?

I love cinema.

Have you a video?

Do you mean a player?

Of course.

Rather than a camera?

No, they're awful.

Who's being self-righteous now?

Do you have a video?

Yes.

Tell me your favourite film.

Tell me your confession.

This is it.

What?

I watch television game shows.

What else?

What else what?

What else do you watch on television?

Anything. I am a TV addict. I love it. I'll watch anything. I like being sick and stay in at the slightest excuse, even on Saturday night when programmes are terrible, I stay in to watch TV. But when I'm sick I get all wrapped up, lie on the couch and watch television all day long. And it gets worse before my period; I eat chocolate and drink red wine watching television, then I'm sick.

Honest?

Sorry.

And that's your confession.

I thought you ought to know.

I appreciate the gesture. Tell me, why don't you have a television in the bedroom?

Because it's decadent. Your favourite film?

Don't know.

Jules et Jim.

Not bad. Pretty good actually. Better than most

French films. I think the trouble with French cinema is that their films don't have an ending. Tell me two French films with endings? You know their films are at an end when they've been going for an hour and a half. Like a football match, ninety minutes and it's all over; extra time for stoppages and injuries.

I hate football. *La Grande Illusion*, do you know it? Or, better still, *La Règle du Jeu*? Jean Renoir. I think *La Règle du Jeu* is my favourite. What about your favourite film?

I'm a bit like you, I don't know that I have an absolute favourite film, any more than I have a favourite book or a favourite piece of music. I suppose one of my favourites would have to be *The Producers*.

Mel Brooks. Wonderful. Zero Mostel.

Springtime for Hitler.

That's not so funny now, is it?

She poured the last of the whisky and lit a cigarette. We'll share them, she said.

We can share the whisky, but you have the cigarette. It wasn't a good idea.

What wasn't?

Me smoking again.

I started to clear the cups, plates and stuff onto the tray.

Leave it, she said. Leave it till morning. Let's go to bed. God, I'm sorry.

What for?

Saying that about your song.

What song?

Springtime for Hitler.

You're right though. It never is far away. Open a newspaper, turn on the television and there it is.

I know.

Is that why you watch game shows?

I told you why I watch game shows. Which side of the bed do you want?

It's your bed.

I know whose bed it is, but I am being hospitable, sharing it with you, darling.

Which side do you usually have?

This side.

Then I'll sleep here.

Do you snore?

I have been accused of snoring in the past.

Would you like another confession? Put that light out; keep this one on. It's softer.

That better?

No. I'll turn them both out. I love to lie here with the light from the streets. How's that?

Pretty good.

Do you want another pillow?

I'm fine. Next confession?

I've forgotten what it was.

Snoring.

How do you know?

That was what we were discussing.

You'll want to sleep next door.

I don't think so.

Can I whisper?

No. It's a confession. You must tell me. You can close your eyes, but you must tell me. And leave that alone. Don't try to divert me.

I was only checking.

Still there.

Good.

Confession?

I snore when I'm drunk.

How do you know?

I was in a hotel room once and wakened in a panic, wondering who I was sleeping with because I thought I had gone to bed alone. Obviously, I was alone, but thought I was with someone because the snoring had wakened me. I sat bolt upright and realised I had been snoring so loudly I wakened myself.

Are you drunk now?

Don't you have a word for it?

A Scots word?

Of course.

For snoring?

Yes.

Soochin.

I don't believe you, but there must be some for drunk.

As many as the Inuits have for snow.

Tell me.

My favourite is galraviched. Waistit is quite usual. Some of the Glasgow ones are good: bellosis, maroculous, lummed up and stotious. My mother used to talk about somebody being hauf smeiked.

What does that one mean?

What one?

That one.

Hauf smeiked?

Yes.

Drunk.

No. In English.

I think smeik means smoke.

As you smoke a cigarette.

I've stopped smoking.

You know what I mean.

I think it means more like what you get from a fire or what you might do to a fish.

Very functional. But why does it mean drunk?

I don't know. Are you hauf smeiked the noo?

The bed's spinning.

It's not, is it?

Just a little. When I close my eyes it turns slowly. Talk to me.

What about?

Anything. Your favourite word.

Why?

Because I want to see how quickly you can make it up.

Cooried, fankled, scunnered.

The last one.

Scunnered.

You've made it up.

Not at all.

You must have. I can't even say it.

Scunnered.

No. I can't say it. What does it mean?

A dictionary definition would be something like disgusted.

But because you made it up it's not in the dictionary.

Listen. It is one of the words that makes the case for spoken Scots. To understand it you must hear it used in conversation.

Give me an example.

I can't.

Why not?

Because this isn't a conversation.

Well, give me an example of how it would be used in conversation.

It would be used the way I've said, according to the definition; but, and this is very important, it is always said in such a way as to denote disgust, or contempt. You have to do it. The form of the word dictates it cannot be used in polite society.

All right. You do it.

What?

Say it. I'll ask a question. Okay?

Try me.

How are you?

Scunnered.

That's wonderful. It doesn't sound like what you said. It's more like a sound than a word. You've no hairs on your chest, she said, and kissed me.

Later, when we'd remade the bed and drawn the curtains, when we had brushed our teeth and were ready for sleep, I was thinking of Coire Fhionn Lochan, up the hill from North Thundergay on the Isle of Arran, dark and still at the head of a brae, in a horseshoe of hills. It was impossible to tell the reality from reflection, the water like plastic, bearing the strain of light, the glitter of stones and pebbles shining from below the resin; the air still as stone, suddenly clear after four days of cloud.

AnnA turned and kissed my arm: Are you married? she asked.

No.

But you've been married?
Uh-hu.
Are you too tired?
No.
Don't you want to talk about it?
I don't know.
She was about to turn away, when I pulled her back and told her about Irene and Janie, about the job and the conference and coming to Paris. I told her I was lost and always had been, then fell asleep almost as soon as I told her, wakening when I felt the shudder of her sob.

My mother-in-law has sold her house.

I thought about it, dear, and spoke to no one. It's a decision I made for myself. A friend has moved into a retirement complex and I thought, why am I in this big old barn of a place when I could be in a lovely little flat that doesn't cost a fortune to heat? They have a res-taurant and a hairdressers, an activity organiser and other residents just like myself. Is there anything you want here? If there is, come and get it. I wondered if the kids wanted anything. Would Janie like some furniture for her new home?

I said I'd ask, but didn't think so. She seemed to have everything she needed.

There is something I read in Paris, but can't find here. I thought I had it with me, but it seems to have gone. I now cannot decide if I ever read it, or thought I read it, if I made it up.

It concerns a manservant Casanova hired who, in dis-tressed circumstances, writes to Duchov. Casanova's pride will not let him answer. The servant then wrote to the Waldstein family, inquiring after his old master's health, and if he is still with them, still alive. His third letter comes from a lawyer, claiming part of the Casanova estate. It arrives as Casanova is dying. He sends a will to the lawyer, leaving everything to his former servant, providing the servant can prove he worked for Casanova. Did he, for example, save any of the piss he emptied from the chamber pots? Can he read a document written in his master's hand, describe an item of clothing, or remember a kind word? Provide two items from a similar list, says Casanova, then come to Duchov to claim your inheritance.

This is a fragment, torn from something longer. It was one of the first things I saw, in a brown manila envelope, out of place among the stiff papers and varieties of black ink.

It opened like a present, as though an unknown researcher, someone with me in mind, had left it as a small delight, a single sheet, wrapped in red ribbon, the writing dark and rococo, like the trail of an adder through dust.

INTRODUCTION TO THE DEAD

The fool says he is come to run a lottery. I am certain that either he does not know, or thinks we will stop using the couple already in progress and fall upon his scheme to give him the wealth his love of the table desires.

He carries a letter of introduction to the dead Egremont. Since his arrival he has been enamoured of a whore, something that happens frequently, I understand. She wants nothing to do with him, silly old fool, and he has spoken frequently of ending it all in the Thames only to reappear in Mother Jane Douglas's Cattery in Covent Garden, the Star or Turk's Head in the Strand. He has, of course, met with Pembroke in Mrs Cornely's in Soho Square, and has appeared at Clerkenwell for debt, one of many. He spent some time in Newgate, but was eventually bailed.

He is poxed, and different from what we are used to; he brings a foul strain from France which will cause 'Plague!' to be cried throughout the city. He is known to be anxious but not always able, which seems to have been the cause of the Swiss Jewess's frustration. She is no better than she should be, is called La Charpillon and has been known to plead her belly across London for some time now.

He was with she I am forbidden to name, having been given a fine ride in her coach from Ranelagh. They met again in Lady Betty Germaine's and he was foolish enough to speak with her. She, of course, said they had never met. He asked if it were possible she did not remember him. 'I remember you perfectly well,' said m'lady, 'but such folly does not presume an acquaintance.'

He left his whore with a parrot which said, 'La Charpillon is a bigger whore than her mother.' Grosvenor bought it for the girl, who wrung the bird's neck.

I had never watched death.

Every night I slept in the little room along the corridor. I wore my watch because there was no bedside table; just a narrow bed, two chairs and a wardrobe. There was no bedside lamp.

I used to wonder if it had been meant as a bedroom and decided I didn't care. The overall impression was a communal grief that lingered, something previous residents had left and to which I would contribute. It was a remnant of worry and pain, the ache of longing, the stupidity of wanting the loved one well, knowing they will never again be well, where out of pain means death.

Sometimes plumbing echoed from the sink in the corner. Every night I piled my clothes on one of the chairs, lay naked in bed and tried the *Independent* crossword, knowing I would have to run across the room, my bare feet slipping on the linoleum tiles, put out the light, run back in the dark, coorie in and close my eyes, hoping to cry, knowing I would not. I wakened every morning when thin light dulled the curtains, having slept like a sickly child.

No one had wakened me. Irene was alive.

Her life never had such significance. Here it was impossible to take her for granted. Yet any place other than here was like an imagined city glimpsed through the windows of a Renaissance painting.

Every morning, before going to the ward, I went downstairs, ate a bacon roll, drank a cup of coffee and checked the answers to the crossword I did not complete. Then slowly I went up, back to the ward, in time for the nursing changeover at eight o'clock.

Irene was always awake. She seemed anxious to hear

my news. I had nothing to tell her, but read the news-paper, choosing items she might want to hear.

Would you like to hear about the government?

She shook her head.

Days were never the same. I knew my wife was dying. Everyone seemed to know except Irene. Every day I wondered if she maintained this little pretence for me, as I surely performed my rites for her. We did not mention the possibility of hospice. No one suggested we should.

It was all too sudden, like a squall of rain, angry and ill-defined. No matter how well prepared one may be, the rain came sideways or up from the ground and soaked you just the same.

What do you need to know? Nothing other than how did it happen. I cannot tell you how it happened. I know the beginning was a series of headaches. I'd find your mother pale and tired, lying on the sofa with a wet cloth on her forehead.

Jimmy Ramsay, the doctor who partnered Irene at the bridge club, said he was sure there was nothing to worry about. She had blood tests and seemed to be well as she waited for the results. Doesn't seem much there, said Jimmy, who added that she should stick to the Paraceta-mol if the headaches continued.

Try the soluble ones, he said. They're better.

Then she was crying in the night, frightened to go to bed, scared to sleep, when she said there was always pain, that it did not go, and this in something like two or three weeks, certainly less than a month. Looking back, I can see that for maybe five or six months before the headaches she had been forgetful. Silly things. She'd open the fridge door and say, What did I want in here?

Would come back with half the shopping done, start a conversation and forget what she was saying. The headaches were the end rather than the beginning.

A scan, said Jimmy. That'll tell us what we need to know. Trouble is, the waiting lists are as long as your arm. Best to go private.

The hospital was like a hotel. The doctor told us immediately. She needed an operation. He would take her into his National Health Trust hospital. Never mind the waiting lists, he said. This is an emergency. Phone me in two days.

On the day we arrived a man in a suit, with a dark tie and bald head, told us there was no bed.

The consultant came out of his office, ignored him completely and told the ward sister, who wore a badge saying Ward Manager above her Christian name, to take my wife to bed and that he would be operating in the morning.

The operation was four days later. Sorry, said the consultant. Administration difficulties. We never used to have them. Now we have them all the time.

The operation took six hours. The consultant saw me and said he would tell Irene himself. He looked at me across the desk. I've done this before, he said. It never gets easier. It's something they don't understand. They don't teach this stuff at business school, any more than they teach the nurses how to sit with an old man who's dying and whose relatives can't be bothered sitting with him. I'm sorry. There's nothing we could do.

She was dead less than three weeks later. Every day, someone from administration phoned to check if the room was still being used.

It was as if she had been given a sentence. I watched her grow thin and tired, pale, her hair straggly, her voice weak, her eyes dull. She was run down and fallen, but every day she put on make-up, listened to the radio, made me talk, forced me to tell her what was happening, did I check the central heating, was I feeding myself, not just canteen food, I should eat more fish and salads and had made a nice job of ironing my shirts.

I refused to recognise the changes. Twice a timid knock wakened me immediately. We think you should come, the nurses said. And in the morning, by the shift changeover, Irene was fine. Only once did she say, only once did she even suggest: I made it, she said, and kissed my hand.

Then came the coma, lapsing in and out of sleep, the small gasps, the laboured rise and fall of the chest the only indication of life. That went on for forty hours.

I sat in the evening. It'll be soon, they said. The nurses told me, It's only time. I was scared to ask how they knew. It was then I realised how we make token gestures in their direction. In circumstances too awful to contemplate, too terrible to bear, they remind us how society ought to be.

It was maybe nine o'clock at night. I had been with Irene since early morning. I know that if I speak, her eyes will open. She will turn her head and try to focus. She will be coherent. It will be hard work. She needs to concentrate on breathing. I am happy to say nothing and assume she knows I am here.

The Ward Manager opened the door. Irene stirred slightly as the head came round the corner. She beckoned me into the corridor.

I don't want to chase you, she said, but you look knackered.

I am knackered.

This is not an offer, but I don't suppose you want to go to bed?

I loved that. It was exactly right. She was Irish, maybe in her thirties, blonde.

It's just that we're changing shifts soon, she said, and you've been here all day. Maybe you should take a wee break. Go and see somebody. We'll be here when you get back. Maybe even go for a drive. You can phone if you like. Why don't you wash your face, have a shave, change your shirt and go out for a couple of hours. Whether anything happens or not, you need to get away.

I did as she said, drove out the hospital and phoned Rhona from the call box across the road.

Sure, she said. Up you come.

She was watching television. I'll make you something when this is finished. It's good. Have you been watching it? How's your wife?

I fell asleep, and wakened with Rhona in her pyjamas.

Some company you. If you want to go to bed, come on, otherwise beat it. I've got work in the morning.

I knew as soon as they opened the door. When the small Highland nurse looked at me, I knew the black boat had called.

Half an hour ago, she said. Very peacefully. I was with her.

I saw her again today. Standing at the traffic lights, wearing her grey trousers, suede shoes and red jacket, not a rory red, but a darkish, softly muted red: Not the sort of thing I wear at all, she said when she bought it. But this is the basis of my new wardrobe.

I kept looking up. The traffic was thick. When the green man came, I ran across. She was gone. I went into the fruit shop. A patient face smiled at me. I knew it was useless. She was gone.

I've seen her many times, always on the other side of the road, on the pavement when I am driving. I have stopped the car, but she'd gone again.

I tried to speak about it, but could not. When I told AnnA she did what she always did; she took my hand in her hand, raised it to her mouth and kissed it. But even then I did not say what I wanted to say, did not really tell what I had seen. I said I knew she would always be on the other side of the street.

There's another fragment in the manila envelope. Why they were together I have no idea. Someone must have meant to remove them. The pair seem unconnected, apart from the subject and the fact that this is also part of something longer.

This is not original. I remember it was one of three pieces that were photocopied, the originals removed for whatever reasons, maybe stolen and copies left in their place. It has been translated from Portuguese.

FROM THE EDGE OF THE SEA

I am writing from the edge of the sea, having strolled across the square whose centrepiece resembles a Saracen war tent. We arrived safely, avoided the pirates, sailed through the Porto de Choggia to the Porto di Lido, were piloted through the islands and docked sometime around seven in the morning.

We had an old man on board, a passenger we collected at Pesaro, who had travelled from Bologna and asked to be given permission to board the first ship sailing to Choggia and into Venice.

He said very little, stayed in his cabin, took meals when they were offered. I asked why he was with us: 'The only way to enter Venice is from the sea,' he said. The voyage was uneventful, the sea was calm.

He wakened, I think around five, was dressed and appeared on deck as we crossed the Porto di Choggia, staring unmoved, straight ahead as we crossed the Lido bar. I have never seen anything so extraordinary. Sailing across to the port itself, the punctual sun rose in the east, lighting the city and the water.

There has never been a sight so beautiful or brief. This was such a morning as I have never seen; heaven on earth for sweetness, freshness, depth upon depth of unimaginable colour and a huge silence broken only by the rush of wind in the sails and the spray of sea.

The old man stood at the prow of the deck, tears running down his cheeks as we sailed into Venice, his body racked in sobs.

EIGHT

If they ask you, Was I running?
If they ask you, Was I running?
If they ask you, Was I running?
Tell them I was flying.
Tell them I was flying.

Take This Hammer,
Huddie Leadbetter

They want to see you, she said.

Fine. We'll go. I haven't met all that many folk recently and I find it a bit daunting; that and the fact they'll be speaking French.

Most of them speak English.

So they'll go out of their way to compliment me on my good French accent.

Or correct it. *Merci*.

The *radis et beurre* arrived. We were back in Le Trumilou, among the farming artefacts this time, the black and white chipped terrazzo floor, the smoking and continual chat. The star of the evening was the American woman who asked for a clean knife and fork and complained about the smoking. Take this away then, she said to the skinny waiter, presenting him with an ashtray. *C'est pour la table, Madame*, he said.

God, I hate stuffed animal heads on walls, the American lady said to her husband. They're so masculine. He looked out the window and sighed.

We had seen something like them earlier in l'Orangerie, cheaper on a Sunday. A party of American women in pink and yellow, with heavy faces and patterned clothes, all with white hair, some in trousers, others with wide skirts and ankle socks, walked round the Monet water lilies.

He's trying to show the reflection, said one.

You mean like a mirror.

No. Like water. They are water lilies in the water.

I think they're too big.

They're old-fashioned.

Hush, said a small, bright-eyed woman. The others looked at each other and smirked.

And there's Great-grandma, said AnnA.

Will she be there?

No. She ran her finger along the back of my hand. But she wants to meet you. Everybody's been wondering where I've been and what I've been doing. They haven't seen me and want to know what's going on. They're curious. They want to see what you're like. They wonder why I've kept you hidden.

Who's first?

Great-grandma.

Wednesday night. She lived in a very grand apartment near the Pont Marie Métro station, close to the *Mémorial du Martyr Juif Inconnu*.

Do you know it? she asked.

No. I don't think I've ever seen it.

A tin can with names, but better than nothing. We know that because Le Pen wants it removed.

She was small, wiry and frail, her white hair pulled into a bun and held together with an elaborate arrangement of hairgrips and pins. She leaned on a Malacca cane and preceded AnnA and me into every room. In the sitting room, she sat on a cream and gilded armchair covered in dark green satin.

I hope you are not hungry, she said. Did AnnA tell you? She has probably forgotten, but I eat very little in the evening. I usually have soup. Tonight we will have *omelette fromage*. You and AnnA will have dessert and coffee. I will have half a glass of wine only and some mineral water. Now I am older I neither eat very much, nor see many people. Lunch is my main meal. I am sure you will enjoy your food. Josephine is very good. I am telling you these things to avoid silly conversation. I may be old, but I am not stupid. I am, of course, blaming you for the faults of others.

Josephine came into the room. She did not speak.

Eh bien. Merci. The last people I had here were awful. AnnA is trying not to laugh. Well, you can laugh as much as you like for all I care. She told me what they were like, but I felt it was my duty. It was my grandson and his new woman, I do not know if she is his wife and I do not care. She is awful. Eat up, Grandma, she said. And she insisted on trying to help me walk. What she thought she was doing I do not know. I can walk perfectly well with this cane. All I need is to be left alone. You sit there. AnnA, you are there tonight. You can attend to your guest.

AnnA had told me. She doesn't mean to sound that way. Her English is not very good. But she is wonderful for her age, though, for God's sake, please don't say that to her.

Grandma talked about her family while we ate a clear dark soup that hinted of fish. There were three cheeses blended into the omelette and a lemon tart to finish. She ate very little, roast potatoes and salad, wine and mineral water, and led us into the sitting room for coffee.

I enjoyed your account of meeting Rilke. It was now after nine o'clock and I knew we would leave before ten.

Hmph. Tell me how he lived and how did he die.

301

Sorry?

Bernard. AnnA said he lives in Jean Nicot, is that by *l'Eglise Américaine*?

She appeared to have a prepared agenda, a list of questions. She turned her ear towards me when I answered, nodded when I finished and shooed us out at five to ten.

AnnA kissed my hand on the Métro. She likes you, she said.

How do you know?

Had I gone on my own, she would have been exactly the same.

You are becoming Parisian, she said, looking at my hand as it raised the handle to open the Métro doors before the train had stopped.

I wonder now who hears me calling. Does she turn in her sleep, reach out to touch me? How is she when she finds the place empty? Does she still lick her right forefinger and run it down the CD rack, say *Voilà*, then stand with her head cocked like her great-grandmother deciding to play the disc or search for another? Does she still run out of ingredients, read the paper standing up, smoke, wash her hair with washing-up liquid, need nine hours' sleep a night, sing Mozart in the bath, buy fresh flowers every third day and believe she could not live in Scotland because of the rain?

AnnA, I said when I thought she was sleeping. Do you know that I love you?

Saying made it clearer, solved a puzzle.

She turned.

Is it that simple?

I think so.

Good.

Line 4 from Vavin to Gare du Nord. Line 5 to Bobigny-Pablo Picasso on the edge of the system.

I had, as usual, wakened with the garbage trucks rolling by the pavement, made the coffee and showered. AnnA shouted: Put on Jelly Roll Morton, *Kansas City Stomp*. Me wet and both of us naked, we danced around the living room, the volume turned up full, till a rapping from somewhere spread us onto the sofa.

We are expected for lunch, she said.

Which means?

They won't eat till one. We can arrive any time before then, I'd suggest around half twelve.

What'll I wear?

She gave a little cry and ran into the bedroom, returning with a carrier bag filled with tissue paper, a blue Ermenegildo Zenga shirt and a silk Ungaro tie.

Un petit cadeau, she said.

Why?

Do I need a reason? I bought them because I thought you'd like them. I thought the shirt would match your eyes.

I don't know what to say.

Yes you do.

Nice labels.

Try again.

AnnA. This is lovely. Thanks very much.

Press your cream trousers and brush your suede boots. You'll look lovely in your jacket. Now what about me?

Your dress.

What dress?

303

The blue patterned dress.

I think I wore it last time.

Then wear another one.

At the door she ran into the bedroom and returned with a lilac silk handkerchief which she put in my top pocket.

There you are, she said. Man at C&A.

We bought flowers and chocolates and Saturday's *European Guardian*, which we read on the Métro.

AnnA was confused at Bobigny, where the Métro, bus and RER stations converge, where the streets are called after Salvatore Allende, Yuri Gagarin and so on. I think it's down here, she said, before you come to les Chambres des Métiers on rue Hector Berlioz. We tripped on the uneven slabs of concrete paving, especially near the trees.

I don't know which it is, she said.

A row of medium tower blocks ran to the left of the street. She tried two before announcing: This is it, definitely; here.

The door of the sixth-floor flat was opened by a tall man with a beard. AnnA, he shouted and shook my hand, propelling me into the house as though we had arrived unexpectedly, called in because we were passing, as they do in Ireland.

As soon as the introductions were made, I forgot the names. There was Beard, who was, I think, a journalist, and Glassesman, who was a doctor; Glasseswoman was with Beard and worked, I think, in publicity, and there was Ribbon, who owned Par Essence where AnnA worked. Glassesman and she may have been lovers and I knew her name was Hélène. There was AnnA and me.

We were listening to Jelly Roll Morton this morning, said AnnA.

Glassesman asked about the Red Hot Peppers' line-up and my favourite tune.

Deep Creek.

Don't know it.

Deep Creek, said Hélène. We play it in the shop. Do you know this? And she produced the digitally remastered BBC recording.

That's the one we played.

She smiled. I felt there was nothing left to say and because I hate the silences where everyone searches for conversation, I looked around the small living room, crowded with furniture and ornaments, mirrors, candlesticks and pictures.

Things are a bit disorganised at present, said Hélène. We have another place, which is being painted. This is Jacques' place. The two of us are living here for the time being. It gets a bit crowded.

She untied the ribbon at the back of her head, gathered her hair and retied it. Lunch is almost ready, she said.

Do you know Paris? asked Beard. I told him why I came, what had happened with the paper and how I met AnnA.

When are you going back?

I'm not sure. Next week, maybe the week after. I don't know what's happening at work. I don't know if they expect me back or when. I've got to give these things some consideration, which I may be staying here to avoid.

Will you work for another newspaper?

I don't think so.

What will you do?

Right now, I fancy something as far away from newspapers as it is possible to be.

Is he telling you about his plans? said AnnA.

Beard smiled.

A *table*, said Hélène.

What do you think he could do? asked AnnA.

What did he do before? asked Glasseswoman.

He was a political journalist, said Hélène, who smiled at me. I know that because we have obviously discussed you. Thoroughly.

I seem to be at a disadvantage, which is not entirely linguistic.

AnnA was pouring the wine and when she came round to fill my glass, she kissed the top of my head.

Of course they knew about you. If I couldn't tell my friends, who could I tell? But it hasn't solved the day's main problem, said AnnA.

A schoolteacher, said Glassesman.

Too old.

Why can't you be a political journalist? asked Beard. The fact that you do not have a newspaper to work for could be seen as a disadvantage, but there are compensatory advantages. For example, you have experience and could, I imagine, work on a freelance basis, writing the sort of article which is popular here, simply give your opinion on the political issues of the day.

I'd like to get away from that.

Why? It's your bread and butter. More soup, anyone?

Yes, please.

Why do you want to do something else?

For one thing, Scottish politics is a very specialised area, where you see the same people and hear the same things over and over again. On a broader level, I have served these people, taken them seriously, made a living by feeding from their trough. They, on the other hand, have courted and used me. This has cost me my family. I worked nights and I worked away. I never saw my children grow, became a stranger, and we now find it hard to communicate. My wife died before I got to know her because the job came first. I am now trying to communicate with my children, but it's difficult. My daughter is a drug addict. I don't know if she's alive or dead and can't remember the last time I saw her, though I remember the state she was in. I know it's a silly point which cannot be substantiated, but I am talking about responsibilities here. Local politics in our country has been effectively removed and replaced by quangos. Inner-city areas have become like medieval fortresses, controlled by the barons of the drug trade, who wander round the heart of our society doing what they like because cost-efficiency has removed the means of stopping them and the politics of expediency and abandonment has left a blank-eyed, pale-faced generation who don't know who they are or what they want; they are being followed by a generation of children whose role-models are steroid monsters.

Everyone had stopped eating. They were staring at me and looked as if they had barely understood what I said, except AnnA, who smiled.

Don't let your soup get cold, I said.

Is that one of your words? asked AnnA.

What?

Trough.

I'll get the fish, said Hélène.

Glasseswoman went to help. We took our portions a little too heartily. AnnA told them of a report she read from the Venetian Archives. Casanova met someone who boasted of his friendship, claimed he knew him and did not recognise him. He asked the stranger about himself and was told a range of sordid little incidents, which he later claimed were untrue. Asked why the stranger was pleased to have met him, he said it was because he had put flesh to the stories. Casanova related what he saw as the grander moments of his life and asked the stranger if he thought they were true. Not at all, said the stranger, though I am sure he would like to believe they were true.

The interesting thing about this document is that they spoke in a merchants' argot which is fully related with a translation. The other thing is the writer's conclusion that Casanova could not decide if the stranger was a spy sent to worry him or a fool.

My cat caught a mouse yesterday morning, said Glasseswoman.

Then they turned to Roger, who came home from work, saw the dishes piling in the sink and knew his wife had left him. He phoned all the women he knew asking if they would iron his shirts.

Has anyone done it?

They must have, but no one will own up.

How do you know?

Because his shirts are always ironed.

Maybe he does them himself.

Last time he phoned here he asked if he could come for lunch.

You should have invited him today.

After lunch we sat on the steel and leather sofas. We drank coffee and liqueurs, we smoked and ate chocolate truffles, and for the first time talked politics. This discussion was different from any I had with AnnA.

Perpetual opposition, said Beard.

Their tactics, of course, are now established, said Glassesman. They will recede and return, gathering strength while they're away.

They seem to be reforming under new banners.

With the old guard and their ideas still intact.

Perpetual opposition, said Beard.

We left around four. At the door Glassesman shook my hand. I hope we'll see you again, he said.

I'm sure we will, said Hélène.

Glasseswoman kissed my cheek.

Good, said Beard, pulling me aside. I'm glad you're here, you know, you and AnnA, it's great. I'm pleased, for her sake. I think it's what she needs. She's been through a tough time, as I'm sure you'll know, and I think you're exactly right.

At the Bobigny terminus a drug addict lay by the carriage door. Passengers turned away. The other carriages were almost full. The needle was in his arm, blood in the cylinder and his face parchment white. Two attendants opened the door, dragged him onto the platform and the train left.

What did Maurice say? asked AnnA.

I told her.

I thought it was something like that. He means well. Do you want to know?

Only if you want to tell me.

I don't know.

I'll understand if you don't.

I don't think you will. You've been a diversion. While you're here I don't have to think about it. I can hide in you.

I know what you mean.

I know you do. And you know what it means if I tell.

Reality and Glasgow.

We'll see.

Gare du Nord, then Line 4, Porte d'Orléans, to Vavin.

It rained today.

And just when you thought it was over, water dripped from trees and lamp posts, ran across the road in sheets. It swirled from a sky black enough for snow and ran round the city changing everything it touched.

In my mind, I huddled by the fire with tea and whisky, buttered toast and a blanket round my shoulders. Wind wrapped the house and rattled the door. I sheltered in one of the overpriced antique shops that have grown round the Bath Street auction rooms: Just looking, I said.

The girl smiled and glanced at the weather.

Are you thinking of going out for lunch?

She smiled again.

I tried to look interested in the prints and piles of furniture. In a corner on a small card table which was perched on an art nouveau sideboard with green glass and copper inlays was a small jug, signed and dated by

William Reid at Musselburgh Pottery. It was a lovely thing, beautifully shaped and unusually decorated, with a gilded rim and a basketweave body.

It had been bought at auction as part of the lot and was waiting to be priced. I could probably have got a bargain, but wondered why I was buying it, and, arriving at nothing approaching an answer, I walked home in the rain.

I've got a cold coming on. I had a big whisky, watched an afternoon quiz show, then poured another whisky with warm water, honey and cloves, which I drank lying in the bath listening to Shostakovich's Fourth Dance Suite.

A line of white to yellow and mustard, grey, pink and red with the sun in the centre like a lamp taking us home. Gradually the grey closed in, leaving a line of yellow and pink like icing, and we were in Venice, someone wrote, I don't know who.

It is one of a number of fragments piled on the edge of the desk. I thought we had located everything, that we had separated the documents, divided them by subject or location and put them into their relevant folders.

I have kept this fragment because I hoped to find a relative, other than Professor Meissner. We have pieces I have yet to translate, as well as a number of illustrations.

Meissner was a Professor of Music at the Prague Conservatoire when *Don Giovanni* was first performed at the Estates Theatre on 29 October, 1787, after several delays. His grandson published the professor's memoirs, which include the story of Casanova locking Mozart in an upstairs room, away from the women, so that the Overture could be completed.

This piece concerns the second Mozart opera to be premièred at the Estates Theatre, *La Clemenza di Tito*, composed for the Coronation of Leopold II as King of Bohemia. Mozart conducted the first performance on 6 September, 1791. Entrance was free and many tickets were distributed, says the *Coronation Journal*, so Casanova could have attended. He was around at the time.

It has an autobiographical feel, memoirs constructed by someone who feels we should be interested in his life and opinions.

INVISIBLE AS MUSIC

I should say he commented all too fully on Mazzola's libretto, discussing at great length its superiority to the offering from the rascal da Ponte. He seemed unaware that Mazzola and da Ponte were friendly, asking if I knew Guardasoni, who, in his opinion, had written many pieces which he was sure could be turned into opera by a hand as competent as Mozart.

This, I stress, was at the Estates Ball which followed the tedious performance. Now, of course, we know so much more. The *opera seria* was under-rehearsed and the castrato Domenico Bedini breached every notion of credibility, the mass of flesh bearing no relation to his fragile voice.

He obviously attended more than one performance of *Don Giovanni*, for he was entirely familiar with the libretto, referring, I seem to remember, to what he stated as the obvious fact that Cherubino from *Le Nozze di Figaro* could be the young Don; though, again he stressed, the libretti were as separate as Mars and Venus.

'The Figaro text was taken from a play. It is based upon a superior work by Beaumarchais,' he said, 'so da Ponte had little more to do than copy what was already written. What other works of distinction has he done? None. It is Mozart who makes these operas, especially the latter, which is one-dimensional and confused. There is no philosophical basis for the character of Don Giovanni.'

This was his mildest criticism. He claimed it was impossible to amalgamate the theme with the genre and that the opera could not decide what it should be, *seria* or *buffa*. The presence of Leporello suggested one thing, but the murder of Donna Anna's father and the death of the Don suggested another. Leporello undermines the seriousness of the final confrontation. This confusion was because da Ponte had no intellectual base to launch the libretto. He had probably seen the Molière play and had certainly seen a play on the same subject by the Venetian Goldoni.

'Ask yourself,' he said. 'Whoever heard of a great lover who fails to seduce a peasant girl? And who would tolerate a servant such as Leporello?'

Opera, he said, should be morally uplifting, about gods and goddesses rather than commoners who are dressed as commoners. He did not mind the poor performance and said he hated singers rather than the opera. These operas are concerned only with ordinary people, our servants, something for which the Abbé da

Ponte was to blame. That old fool could not write a classical story if he tried. Grandeur and honesty, encouraging others to aspire to greatness, or at least to do better, was never for him.

He had an acquaintance of Mozart, was in Vienna in 1792 when one could not get a ticket for his subscription concerts, and like many another he had gone to St Stephen's Church when Mozart was here previously, waiting for the maestro to turn up daily to play the organ. He did not know the Duscheks, other than as performers.

I confess, I felt sorry for him, with his painted face, silly old clothes and dead ideas. He was neither a terror nor a rake, no threat to Count Waldstein nor to anyone else. He was a dull old man.

He told me he had been standing at the back of a church, hearing mass, when he wept for Judas, without whom there would have been no resurrection. There is, he said, but did not say where, a bleeding crucifix which weeps when it witnesses a beheading, and there is a dog who has been known to sing.

AnnA was distant. She left in the morning and came back late at night, firstly apologising, saying it was work and study and the pressure of both; then she said nothing.

She occasionally reached out. When this happened it was always wine. She never found me without help.

Are you mine? she asked one night.

Your what?

My boy. Do you belong to me?

314

If you want me to.

I want you to want to belong to me.

I'd like nothing better.

She laughed. We'll see, she said.

I have notes, her wonderful handwriting summarising pages of documents, cataloguing and beginning an index. That time seems to have been spent working, as though there was a pressure to finish, to get what brought us together out of the way, in order to move on to something else. In the end I left before it was done; I brought work home with me.

It isn't all clear. Some was returned with a summary intact. Other pieces were returned with nothing done. I have AnnA's notes of a letter from a woman in Rome: He has been gone for more than a month, she says. Already his image is fading.

I wait for his letters, like cargo from a foreign port, like the gift of sight, like a decade of the rosary or the walk of a seaman approaching the shanties. They will mark my sorrow, expose my sin. Their absence is a name shouted in the wind.

It is wonderful to touch this paper, to feel where her hand rested. I can see her working, the way she bit her bottom lip and looked at what she had written as though inspecting a drawing, as though there was a detail, something she had lost.

I remember Le Caméléon Bistrot, rue de Chevreuse, along from the flat. Electrified gas lamps, flowered wall-paper against a black background, an extraordinary range of photographs, cartoons and a child's drawing in green felt-tipped pen, a newspaper cutting, posters for out-of-date art exhibitions, two paintings of cafés on either side of a mirror beneath the rounded wooden arches. Langoustine soup with lentils and cream as part of the fish base, with half a dozen langoustines decorating the centre, duck that fell off the bone, roast potatoes, perfectly chilled mineral water, green salad, vin Cairanne, Côtes du Rhone, rich and dry and delicious. Individual lemon sponges and *chocolat à la maison*. The staff had a glass of champagne at the end of the night.

I have the notes she made then: We achieve a closeness to God through sinning. If we indulge in sexual excess and repent then God will forgive us. Obviously the urge to sin will return. We are composed of three elements, a triangle of body, mind and spirit. Why do we persist in nurturing one in neglect of the others?

The last of these is in a folder of what look like anatomical drawings, lips, eyes and hands, feet and buttocks done in chalk and charcoal. I have AnnA's notes and nothing of the original documents: There is a lovely moment around seven of a summer evening. We take the lamp down from the shelf and watch it silently transform the room, turning the air from nothing to yellow to pink and yellow until a yellow and grey light fills the place. This is when I work. I pull the table over to the fire, carry the lamp to the table and with pen, ink and paper scratch away, the cat by the fire, the room alive with shadows.

What was the worst time? she asked.

Leaving because I could not stay. She was in a side room. I sat for hours asking, Why am I here? What am I waiting for? I phoned a girl friend and went to see her. She lived in the Whiteinch flats, which have a view of what used to be the working river, the cranes and the shipyards, mostly defunct, foreign-owned or building warships. You can see the Parkhead floodlights when a game's on.

Is that good?

It's great. We used to watch the sun come up across the eastern end of the city; we'd watch it creep across the buildings and turn the river to solid gold. The night I visited her, I fell asleep. Back at the hospital, my wife was dying.

The Ward Manager asked, Would you like to see your wife?

Yes.

And would you like us to make the funeral arrangements?

A young man arrived. He had dark, unwashed hair and was wearing a Rangers strip. Is there a deid body here? he asked.

The Ward Manager pointed to her office.

Eh?

In there. Now, she said.

She went into the office when I went into the room. They had opened the curtains.

Irene. Jesus God Almighty, Irene. I'm sorry.

I don't know when the Ward Manager came in with tea. Oh my God, she said.

Leave me. Please.

I kissed Irene's hand and brushed her hair.

AnnA was sitting on the floor, her arms wrapped around her legs. She sat that way for a very long time. Then she kissed my forehead. Goodnight, she said, and went to bed.

I slept on the sofa. In the morning there was a note on the kitchen table: Sorry.

I got as far as phoning a travel agent and asked about flights. In the end I phoned the office.

All's well here, he said. How's things with you?

I told him a little.

Sounds interesting. When can we expect to see you?

I told him.

Give us a ring when you get back. There's a couple of things I'd like to discuss. We've used that piece about the Mackintosh stuff in the Musée d'Orsay, and I believe there's a couple of books coming in you might want to look at if you fancy doing reviews.

It was after nine when AnnA came home. Her face was flushed and she had been drinking. She said Hello, threw her coat over the chair, went to the kitchen, opened a bottle of wine and brought two glasses into the room. I was reading *Out of Africa*. She poured a glass of wine, took the book from my hand and handed me the glass. She threw the book on top of the coat and poured a glass of wine for herself: I thought you'd be gone, she said.

I didn't want to go without seeing you.

Why not?

It seemed as though I was creeping away.

I wouldn't have thought that. I expected you to go, but I thought you'd get in touch when you were back in Scotland.

I'll do that if you like.

Don't be silly. I was only hoping you'd go because that would mean I wouldn't have to face this.

What?

I've been trying to tell you and can't. Even now I can hardly say it. I had a son. He died. That's it.

What do you mean?

He was six years old.

AnnA. I'm sorry.

I always do this. I can't talk about him.

Do you want me to ask you questions?

No.

Light from the doorways and windows, light from the street fell on her face, giving it a lustre. Everything seemed to come from outside; the room and the lamps in the room, the furniture and wallpaper holds her attention with its knots and whorls and repeated patterns of brown and shades of brown. The little pine-framed mirror by the kitchen door sent back her image, face flushed, her hair flat and damp. The kitchen light showed dishes in the sink; the light in the hall caught a bunch of flowers wrapped in white paper and spun away from the glass in her hand. When I think of her in that room, I think of something I have never said, something that comes from fable and mystery, something that is used for poetic effect, a rapturous invention whose existence I barely even imagined; thinking it came from a badly written novel, where sentiment is used for cheap effect. It could still be said in a film, where people act, pretend to be real, make us think they are speaking to each other in soft, intimate ways, make us believe we are eavesdropping, make voyeurism a pleasure. It is far too common for poetry or opera, though I believe it could be sung; not in anything one might hear on a broadcast medium, but from a chant, from a part-song or refrain composed in the dawn of polyphony when people learned to sing together and to make their sound interesting, to extend the voice into areas it never knew. It could only be sung then because it needs as much support to sing as it does to say and only makes sense when one is learning and does not know how to proceed.

I was living with a man, she said. It was awful. Well, it wasn't always awful, it became awful. I was living with this man for less than a year; six, eight months, I don't know. His name was Robert. Do you want a cigarette?

I've stopped.

Of course. I always do this. I find myself involved and think it's what I want and then find out it's not what I want at all. Not that he was like that. I thought we wanted the same things, but we didn't. He wanted to be with me and be a bachelor at the same time. He was constantly criticising me, constantly making me feel silly. I reached a point where I was always asking what I should do, because whatever I did was not good enough. Then he'd criticise me for that too: Can't you even make your mind up about what to wear, he'd say. He was just a big baby, who wanted someone to do what his mother did and sleep with him as well.

I'm sorry.

Why should you be sorry? It's got nothing to do with you. I just left. I got up one morning, packed my bags and phoned a taxi. I came here and lived with my father. I was here a month and knew I was pregnant. I was a schoolteacher, so I applied for the first vacancy I saw outside Paris and that was where we lived, André and me, where he was born. It's where he died.

Where?

Olonzac.

I don't know where that is.

Languedoc. In the Minervois region. Near Homps on the Canal du Midi.

I've never been there.

It's not far from where my mother is now.

Do you want more wine?

I've drunk too much. I'm not going to finish this. And I can't smoke any more. Can we go to bed?

I pulled her up from the couch. She put an arm around my neck and we moved towards the bedroom. She stopped by the door.

I have to brush my teeth, she said.

You'll manage that yourself?

I think so.

You're naked, she said when we passed in the hall. I'm going to have a naked man in my bed.

You've had one in your bed for a few nights now.

She kissed me. Gorgeous, she said.

When I got into bed she kissed me again. You taste of toothpaste. What do I taste of?

Toothpaste.

And?

Cigarettes and wine. There's a hint of garlic in there.

That's horrible. I won't kiss you.

I didn't say it was unpleasant.

It's not very nice.

It's lovely.

I'll kiss you here instead.

And we lay that way for a very long time, her head on my shoulder, my arm round her back till it was cramped and sore, but I felt I could not move and was waiting for her to move when I drifted into something that could have been sleep and was wakened by her voice, her breath beside me as she whispered, giving her story the qualities of dream, something that belongs to here and there.

I will tell you a little. There are hundreds of photographs. I'll show you the photographs. You can ask about the people and anything else that takes your fancy. That way you can see and discover at the same time, always the best way to learn.

We lived in a house on the outside of town, on the edge of a vineyard, a house at the top of a dusty path that was hardly a road. The bread van used it every morning. André ran down the road to catch the school bus. He ran between the vines. He went to one school and I went to another. He and I and the bread van were the only people to use the track. Our mail was left in a box by the main road.

I have gone over this bit many times. I know this story, especially this bit; I know this bit very well. I do not need prompting, nor to set it up, I can enter this story at any point. It's like a film or a loop of film I have played many times. I do not know if it is accurate. I do not know if it is true. I know it is mine. I know I have kept it and I need it now, can't live without it, my little film, though I like to say when it will run, and can say that now. It used to run of its own accord. We'd have a showing in the middle of the night or in the supermarket, crossing the road, anywhere. Now I call it up and arrange the showing. No one else has seen it. No one else could see it. I will describe it to you. I have never described it to anyone. I have told little bits, but never described the film.

She was quiet. Again, I thought she might be sleeping.

The school bus came at the same time every day. I got away from school early and thought about calling into the supermarket to get some things, then I thought I'd wait till André came home and take him with me because he liked to go. It wasn't a big shop, quite small actually, but it must have been like a treasure store to him. He picked up his favourite things, apples, yoghurt, biscuits, stuff like that, knowing some would get through; I think that was the pleasure, seeing him choose; it was always the same. Anyway, I parked my car in the dusty road facing Olonzac. The school bus came the opposite way, facing Azillanet. It dropped him off on the other side of the road. He must have seen my car when the bus pulled away. He knew about looking both ways; God Almighty, he did it every day. But he ran across the road shouting and smiling to meet me, his arms outstretched shouting, Maman.

I never really saw it. Maybe I did see it. Perhaps it's a memory I imagined. But I know I heard his scream and the screech of brakes. The man said he saw him as he turned the corner when the bus pulled away, he saw him standing on the opposite side of the road and thought he was going to let him past. But he just ran out. He was frozen to the spot and the car hit him, sending him into the air.

I knew he was dead. That was it. I couldn't really stay any more. Leaving André was the hardest part. I decided to try to make a new life for myself. It was the only decision I could make. André was gone, but my life could continue.

I saw the driver for a while, the driver of the car that hit him. I knew him slightly before the accident. He had a restaurant. Does this sound crazy or terrible?

What?

I felt sorry for him. He was ruined. The restaurant ran down and he was forced to sell for a fraction of what it was worth. He tried a number of jobs, sales representative and stuff like that, but couldn't do it; he simply could not work. He had branded himself as a murderer. He was married with two children and when his marriage broke up he came to see me, to tell me he was leaving and to ask my forgiveness. I asked where he was going and he said he did not know.

We slept together only once. He was the last man I slept with before you. I don't think it meant very much to him and it certainly meant nothing to me. It was comfort for us both. We were joined. Still are; at the time it was painful for us to accept. I had given life and he had removed it. He left in the morning and I never saw him again. Thank God it didn't happen here. It was in Olonzac, before I left.

She kissed my chest. As I fell asleep I was sure I heard her snoring.

This is the last thing she did. I know because she has dated it, a statement from Wilhelm Roth's sister Maria on the death of Casanova.

'Not so cocky now, are we?'

My brother used to shout at him every morning. 'Are you alive or dead yet? You are at my mercy. I can do what I want and there's nothing you can do about it.'

I hardly saw him then. He was always so proud, so well groomed. To see him dependent, struggling for breath was terrible. No matter what one thought of him, and I quite liked him, I liked the fact that he was different, that he knew his own mind; no matter what you thought of him, it was a shame to see him like this because he was obviously used to better and deserved to die in peace, as we all do.

'This is my loneliest journey,' he said one day. I had looked in to light his candle. He was wheezing and struggling. 'Tell them I'm dead,' he said.

I think he thought I was someone else. Another girl used to see him. He gave her a book and she could not read. I think she thought no one knew about them and everyone was laughing behind their backs, so I suppose he thought I was her.

He asked if I could dance and I told him I could do a little hopping dance I learned in the village, not unlike the polka. I danced a little and he smiled at me from the high bed.

'Lift your skirt for me,' he said, so I lifted my skirts and danced.

I went to see him when I knew he was alone. I did not like the idea of an old man dying alone. When a horse is dying someone sits with it in the stable, but they were prepared to let this old man die on his own. I thought it was awful and went in to see him.

My brother mocked and taunted, shouted and tormented him.

'You'll never see Venice again,' he said. 'Napoleon's got it. He's taken the golden horses off to Paris. Venice is in ruins and you're next. He's coming for you, coming to free us and coming for you. Napoleon's coming to get you, Napoleon's coming to get you.' He chanted on and on like that. I danced for him that night, but he fell asleep in the middle.

That was the last time. I felt as if an old knot inside me was being untied, slipped from my limbs and fell to the ground.

From the back of nine in all weathers they gather on the right-hand side of Paisley Road, just before you get to the Toll, outside what used to be the Kingston Halls and Library, built at the turn of the century by Robert Horn of the City Engineer's Department and Glasgow Corporation's Director of Housing for three years from 1928. He designed the Mosspark cottages in our first garden suburb, and remodelled J.J. Burnet's Old Ship Bank building in the Saltmarket, giving the pub a pilastered front and glass windows, engraved with a likeness of the old bank building.

For the Kingston Halls he copied Burnet's Athenaeum at the top of Buchanan Street, with a three-bay front for the halls and a one-bay front for the library, which also got carved art nouveau lettering.

Now it's a night shelter, open at the back of ten. Regulars come early.

It's warm and dry and there's food, soup and sandwiches, bakery left-overs and stuff that's past its sell-by date.

The shelter is mostly run by volunteers. Their clients are depressives and schizophrenics, folk who forget their medication, drug addicts, alcoholics and homeless, some who came to Glasgow looking for work. In any one night you find those who do not sleep, who walk around the place singing, shouting or talking to themselves, or stare into space, as well as those who want to fight, shoot up or get someone to listen to what they have to say.

Davie was a chef in Cirencester. He is married with two children, who live with his wife outside Perth. He had been in the hotel since summer, travelling back to see his family every month or six weeks.

His wife works two evenings a week in a local pub and spends at least three afternoons stacking supermarket shelves. Her mother usually looks after the kids, and takes about a third of what her daughter earns.

Just before Christmas, the hotel owner took Davie into the office: That's it, he said. Here's what I owe you, including the two weeks' lying time, and that's the documentation. We'd like your room cleared in an hour.

Two hours later police removed Davie from the premises.

If you don't like the arrangements you can sue or try taking us up before an industrial tribunal, the boss said.

Next day the hotel was staffed by students from the local college who worked Christmas and New Year for less than half of what the previous staff had been paid. Before the owners went to Florida for January and February they put an advert in Job Centres across the country recruiting new staff for the grand reopening banquet at the end of March.

It took Davie three days to hitch-hike to Glasgow. He wanted to get home for Christmas, but thought he might find work. He said he'd do anything. Look at me. I can't get a decent shave and I can't wash my clothes. Would you give me a job?

Alec showed him how to beg.

Just sit, right. Don't try nothin like askin for dosh to take ye hame or get the weans a Christmas. Just sit. Don't move nor fuck aa. Sit. It's good if you've a wean or a dug or something like that cause folk'll gie that money. Don't look or ask for fuck all. Just sit. Watch how I do it. And don't leave the money in the box. Keep a few coppers in it, that's aa. I'll dae an hour and you dae an hour and we'll see how we get on. It's a good pitch.

Rhona asked me round for dinner.

Her flat was small, little more than a room and kitchen with a bathroom and a bit of space in the hall. She took me on a tour, as though I was a prospective buyer, occasionally telling me how her smaller place was cosier than my larger, more expensive place.

She slept and worked in the front room, but otherwise seemed to live in the kitchen. The bathroom was warm and luxuriant with hanging plants and towelling robes, soaps, sprays and pot-pourri.

She had a few books and back issues of film and

fashion magazines in a bookcase in the hall. The kitchen was a table and an assortment of shelves and plates, framed photographs and small prints.

I went climbing, she said in front of a board of pictures of herself. One or two of us went up Dumgoyne. We're going hang-gliding next week. Something to do, isn't it? Gets you out. It uses the countryside and is good for the local economy.

We were having dinner to celebrate her short-term contract with the paper.

It's nice being back, she said. Lots of happy memories for me. I'm sorry you're not around. Have you seen the paper recently? I've done some political articles, assessments and the like. No one else seems interested in that area and the powers that be seem to appreciate what I do, so I reckon there's an opening, the voice of youth and all that. You seem quiet.

I'm listening.

You always did that; but there's something more.

How do you think I've changed?

It's hard to put my finger on it. A bit detached, but nicer. Anyway, what's going on?

Nothing much. I have neither job nor family.

Would you like to be married again?

I don't know.

I'm sure it wouldn't be hard to find someone.

That's as maybe; I decided to try things another way.

What do you mean?

It's a bit difficult to describe without sounding trite or stupid, maybe even sentimental, but it's what I'm doing down at the shelter.

What shelter?

Homeless folk, down-and-outs, schizophrenics and the like.

What do you do?

Give them tea. Listen. Not much really.

Is that why I couldn't find you?

Probably.

Bit pretentious, isn't it? Retired man with a private income and lots of time decides to help those less fortunate than himself.

Is that what it sounds like?

People could take it that way.

Let them.

Doesn't it worry you?

I'm not doing it for anyone else. I am doing it to learn about me.

Why the change?

I'm not sure it is a change, any more than I am sure it'll last. It's just another way of doing things. I don't think it would suit everyone, but it suits me. Every night I wonder if I'll see my daughter or anyone who knows her, maybe even knew her, then as soon as things get going, as soon as the place begins filling up, as soon as I am doing things for other people, it becomes simpler.

There's no answer to that, is there?

I don't know. As far as I am concerned it eases my confusion. I am often confused, especially about my motivation.

I never think about it, though if I was in your position I might. What I mean is that I don't understand. I might help others after myself. Does that sound selfish?

I smiled. She reached across and squeezed my hand. You have lovely eyes, she said.

I don't suppose I thought about it. My reaction was purely instinctive. I took her hand in mine and kissed it. She smiled across the table.

Coffee? More wine?

I'd best be going.

Where?

I said I'd be down at the back of eleven. You can come if you like.

No thanks, I've made other plans. For one thing, I thought we might spend the evening together, have a few drinks, relax. I thought you'd stay and I can't believe you didn't know that. Why do you think I asked you to come here?

Why do you think I am going?

Do you think they're related?

Could be. Anyway, I must be off.

Have you stopped fancying me?

Of course not.

Then come back later?

I don't know when I'll finish.

Can I phone you?

Of course.

Are you going away, leaving Glasgow?

It's possible.

Listen, sweetie. She put her arms round me. She kissed my cheek. I'm sorry to ask this, darling. You know how much I love you. She looked past me, buried her face into my chest. Can I call on you, ask your help? Can I phone you up and ask you things? Would you mind? I think I'm a bit out of my depth. Some things are okay, but I've been reading a few of your old pieces and they're so clear. I know I could get this job. It's a wonderful opportunity and I don't want to lose it. Will you help me? Please.

No. I'm sorry. I don't think I could do that.

You don't mind helping down-and-fucken-outs but you won't help me.

Sorry.

Why not?

Can't do it, Rhona. Sorry. I'm sure there are others who'd be only too pleased to help.

Don't think they haven't offered.

Take them up on it.

I might.

It would be good for your career.

Tacky, isn't it? Same everywhere. Off you go and have a nice time.

Andy and young Tony were fighting over a piece of bread. Mary was crying. Bobby sang *The Bonnie Wells o Wearie* and we all joined in. Willie preached eternal damnation and Gerry was going back into training. Jackie had a vision of the Kingston Bridge on fire and his mother rescued him. Pat sang *Pal o My Cradle Days* and Geordie joined in. Dick was anxious to get back to jail, where he had a good wee job and felt safe. He tried to smash the place up hoping we'd phone the police, then left at two in the morning.

I'm glad you're here, said Jessie. I think I'm pregnant.

The Social are trying to take my weans, said Alice. Just because they're in care doesnae mean they can take them, sure it doesnae?

Irene's mother phoned this morning.

I was wondering if you were thinking of coming through? she asked.

Not really.

It's just that there's a lot to do.

I thought you were settled.

Of course I am settled, but there's still a couple of things that need to be done. Mrs Hendry would like a cabinet of mine and I wondered if you could deliver it.

Doesn't Mrs Hendry have a car?

Don't be ridiculous.

Does she have a family?

What are you getting at?

I would have thought the onus was on Mrs Hendry to collect rather than on you to deliver, especially since it involves me driving through from Glasgow to do so. Where does Mrs Hendry live?

It doesn't matter. If it's too much bother, just stay where you are.

What else did you want?

Nothing.

Pardon?

I only thought that if you were coming through you could have taken me to Perth.

What's happening there?

It isn't Perth actually, it's Gleneagles. I thought we could have lunch in Perth then you could drop me at Gleneagles on your way back to Glasgow.

So you wanted me to drive to Edinburgh, load and deliver an item of furniture, take you to Perth for lunch then drop you off at Gleneagles in the afternoon, is that right?

She was silent.

Have I understood you properly? It was a round trip to Perth, via Edinburgh, you had in mind?

You're obviously too busy. And I don't like your tone of voice. There's no need for sarcasm. It was a straight-forward request. You could have said no.

I am sorry if I sound sarcastic. I am simply trying to remember the last time you phoned here to ask how I was, or to ask for the children. Any time you call, it is to ask me to do something.

It isn't true.

I think it is true. I am sorry I won't be able to take you to Gleneagles. I am rather busy at the moment.

Couldn't you have said that in the first place and saved all this aggravation?

Finally, from what the researchers tell me is the unfinished manuscript of a novel believed to have been written by Eduard Mörike. It was discovered in Cleversulzbach earlier this century. Mörike was parson there from 1834 to 1843. During this time he wrote and published many of the lyrical poems which were later set to music by Hugo Wolf. His novella *Mozart's Journey to Prague* was published in 1855, the year his first daughter was born.

IN THE LIBRARY

Casanova is dancing.

He bows to his partner, holds himself erect and marches to the music, hand on hip, head aloft, eyes front, pausing to frill a step or two. He is aware only of being watched, of seeing and of being seen.

And what of the women who watch? What of his partners? Who are they and what do they want? They want to feel loved, want to feel better, to be normal, the same as other women, secure. They want a safe escort.

Casanova is writing.

By the light of a single candle at a high desk in the unused library, he is reconstructing his life. It will not end with insults and tremblings, in a place where peasants jibe and call, where they hang his picture on the lavatory door, assault him in the street, treat him no better than a common servant.

He is the Chevalier Giacomo Casanova de Seingalt. His life is epic.

Peasants who have never been further than ten kilometres from where they were born reduce him to their understanding, mock his manners and his accent, insisting he is no better than they, saying he is also a servant.

The aristocracy continue to ignore him. They defy his talents and contain his life. They have thwarted his dreams and kept him to heel. At times they have reduced him to little more than a toy for their amusement. He has served and entertained them, yet they continue to ignore him as they have always ignored him, squandered his talents, denied or denigrated his worth, used him for their own ends, then plotted, gossiped and conspired against him.

'Better to be wherever you are than here, where all manner of unspeakable atrocities are a daily occurrence, where we live in fear of our very lives,' wrote Mariscallo, the negro acrobat who stayed in Paris. Casanova believes the reply was his last. If Mariscallo had money he would have sent what he could, knowing it would hardly have arrived intact. He would have sent something. Mariscallo would have responded.

It is winter. Snow covers the forests. Roads are blocked, ice in the buckets and the fire is low. His Grace Count Joseph Charles Emmanuel Waldstein is not here, nor will he return for months. His Grace is in Antwerp, avoiding the Bohemian winter. So while complaints and anguish fester, Casanova is writing.

In a woollen hat, a long scarf and fingerless mittens. There is a blanket round his shoulders. He makes his own ink and steals the parchment. Every day, instead of filing and shelving his master's volumes, cataloguing and rearranging books no one will read, collating manuscripts and seeking new treasures to delight and entertain the gentlemen after hunting, something to shorten winter's fears, Casanova constructs the story of his life.

Now he can live as he wanted to live. He can be remembered as he would choose. He will tell all, what they made of him; ruined and wasted him and his worth.

History beckons. She taunts and dances on and on, turning to glance over her shoulder, to wink and point her tongue at him.

His life has taught him to entertain. He had to tell stories to shorten the hours in hard, springless carriages that trailed across Europe. He could take the merest suggestion and turn it into Homeric proportions, could keep a weary audience awake. With poems, plays and novels behind him, this, his life, will be his last, will be best of all. For he has learned the way to entertain gentlemen, learned to be a man's man, to drink and gamble, smoke and swear; he knows when to joke and when to nudge, when to laugh and when to make others laugh, when to be proper and keep peace. He knows a good tale and his life will tell it, showing what they missed, following history wherever she leads.

Casanova is writing. He has chosen French, the language of the court. The language they will read.

Now that it's over I don't know where I'll be. Look and you'll find me. If you search, I'll be there; in the pubs and bookshops, the supermarkets and football terracings. I'll be there or thereabouts and you'll find me if you look. I will not be here.

I know how I'll get there. I'll walk across the Rannoch Moor and climb Buchaille Etive Mor. I'll launch myself out. I will jump from the top and just as I seem to be falling, tumbling and about to crash, the wind and the souls in the wind, the spirits of the dead departed, those angels who are in the air and the land around us, who cannot live here or there but return to the sites of their former existence, they will lift me, carry me up to be borne by the wind, and that is how I will fly without feathers, take myself off, dip and soar across Rannoch Moor.

Fly away.

We returned the papers in her great-grandmother's

name, photocopied them in four days, working in relays, taking half a dozen a time down to the shops.

What now? I said on my final evening.

Now I miss you.

I know.

But it's necessary.

I know that too.

And you'll write?

Of course.

And phone?

Regularly.

And come and see me?

Whenever you want.

No. Not when I want. When we decide we can see each other. When you're settled and my studies are over and we can begin to live.

Things could change.

I settled for what I thought I could get, for what I thought was possible rather than for what I wanted because I believed I would never get what I wanted. I thought I had it and bits kept falling off, so I retired into myself like a tortoise. That's changed, but nothing else has changed, it's only become clearer.

Will you come and see me?

I'm thinking about it.

Really?

I want to see your home.

Is home where we are or where we come from?

She raised her glass. To an unsolvable question, she said.

Next morning she waved as I went into the Métro

station. I ran back upstairs because I knew she was crying.

Something in my eye, she said. Just a speck of dust.

I smiled.

Let me know you're well, she said. I turned and she was gone.

Struggling with my bags, I thought I saw her. A young man jumped the barrier in front of me when I put my ticket in the slot, and as I stopped I thought I saw AnnA.

On the train north my mind is stone smoothed to pebble, levelled as the pebbles are washed to sand; sand, water and lime are mixed to stone again. It was a circle with depth on the surface. Coming northwards even the trees trembled a little, the sky like ashes, till she was a memory, a line in the distance.

Please, she said at the station. I would like you to have them. Richter playing the Brahms Quintet and something to read on the train, Mandelstam's poems and *Out of Africa* by Karen Blixen, whose last sentence is mine: The outline of the mountain was slowly smoothed and levelled out by the hand of distance.

Acknowledgements

Two texts were indispensable. They informed and maybe even inspired bits of this novel.

First of all, the man himself, Casanova's *L'Histoire de ma Vie*. I am grateful to my friend John Bampton for this, one of his many surprises, and happily thank him here in the knowledge that he will remember his place in these pages. Secondly, there is John Masters's biography, *Casanova*, which takes the autobiography as a starting point, tempering it with enthusiasm, reasonability and erudition.

I am also grateful to those who bought me time to write a book which has taken too long. Firstly, again, to the Scottish Arts Council, as well as those whose titles defy anything other than simple statement – the Glasgow Arts and Cultural Development Office, South East Area and the Glasgow City Libraries, South Division.

There are other references too numerous to mention, ut I am happy to acknowledge my debt and gratitude.

The pastel portrait by Francesco Casanova on page 10 is from the Dashcov Collection in the State Historical Museum, Moscow.

The Osip Mandelstam poem quoted on pages 226 and 227 is from the *Selected Poems* (Penguin, 1977), translated by Clarence Brown and W. S. Merwin.

And finally, the story of Rilke and the violets on page 141 is true and was given to me a long time ago by Maryann Scott.